Ma

SERENISSIMA

ERICA JONG

Serenissima

A Novel of Venice

GUILD PUBLISHING LONDON

This edition published 1987 by
Book Club Associates
by arrangement with
Bantam Press
a division of Transworld Publishers Ltd

Printed in Great Britain by
Mackays of Chatham Ltd, Kent

For

My Mother and Father
who loved Italy and Shakespeare
before me

For

Molly and Margaret
intrepid coexplorers

For

Liselotte and Manfred
who gave me the glittering keys
to their watery city

and

For

All the strolling players who
travel through time

For more than a thousand years Venice was something unique among the nations, half eastern, half western, half land, half sea, poised between Rome and Byzantium, between Christianity and Islam, one foot in Europe, the other paddling in the pearls of Asia. She called herself the Serenissima, she decked herself in cloth of gold, and she even had her own calendar, in which the years began on March 1st, and the days began in the evening. This lonely hauteur, exerted from the fastnesses of the lagoon, gave to the old Venetians a queer sense of isolation. As their Republic grew in grandeur and prosperity, and their political arteries hardened, and a flow of dazzling booty enriched their palaces and churches, so Venice became entrammelled in mystery and wonder. She stood, in the imagination of the world, somewhere between a freak and a fairy tale.

James (Jan) Morris
THE WORLD OF VENICE

But Time, unfortunately, though it makes animals and vegetables bloom with amazing punctuality has no such simple effect upon the mind of man.

Virginia Woolf
ORLANDO

SERENISSIMA

1

Between Freak and Fairy Tale

THE WAY WE LIVE now, jetting from palmy LaLa Land to gray and frenzied New York City, to azure Venice, the Serenissima of all Serenissime — the most serene republic of our dreams — we might as well be time traveling. And we are.

It is already midnight in Venice when my six P.M. Alitalia flight takes off from JFK. Gondole are slithering through the narrow canals. Somewhere in Cannaregio, a violinist from the Fenice Theater sits upon the painted prow of a leaky Torcello fishing boat, playing Mozart on a Guarnieri, while a beautiful young man rows along the back canals — for he has studied rowing in a school for gondoliers, and he is proud of his biceps. The water is black, aubergine, bluish, slate gray. History drowns in it. There are two women in the boat as well — one a slender dark-haired actress, one a honey-curled painter who is older and wiser (though not about her own affairs).

The fishing boat shimmers along the back canals. From time to time a window opens and a shadowed figure steps out on it to shout "Brava!"

"Brava!" we also shout, for Venice is ever the fragile labyrinth at the edge of the sea and it reminds us how brief and perilous the journeys of our lives are; perhaps that is why we love it so. City of plagues and brief liaisons, city of lingering deaths and incendiary loves, city of chimeras, nightmares, pigeons, bells. You are the only city in the world whose dialect has a word for the shimmer of canal water reflected on the ceiling of a room. But, alas, I forget that word. It is not *riflesso*, nor *scintillio*, nor *gibigianna*. No matter. It will come back, for I am flying back to Venice.

I had come to the Venice Film Festival for the presentation of my last film, *Women in Hell*, and was staying on to begin filming the next, *Serenissima*. I had never been to the film festival before, though I had been to Venice often enough from adolescence on. The festival was pure madness — *paparazzi* everywhere, my director booed in the Sala Grande, journalists, hangers-on, and all the skinny little actresses in sequins, trotted out, poor lambs, to be sacrificed to the crowds . . . the kids on the beach rushing for autographs.

"*Chi è?*" they chirp, coagulating on the sand.

"*E famosa?*"

They flutter down like hungry little birds with pieces of paper in their beaks. What do they *do* with these pieces of paper? Sell them? Lose them? Trade them? These overfed Italian *bambini* rush at you, proffering their bits of paper, brandishing their plastic pens. If you are being photographed, giving an interview, talking to someone who *looks* important, they descend, terrifying in their efficiency, but utterly oblivious of your identity.

The whole festival is an exercise in the madness of crowds. The way a crowd accretes around a would-be celebrity, attempting to find a focus for its crowding, gathering centripedal force, then endeavoring to crush or dismember the personage at its center. Finding the scene at the Excelsior somewhat daunting, I took to navigating a peripheral route through the lobby by walking crabwise behind the elegant glass cases displaying perfumes, Italian fashions, expensive smoker's gear — as if I were an ancient Venetian galleon hovering along the Dalmatian shore on my way to Greece.

They had invited me to be on the jury of the film festival — the *giuria* — the only woman, the only American, the only actress. I was decorative. I spoke Italian. I represented America, women, the postwar generation.

It was known that I was staying on to begin a film about Venice — and that gave my presence added piquancy, for Venice, by definition, loves everything Venetian. It is not surprising that Venice is known above all for mirrors and glass since Venice is the most narcissistic city in the world, the city that celebrates self-mirroring.

When had I first come to Venice? I wondered, as I unpacked my own sequins (and blue jeans) in a huge spun-sugar-chandeliered suite at the Excelsior, the Adriatic gently lapping outside my fourth floor window. It was probably around the time that my mother married stepfather number three, the Italian. In fact, I seem to remember my childhood summers in conjunction with my motley assortment of stepfathers. Their nationalities and eccentricities determined where we stayed, and their solicitude, or lack of it, determined the state of Mother's mental health.

Winters, it was Chapin School for me, and Buckley for my brother, Pip, and the huge dark apartment on Park and Seventy-third where Mother slept until four every day, waking up just in time to dispatch us to do our homework. (For her, breakfast, brunch, and cocktails merged into one meal.)

Sometimes we'd be trotted out at cocktails to entertain the next prospective stepfather — though less and less as the years went on, and Mother seemed, after three divorces, to give up on the myth of conjugal bliss.

Stepfather number one was French, number two English, number three Italian, as if somehow, by never duplicating nationalities, Mummy could sidestep her cursed marital horoscope. (Daddy, of course, had been a seductive Southern gentleman, the archetypal charmer who marries for money and is the last one on earth to know that about himself. After my mother, he went on to wed five more heiresses, while she took on a whole NATO alliance of husbands.) The Italian proved the worst — a blond, blue-eyed Venetian with a taste for black-eyed wives. He was not rich, though his tastes were, and he had inherited a crumbling palazzo on the Grand Canal that devoured money like an ocean-going yacht. I first came to know Venice because of him — Gian-Luigi Mocenigo-Loredan, he was called — and doges, diarists, *assassini*, soldiers of fortune, and world-class heiress hunters ran in his family.

Mother must have married him somewhere in my preteen years

because I remember being fifteen that Venetian summer she walked out on him. Pip, my "baby" brother, was twelve. I see myself in pictures from that period — a slender, titian-haired girl with huge, brown almond-shaped eyes — almost as if I had become Venetian to please my stepfather. (What the pictures do not show are the daydreams, the longings, the reveries to which I was prone, then as now. I lived in a world of costumed courtiers, magic rings, and fairy godmothers; my face always hidden in some book, my diary full of cryptosexual longings.)

Before our Venetian period we'd spent summers in Anjou — at the castle — or "kaa-sel" as my second stepfather used to say. He was English, stiff-upper-lippish, and had not married my mother only for her money.

The castle had actually belonged to my *first* stepfather, who was French, loony, and had the same mad eyes as all his ancestors (whose portraits, costumed appropriately for all periods from the thirteenth to the nineteenth century, filled the ninety-seven-odd chambers of the chateau). When he shot himself with his hunting rifle, Mother got the chateau — though not, as you might imagine, without a struggle, since his relatives tried to prove she had shot him. But that is another long story best left for another time.

The chateau at Anjou was a peaceable-looking place, considering that it had been built on so much bloodshed. It had sloping gray slate eaves, a clock tower whose clock had stopped working in the eighteenth century, and a moat Pip and I could paddle around in a rubber canoe. In July the moat was choked with water lilies at one end, and you had to paddle deftly through a watery labyrinth. My brother would vie with me to see who could get through the weeds faster. I remember the golden water lilies that grew in the lily pads and their extraordinary aroma. For years that aroma gave me back my childhood.

Why Mother broke up with the Englishman I do not know (perhaps he was gay, or perhaps he really loved her and she was too wounded within to be able to tolerate such love), but break up with him she did — in favor of Gian-Luigi, the world-class wife beater. It was then that Venice came to replace Anjou as our summer place, and not so long after that the whole world fell apart for me.

4

That last summer in Venice, I was fifteen and my mother fifty, and all those marriages and divorces had taken their toll. At fifty a woman can either be in her prime or a ruin — or, still worse, she can be a hidden ruin with eyes so hurt they go back in her head like the eyes of a hunted animal. My mother turned that kind of fifty. A month later she was dead, and at fifteen I was set to inherit half of it all — trust funds, tax problems, half a crumbling chateau, half a rotting palazzo, half a dark Park Avenue apartment, and the deep and abiding melancholy that comes from knowing all your life what money cannot buy.

How I lost most of it, and wound up in the Land of LaLa — Hollywood — among people whose curse (or blessing) it is *not* to know that, is one of the tales I have to tell. I don't know if I'm adequate to that epic — but what storyteller is adequate to her story? The story carries us along, bottles on the tide, each with our secret message and the fervent hope that it does not turn out to be blank.

As I unpacked my sequins in Venice, with the Adriatic making its mysterious presence heard outside the window, it was inevitable that I be flooded with those memories of Mother. Her suicide had left me with a ghostly companion from the age of fifteen on, an insufferable burden for a child. If parents die in their own good time, we learn to shed them and go on; if they take their own lives untimely, they cling to us forever, whispering their good-bys. My mother had clung that way, obliterating all other presences: defeating suitors, lovers, even a husband and the daughter he stole from me. In vain I tried to shake her off; she clung the harder. Sometimes I thought I had accepted this prolonged gig in Venice in part because I hoped that somehow I could find her here (and perhaps also lose her for the last time).

Some artists need to wallow in self in order to create. I, on the contrary, was always fleeing myself — the very opposite of the writer's craft. When the lights come up on the stage, when you are isolated in the little circle of heat and brightness that insulates you from the crowd, you are also insulated from past and future. There is only that moment and the character that consumes you.

You feel the audience also as a source of heat, and there is the heat within you — panic, ambition, dread — that propels you into the part, that makes you embrace it as if somehow, through it, you could find home, mother, completion, peace.

I had begun with Shakespeare — with Shakespearean roles, that is. Shakespeare was my home, my substitute mother, also my escape. In high school I discovered the sonnets. In college I acted Juliet, Portia, Cordelia, Rosalind, even Lady Macbeth (though I was much too young and green to understand her). But I had never acted my namesake, Jessica. It was ironic that I had been named for Shylock's daughter, named for her by a WASP mother who also loved Shakespeare. The name Jessica is all the rage nowadays with four-year-olds, but in the forties it was still an odd name — almost as odd as Nerissa or Cordelia. I always found it strange that I, who felt almost like an imaginary Jew (the very definition of the outsider), should be named for the young Jewess who renounces her faith and her father for a facile Christianity and a foppish young man.

Now, after all these years, I was going to get to play my namesake, for *Serenissima* was nothing less than a filmic fantasy based on *The Merchant of Venice*. My director, the nearly mythical Swede Björn Persson, had announced it as his last film — the climax of a career that had included a film about Tchaikovsky, a film about Byron, many films drawn from his own tortured Swedish life, and, just recently, a brilliant and controversial film about Mozart. It was rumored that in *Serenissima* Shakespeare himself was to appear as a character representing the director, as Prospero represented Shakespeare in his last play — but that remained to be seen.

Björn was legendary for never allowing even his most celebrated international stars to see the script before commencing to shoot. You worked with Björn because it was an honor to work with Björn, because he was an artist in a world in which artists were an endangered species, and because you knew that the script you would receive when you arrived on location would be a masterpiece — or at least an ambitious and beautiful failure, more interesting to be seen in than most "successes." You worked with Björn because there was no way to turn Björn down. He was hypnotic, a svengali, a genius.

When he talked to you, when he looked into your eyes with his luminous blue-gray ones and explained your role to you, or anything in the world to you for that matter, you felt yourself to be the only person alive on earth, the only actress, the only woman, in all of time, in the entire galaxy.

This movie of *The Merchant of Venice* was critical to me in a way other actresses my age will immediately understand. It was my last chance to play the lover before I entered that desperate no woman's land between *innamorata* and grandma, that terrifying no woman's land from forty to sixty that all actresses wander into sooner or later. It was true that I had staved off the inevitable longer than most because I looked young — but it was only a matter of minutes, I felt, before the best roles would vanish, and with them my career. So I was looking forward to working with Björn again, though his very presence gave me pain.

I had had my obligatory fling with him — if an affair with Björn could be called anything so frivolous as a fling — several years ago, when we were both between marriages (his sixth and seventh, my third and fourth), and it had left me raw and amputated for a year. But there was no way I wasn't going to work with him again. He was undoubtedly the greatest director of our time, and saying no to him would have been like saying no to Shakespeare if you were an Elizabethan actor. He was brilliant, maddening, mercurial — alternately gregarious and reclusive. He required a woman to care for him like the giant baby he was, to keep the world at bay when he was working, to nurse him through breakdowns, depressions, fits of writing or blockage, starts at films that never got off the ground.

Though he was the most loving and maternal of directors on the set, in life he used up all the air in a room; his genius permitted no one else's to exist. He fell in love with creative women and then tried to strangle them or make them into nurses, killing in them the thing he first had loved. It was an impossible dilemma which he had not been able to resolve until the age of sixty. Nowadays he was married to a wife who understood, possibly even enjoyed, all of this — wife number seven — a beautiful, green-eyed, gray-haired matron who sailed through the world like a great galleon of the sixteenth century, accepting Björn's awards in foreign countries, nursing him through bouts of writing in their hideaway in the south of France (Villa Persson, it was called), understanding his need to be a genius who transformed women into nannies.

She was a brilliant woman — this Lilli Persson — as brilliant in her way as he was in his, and she understood the fine (all but lost) art of cosseting genius. Without her, nothing would get done in Björn's life these days — not *Serenissima*, not his plays, not the operas he sometimes mounted at Stockholm's Royal Opera House.

I was both terrified and elated at the prospect of seeing Björn again. Björn had turned my life inside out and then departed with Lilli. It was not, God knows, that I wanted to *marry* him. I was not masochist enough for that. It was just that he had stirred me to the bottom of my being and then fled. It also struck me as a sort of karmic joke that we should meet again in Venice, that chimera, that city of illusions where reality becomes fantasy and fantasy becomes reality. Perhaps it is because Venice is both liquid and solid, both air and stone, that it somehow combines all the elements crucial to make our imaginations ignite and turn fantasies into realities.

Each time one comes to Venice, it reflects back another self, another dream, as if it were partly your own mirror. The air is full of the spirits of all those who have lived here, worked here, loved here. The stones themselves are thick with history. They whisper to you as you walk the deserted streets at night. Cats leap out as if they were the embodied spirits of all the dead ones who created here or died here: Byron, Browning, Ruskin, Turner, Tintoretto, Mahler, Stravinsky . . . Shakespeare. Was Shakespeare ever here?

I had read and re-read *The Merchant of Venice* on the Alitalia flight from New York (a studio jet had carried me from Burbank to Teterboro, a helicopter from Teterboro to JFK), searching for some clue that he *was*.

But the play was equivocal, Anglicized, unclear. At first it did not seem to bear the unmistakable scent of Italy as Browning's work or Byron's bears the scent, as Ruskin's and Henry James's work bear the scent, reflecting in the very rhythms of their prose the rise and fall of the sea.

8

Was Shakespeare here? Remember those "lost years" in his life — the years no one can account for, the years after he marries Anne Hathaway and has three babes, but before 1592, when an envious Robert Greene mentions him as "an upstart crow, beautified with our feathers . . . in his own conceit the only Shake-scene in a country. . . ." What was he doing then? Apprentice player? Schoolmaster in the country? No one knows. Then there were the plague years, 1592 and 1593 particularly, when the theaters in London were closed and players had to tour the countryside to earn their bread — or might he instead have voyaged to Italy with Henry Wriothesley, the Earl of Southampton, his patron and (some say) lover?

Who knew? Shakespeare scholarship was rife with petty academic rivalries, outrageous suppositions, the mad hypotheses of good brains gone bad in college libraries, eaten by the maggots of paranoia and thwarted literary ambitions. Stratfordians said "the Bard" (How I hate that orotund, pretentious epithet!) was a simple glover's son; anti-Stratfordians made him earl of this or that, because in their snobbery they could not believe that our greatest poet could lack a title. Piffle.

It was all as Joyce's Buck Mulligan had said, "He proves by algebra that Hamlet's grandson is Shakespeare's grandfather and that he himself is the ghost of his own father."

But what if Shakespeare had been here? Venice, then as now, was the end point of exotic English travels, a place of resort for lusty young men with poetic and bisexual ambitions, a city of sin, decadence, and glamour, a place to expose oneself to new viruses when one's own plagues were either too weak or too strong, a city of fabulous courtesans who wrote poetry, a city of Jews, usurers, Moors, moneylenders, a city of feuding noble lords who dressed in all the pearls of the Orient, who rode the civic waterways in curious boats whose toes turned up like slippers, but who commanded the entire Adriatic, Aegean, and Mediterranean with galleasses and triremes rowed by hundreds of sweating slaves.

How could Shakespeare *not* be drawn here — with his golden-ringleted earl, "the onlie begetter of the Sonnets," the patron to whom he dedicated the greatest stroke poem of all time, that "book of one hand" (as the French say) *Venus and Adonis*? Venice, then as

9

now, was the city of sex and sin to which two lusty young men might sail in a great, wide-beamed Elizabethan galley, searching for future plots and poetry beneath the golden lion of St. Mark. . . .

My suite at the Excelsior is grand. All the members of the jury have grand suites. Having been duly met at the Aeroporto Marco Polo by members of the Biennale committee toting gaudy, cellophane-shrouded bouquets of roses, we have been ushered in state (a private silk-curtained state *motoscafo*, that is) to the fairy-turreted, fake Byzantine fantasy that is the Excelsior. *Paparazzi* accost us as the *motoscafo* docks at the private landing. I am wearing the requisite giant tortoise-shell movie star sunglasses and, of course, the *paparazzi* beg me to remove them.

"Jessica! Jessica!" they call. "Coulda you pleeza remove the *occhiali?*" (It is astounding how the use of one's first name evokes intimacy — even if used by a total stranger.)

I dutifully remove the *occhiali*, strike my best angle, and smile. If my forty-three years of being photographed have taught me anything, they've taught me my best angles — though, of course, I only confess to being thirty-four — simply reversing the digits like a dyslexic. I don't *believe* a woman should lie about her age, but in my profession, it's a question of survival. Admitting to thirty-four, I'm still offered roles I would never be offered if I admitted to forty-three — ridiculous, but true.

I am helped out of the boat by a toady in white (oh, Venetians are so groveling if they think you're important, so maddeningly indifferent if they think you're not), and my fellow members of the *giuria* follow me out of the boat and strike poses on the dock for the *paparazzi*.

I toss my hennaed chestnut hair, open wide my "fabled" gold-brown eyes, smile with lips recently reslicked with pinkish lip-gloss, and try to act as if I *feel* beautiful — although I have never mastered that art. Like most women, when I look in the mirror I see the flaws in my beauty, not the beauty, however much it has been praised. And I hate the photography ritual, though I accept it as part of my job. Much as I *try* to enjoy it, I cannot quite get past the feeling that my soul is being stolen by the cameras. My soul feels none too attached to my body these days anyway. Every August I experience severe distress as the anniversary of my mother's suicide arrives (on September first, to be exact), but this year it has been worse than usual. It is twenty-eight years later and somehow I still cannot believe she is dead. She did not actually die in Venice, but she might as well have, for it was in Venice that she entered her final hopelessness and depression. If her soul is lingering anywhere, it lingers here in this city of mirages, and not in the humid canyons of New York.

The other members of the *giuria* are posing with me — and the *giuria* is heavy with literati this year: a flamboyant Russian poet with arctic Siberian eyes of icy blue; a famous octogenarian antifascist Spanish surrealist poet with long white tresses and a dishy, young girlfriend; a dark-mustachioed German playwright of the radical sixties who bristles — prickly as a porcupine — with ideology, politico-aesthetic theories, and Marxist epigrams; a frail, freckle-faced Nobel laureate who began his life in a shtetl in Poland and is ending it "in Svizzera" (having, in between, written his major books in Brighton Beach); a very vague aristocratic painter from some nebulous country like Belgium, who is trailed by a beauteous Japanese wife in kimono and two exquisite Eurasian daughters of eleven and thirteen. And then there are the film types: our president, a famous brooding intellectual Italian film director with a strange tic like St. Vitus's dance; an even more famous anti-intellectual Italian film director with an actress-wife and an actress-mistress in tow (the mistress and the wife appear to be the best of friends: they share a suite, while the famous film director will soon be seen dallying with starlets on the *terrazzo* and the beach); a famous Swedish actor (also set to be in *Serenissima*) who is an old lover of mine (like my Swedish director, due to arrive in a day or so); and a variety of others who are not yet in evidence.

My photo duty done, I break free of the crowd and am ushered up to my room, informed that *i bagagli* will follow. I am carrying the cellophane-shrouded roses, but my room is already full of other roses: one bunch from the president of the Biennale, another from the managing director of the hotel, another from the president of the *giuria*. I open each card eagerly — hoping it will prove to be a bouquet from a lover rather than an obligatory bouquet from an official who is duty-bound to proffer obligatory *fiori*. Alas, this is not the case. I have no lover at the moment — and this is purely by choice. But apparently the female of the species is psychologically constructed in such a manner that she cannot open the card in a bouquet of roses without wondering whether some new and delicious lover will soon enter (stage left) and audition for a role in her autobiography.

I crank up the shutters and throw open the two giant windows that face the Adriatic. Diaphanous white curtains fly in my face propelled by the wind from the sea. It is still there — slightly tarnished by pollution, but eternal. Polluted or not, the sea is the very embodiment of eternity. "Wavewhite wedded words shimmering on the dim tide," said Joyce — who apparently said everything not said by Shakespeare. And there's the Lido: the Byzantine white tents of the Excelsior, reminding me of Visconti's film of *Death in Venice;* the fat little *bambini* gallivanting on the sand, reminding me how far away I am from all that — cut off from the quotidian demands of motherhood and wifedom; the *paparazzi* reminding me, as they coagulate on the *terrazzo*, of the whole absurd dance of fame and status, starmongering and starmaking, crescendo and diminuendo, which I feel somehow removed from even though it is the context (if not the inner texture) of my life.

Suddenly elated to be alone, I whirl around to inspect my room. I love it! From the great spun-sugar Murano chandelier, to the faintly old-fashioned mirrored armoires for my clothes, to the hi-tech Italian bathroom with its civilized bidet and its big, deep tub, to the "frigo bar" with its parades of little bottles — amber cognac, Scotch, and amaretto, crystal sambuca, deep golden Galliano and strega, pale golden champagne, dark golden Vouvray, Pouilly-Fuissé, and a variety of wines from the Veneto. I strip to my red teddy (bought in London, lavish with loverless lace), pick out a split of Pinot Grigio, my favorite, open it, pour it into a glass, and toast myself and the sea.

"To the sea," I say in my best mock heroic manner, stepping up onto my little balcony and sipping the wine stagily.

"To Byron, to Browning, to Shakespeare. To Venice, the Serenissima . . ."

There's a knock at the door. "Shit!" I say and balance my wine glass on the stone railing. I throw a toweling robe — CIGA-issue — over my bare shoulders and stride (in my high heels) to the door expecting to find my weathered Vuitton luggage and especially my footlocker of books crammed with Shakespeare. Instead there's a flash of lights, yellow spots before my eyes, and when those clear, a dark little man in a brown hat, holding a Nikon aloft.

"Smile pleeza," he says. "Say cheeza. . . ."

Another flash. The camera goes off once more before I slam the door.

"*Vada via!*" I shout from behind the door. "*Vada via!*"

My little private idyll is ruined. The film festival has begun with a flash.

The luggage arrives a little while later and I glimpse the brown-hatted man — the Ron Galella of Venice — still lurking hopefully in the hall. This time I outsmart him by hiding behind the door as my bags are brought in. Oh, what stratagems we are driven to! I calm my nerves as I meticulously unpack, sipping a freshly poured glass of wine. I have brought ball gowns and cocktail dresses, bathing suits and blue jeans, sweat suits and sneakers, to carry me through the autumn filming of *Serenissima*. Most of all, I have brought books — for life on location can be a kind of imprisonment of waiting, and my usual way of dealing with this is to lose myself in books that will help me lose myself in my role. My footlocker is fairly bursting with Shakespeare, with books of Venetian history and Venetian art, with books about the Jews in Venice, Shakespeare biographies, Shakespeare criticism. I unpack it carefully and line up the volumes on my desk as if they could be my wall against the world, my protection, my fortress, my castle.

There, I think, setting out the books, as well as a silver-framed portrait of my much-missed daughter, Antonia (taken from me with lengthy briefs and the lying testimonies of lying witnesses); a Rigaud candle to scent the room so that it smells like home; my little diary, the leather-covered journal bearing — or baring — my heart into the future; and the other objects that give me comfort: my magic rose-quartz crystal, my crystal ball on its little golden stand, the silver casket given me by my teacher and mentor Vivian Lovecraft, the great Shakespearean actress. (Graven on it are the words: "Jessica my girl, catch this casket; it is worth the pains. — Vivian") *There*, I think, I am safe now.

But apparently I am not, for another knock comes at the door.

"*Chi è?*" I shout, wrapping my robe tightly around me to foil my nemesis.

"Maid, pleeza," comes the reply.

I cautiously open the door to discover a huge bouquet of long-stemmed white roses — three dozen, it appears — towering above a Venetian vase of candy-striped pink glass.

The Ron Galella of Venice is still lofting the expectant Nikon, so I snatch the roses and hastily shut the door, promising myself to leave a good tip for the maid later. I put the roses on the cocktail table by the window, dash back to bolt the door, and then collapse in a chair, admiring the blooms. Who could these be from, I wonder. Whoever it is, it must be someone who knows me well, for white roses are my favorite flowers; my garden in Pacific Palisades is full of white roses.

There's an envelope attached to one of the long stems with a white satin ribbon. JESSICA is all it says. Inside there's a piece of heavy parchment which I open to reveal, lettered in beautiful calligraphy, these words:

To the Onlie Begetter
from her humble admirer W.S.

And then, in the same beautiful calligraphy, Sonnet Sixty-one.

Is it thy will thy image should keep open
My heavy eyelids to the weary night?

Dost thou desire my slumbers should be broken,
While shadows, like to thee, do mock my sight?
Is it thy spirit that thou send'st from thee
So far from home into my deeds to pry,
To find out shames and idle hours in me,
The scope and tenor of thy jealousy?
O no! thy love, though much, is not so great.
It is my love that keeps mine eye awake,
Mine own true love that doth my rest defeat,
To play the watchman ever for thy sake.
    For thee watch I, whilst thou dost wake elsewhere,
    From me far off, with others all too near.

A joke, I think. A message from Björn to get me ready for my part (as if I needed it). Björn is full of tricks like this. Posing as "W.S." — how typical of him! Pleased as I am with the roses, I am a little put out by the Shakespearean imposture. Björn should know by now that I hardly need *his* tricks to get me into the part. I am a consummate professional — as professional as he, despite our occasional dives into panic, passion, and near-madness.

Merely arriving at the hotel has been an ordeal. First the photo session on the landing, then the delay for luggage, then being ambushed in my hotel room by the brown-hatted *paparazzo* — who, for all I know, is still outside. Then, these trick roses . . . I am not enough on my guard, I think. I am too vulnerable. And it is all the fault of Venice. Venice is the place where I let go. Venice is the place where I do not feel protection is necessary.

I had been there a mere two months ago, living in a friend's house in Dorsoduro, wandering from the baker to the *gelateria* with no *paparazzi* trailing, shopping for fish on the Rialto, reading my books on Shakespeare and Italy in the sixteenth century, preparing for my role as Jessica. Venice had been jolly in July. We'd had five beastly days of sirocco, but by the time Redentore rolled around, and the garlanded fishing boats bobbed on the Giudecca Canal under the fireworks and the full moon, the weather was perfection. Vivaldi and Monteverdi were heard over the waters as the entire city turned out for this *festa di tutte le feste*, the Feast of the Redeemer, the ending of the plague in 1576 for which Palladio's Church of the Redentore was built.

The Redentore *was* Venice for me — the most serene of festivals. Where else in the world could you float along in an old, leaky Torcello fishing boat, hearing Vivaldi and Monteverdi waft over the lagoon while firework nebulae exploded all around you? People passed food and wine from boat to boat. *Prosecco* poured over the prows, baptizing them anew. The rhythm of the sea, which is the essence of Venice, pulsed in the music of that glorious period when Venice was still the terror of the tides.

Each city has its own rhythm. Venice's rhythm is the Adriatic lapping. New York, my hometown, my springboard, has a whir like a dynamo humming in the night. Driving down from New England, you hit the Greenwich toll and hear it — a palpable whir like a million insects (cicadas or crickets, say — though they are probably really roaches) rubbing their legs together, all wanting to be first, to be best, to be king, to be queen, to be emperor, to be Caesar, to be doge. L.A., the Land of LaLa, my current home, has another rhythm altogether: deceptively calm — with a sort of cocaine frenzy underneath. The air is *soft*. The palm trees wave. The desert is not far off, and the sea — the great Pacific — is there, glorious as always. But wedged between desert and sea, a strange species of agents and moguls and women, who *look* like flesh and blood (but are really bionic), have managed to transform the City of the Angels into a city of very minor demons — demons of "step deals" and "power lunches," demons of "turnaround," "pay or play," "net profits," and "gross from dollar one." People in the Land of LaLa look like expensive wax fruit. And they work hard to achieve that look. They have exercise coaches and psychic nutritionists, surgeons who specialize in tummy tucks and breast implants, lifts and lipectomies, rhinoplasties and rhytidectomies. Their clothes are scantier but in a way just as elaborate as the clothes of sixteenth-century Venice, for they, too, betrayed status. And the Land of LaLa has its own sumptuary laws: starlets wear clothes of one rank, the wives of moguls another, and the stars — the stars create the fashions as Queen Elizabeth, the great Gloriana, once did for her court.

In New York and Los Angeles I was used to being on my guard — but in Venice I let go. I had best remember that the film festival was not truly Venice but a sort of overseas branch of LaLa Land. I had best remember the rules, or I was sunk. . . .

I glance at the sonnet again, then read it over to myself slowly. At first, it seems to be another sonnet about insomnia, Shakespeare's great theme — and lover's insomnia at that. But one line resonates as I read: "To play the watchman ever for thy sake." What is Björn telling me? That he is still in love with me? That he is losing sleep pining for me? Impossible.

And yet it says, "For thee watch I, whilst thou dost wake elsewhere. . . ." Is he waking in Sweden while I am sleeping in Santa Monica? No. Sweden is nine hours *later* than LaLa Land. It doesn't work. And Björn, when he plays tricks, plays tricks that work.

I order a light supper from room service, draw a bath for myself, and soak in it, awaiting my *carpaccio* and *insalata mista*. Aha, I think, I will outwait the little man — my nemesis, my Rumpelstiltskin, my flasher, my personal *paparazzo*. Here I am in Venice, the end point of exotic travels, and Venice has as usual made her doubleness apparent to me from the very moment of my arrival. City of grand illusions and funhouse mirrors; city of high artifice and low trickery; city of astounding greatness and impossible pettiness. City of history, mystery, doubleness, deception. It is all here and I am in its grasp.

2

Festival del Cinema

NEXT MORNING, the international press has my red teddy (and CIGA robe) plastered all over. And my words are blown up to tabloid-size type, giving them a Garboesque resonance I never intended.

> *LA PRUITT DICE COME LA GARBO:*
> *"I WANT TO BE ALONE"*
> *«Vada via,» grida la star internazionale Jessica*
> *Pruitt mentre la fotografano all'apertura della Mostra*
> *del Cinema. . . . «Vada via. Voglio star sola. . . .»*

You can imagine the rest. It is made to appear that I am camera shy and have fought off the good, decent, humble, honest press, hiding behind my haughty "incognita," refusing even a flash of teeth. Teeth, indeed!

The Festival del Cinema opens officially with the *giuria* assembling in the lobby of the Excelsior. Again we are lined up for a group portrait.

"Jessica, Jessica," comes the call of the *paparazzi*.

"Say *denaro*," says one waggish fellow with a Hasselblad on a tripod — a rich *paparazzo*.

"*Soldi*," I say, hissing. Already branded for the world as camera shy, what have I got to lose? Except that I have broken the cardinal rule: Never joke with the press. Irony does not translate into newsprint.

"*Denaro*," I say, relenting. I am caught in that moment of kissing the air with inky lips by thirty cameras disseminating my soul (by wire, in dot matrix) all over the world.

Journalists are everywhere scribbling away. (What could they be writing? We haven't *done* anything yet.) I see the surrealist poet with long white hair (Carlos Armada is his name) giving a lofty quote to an ink-stained wretch and laughing in that mirthless, self-congratulatory way public persons laugh on public occasions. I am acutely aware that all the other members of the jury are male and I the only female.

"You smile all the time," says Grigory Krylov, the tall Russian poet with the arctic eyes. "A typical American."

"I only smile when I'm nervous," I say.

"And when you're not nervous, how are you?" asks Grigory.

"Then I don't smile so much."

"Ah, the glah-morous Jessica Pruitt." Grigory sighs, drawing himself up to his full height of six feet six inches. "Do you know that I'm the only man in the world who can destroy you? Is that why you avoid me?" He puts his arm around me possessively. I step away neatly.

He is making the statement as much for the entourage as for me, but it genuinely makes me laugh.

"Perhaps *that's* why I avoid you," I say. "I'm too old and too tired to get involved with men who want to destroy me. At twenty, I'd have found you irresistible."

"You can't be more than twenty now — Jessichka, my Dzark Ladzy of the Sonnets. . . ." And he begins to quote what seems to be Shakespeare in Russian — a mellifluous sound that quite undoes me, though I know no Russian but *da* and *nyet*.

"Did you send the roses, Grigory?" I ask.

"Call me Grisha," he says. "No — but I shall do it at once if I may lie at your breast with them. . . . But watch out — I have thorns. *Big* thorns!"

Has nobody *told* the Russians that this style of male braggadocio has been out of fashion for twenty years? Apparently not. This is no postfeminist machismo — this is just plain old male-chauvinist pigism of the old days. I find it almost endearingly quaint.

We parade the short distance from the Excelsior to the Palazzo del Cinema, followed by the press. Besides Grigory — or Grisha — Krylov, who has staked me out as his prey, and Carlos Armada, whose dishy Italian girlfriend is along for the walk, there are Walter Wildhonig, the bristling German playwright; Benjamin Gabriel Gimpel, the pale, shrunken Nobel laureate; Pierre de Houbigant, the vague aristocratic painter; Leonardo da Leone, the twitching intellectual film director who is the chairman of the *giuria;* and Gaetano Manuzio, the anti-intellectual film director who has no tic and is accompanied by his actress-wife Elisabetta Grillo and his actress-mistress Barbara da Ponte. Also, there is Per Erlanger, the Swedish actor who is set to play Shylock in *Serenissima.* Like his character, he is a lugubrious and bittersweet Jew.

The Lido sun is very bright as we march to the theater, trailed by *paparazzi,* attracting swarms of *bambini* seeking autographs.

Motorcycles roar by. Taxis barely miss us — for the Lido is not truly Venice, that city without wheels, but a spiritual (if not physical) extension of the mainland. At the Palazzo del Cinema, we are brought upstairs to an office and photographed yet again, this time for our badges. Each of us is given a little golden tag with LA BIENNALE and MOSTRA INTERNAZIONALE DEL CINEMA printed on the back and our names and GIURIA printed on the front beneath our pictures. These badges will be our tickets of entry into the films, the prize ceremonies, and all the major events of the next several days.

When our photos have been taken, we are ushered down to the stage.

"Ladies accompanying, please within," says a functionary, assuming I am just a chickie, because of my gender.

"She's a member of the jury," says Grigory, taking a proprietary interest in me. "See, Jessichka, the smiling American needs the non-smiling Russian."

Grigory is famous for being a survivor, an artful dodger, and (some say) KGB man. The only Soviet poet — except, of course, for Yevtushenko — who has managed to stay in the Soviet Union while still writing anti-Soviet poems, he is the Kremlin's token rebel, the writer they send out into the world to demonstrate Soviet freedom of speech. Consequently, he is suspected of hypocrisy by everyone. Dissident Russians detest him, American writers suspect him despite his charm, and the PEN club welcomes him but not without a subtext of whispers. It is said that he lives in a glorious dacha outside Moscow; is attended by students, servants, and mistresses; drives in a chauffeured car; and shops in those special stores reserved for the Soviet elite. That he travels all over the world I surely know, because I have met him several times at gigs like these — that eternal round of prize-givings, festivals, free cruises, and rubber chicken dinners that are the price, and the dubious booty, of fame.

I keep walking away from Grigory, but he keeps catching up with me. When we are led to our seats on the stage, Grigory takes the one next to me. Resigned to him as my shadow, I decide to make conversation.

"Do you like Venice?" I ask.

"Don't ask empty questions," he snaps.

(But for me it is not an empty question, since Venice is the city of my heart.)

"How Russian and judgmental you are," I whisper.

"How American and trivial you are, Jessichka."

"Is this the Russian way of flirting — abuse and insult?"

"Yes. And then I drag you to my cave."

He smiles for the cameras, striking his best angle. Grigory is movie-star handsome (high, Slavic cheekbones, retroussé nose) and movie-star vain, but the creases in his pale brow (and the darting blue eyes beneath) betray the price he has paid for being a survivor in a country where artists are either silenced in Siberia or speak with forked tongue all over the world.

But then I am a survivor, too; survivor of a system just as brutal to artists in its own way. I have paid for my passion for Shakespeare with movie and television roles so silly that sometimes I wanted to giggle (or weep) when I first read the script. I have been murdered again and again, seduced and abandoned again and again, and now that I am in my "middle years" (though just how middle, I do not say) I sometimes play the *mother* of the girl who gets murdered or seduced, or seduced and murdered. The whole women's movement came and went without murder and seduction ceasing to be the principal fate of woman on film. Which is why I am happy to be working again with Björn. At least his women are subject to fates more complex — if no less brutal.

I cross my legs. A hundred cameras with flash attachments are at knee level. We are on the stage and the photographers are crouched directly below the footlights. The president of the Biennale makes a long speech full of words like *artisticamente, belle arti, cinema come arte*. When people talk about art, I reach for my gun. Every scoundrel with a sinecure prates of art. We who attempt to *do* it (however imperfectly) know that sometimes one has to be murdered on film to pay the rent, and sometimes one works for love — though love doesn't pay for Vuitton luggage nor for the kinds of clothes you need when crossing your legs before a hundred photographers.

I am wearing a purple silk dress full of odd-shaped patches of purple print, gold lamé, and silver lamé — a Koos van den Akker collage. On my feet are golden gladiator sandals; on my toenails, golden polish. I take my sunglasses off and put them on, aware that merely sitting here is part of my performance. I wet my lips with my tongue. From time to time Grigory, also an actor in his way, gives my shoulder a squeeze and smiles at the press. The flashbulbs accelerate dramatically.

The president of the Biennale is followed by the mayor of Venice, who is followed by the president of the film festival, who is followed by some unknown cultural *capo*, who is followed by the president of the jury. As the speeches go on and on, I drift away into another world . . . the movie I would write if I dared write anywhere except in my journal, my own little filmic fantasy of Venice. . . .

> *Two young men are arriving in the Serenissima. They are Elizabethan dandies, men of the world, and they have sailed from London to Southampton, Southampton to Lisbon, Lisbon to Cadiz, Cadiz to the Balearic Islands, the Balearic Islands to Palermo, Palermo to Messina, Messina to Corfu, then up the Adriatic coast to Zara, Trieste, and Venice. The journey has been long, the*

rations at sea half rotten and wormy, and the ports along the way teeming with slaves and prostitutes, escaped criminals, and all the wretched refuse of the earth. They have sailed in a Venetian galley — the galley of Flanders, say, that plied the Atlantic route to Bruges and Antwerp, with stops at Southampton and London. This great, wide-beamed merchant ship sailed the seas in a convoy of three or four other such vessels, great galleys with lateen sails, and nearly two hundred oarsmen as well. . . . An astounding ship for its size and height, at times it was so swift it could make the journey from Southampton to Venice in as few as thirty-one days, except that on this occasion there were all sorts of uncontemplated delays — delays of a sort that a young poet and his still younger noble patron would delight in at first as fit meat for future poesy, but then grow tired of as the delays multiplied and the meat grew less fit. . . .

Many of their fellow travelers do not have Venice as their final destination but are going onward in summer in the galley of Beirut toward Corfu, Crete, Rhodes, Cypress, Palestine, and the holy shrines. . . . The Venetians will accommodate all these travelers, who, along with spice and silks, silver and gold, constitute, even then, the wealth of the Serenissima. But our two travelers are men of the quill, men of the playhouse, and they are stopping in Venice in part to see those marvels unguessed as yet in London — women players, as famed in the Serenissima as her golden-haired cortigiane *(who write poetry), her masked balls and carnivals, her state celebrations upon the waters, and her great regattas.*

The poet is of humble origin, auburn-haired, with luminous, dark brown eyes and one golden earring glinting in his left ear. He's a simple glover's son from Stratford, but his young friend with the flaxen ringlets is a Lord of the Realm, the Earl of Southampton. "Harry" he is called to his friend's simple "Will." The Earl of Southampton, Henry Wriothesley, being well connected, has no need to lodge at the White Lion Inn but is invited to sojourn with a family of Venetian aristocrats in a palazzo on the Grand Canal. . . . Thus, like many young men for centuries to come, these two Elizabethan dandies, in their hose and doublets, daggers and pistols, set foot in the lagoon city, their heads ablaze with fancies of the sights and sins, the sins and sights of Venice,

24

*that capital city of dream and intrigue, that double city (one
above and seemingly solid, one below, wavering and reflected in
the waters), which never disappoints. . . .*

*They have fled England — these two — because the plague
has closed the playhouses, and the young player-poet earns his
living on the stage. His patron finds this a rather mean and low
occupation and prefers that his friend write sonnets, at which he
is unparalleled, or epics on mythological themes, with which he
is on the verge of making a gaudy reputation — but young Will
persists in believing that only on the stage is the word made
flesh, and if the London playhouses are closed then he will repair
to Venice, where plays still flourish and where Englishmen may
learn Italian ways. . . .*

The speeches cease. The lights come up. Suddenly we are all being
herded toward the wings where yet more photographers wait. My
two Elizabethan dandies have vanished and I am back at the film
festival again, playing Jessica, playing myself.

Grigory Krylov puts a possessive arm around my shoulders, beams
at the world press, and in a volley of flashbulbs we go to lunch.

Being a member of the jury at the film festival proves to be no boon-
doggle. It reminds me of touring Southern penitentiaries in a desperate road show of *Medea*. (I did this once and it remains for me
the very nadir of an actor's life.) So it is with film festivals. The
screenings begin at ten A.M. and go on all day until six, excepting
three hours for the sacred Italian lunch break, then more films follow in the evening. Dinner is gulped in the half hour between the
end of the eight o'clock film and the start of the ten-thirty film, and
sometimes there are midnight screenings as well.

Watching so many films, I begin to feel, is like being immersed in
someone else's bad dreams. I seem to slide into the third person or
into other lives not my own, the fitful dreams of dozens of mediocre
poets. I would rather be a character in Shakespeare's dream, I think.
I would rather be making *The Merchant of Venice* — for I am yearning to work again. But no: I am stuck in some endless replay of the

Second World War. If the Second World War did not exist, it would be necessary to invent it.

And so we have. A ceaseless battle between good and evil goes on, embodied by the stock comic book figures of good American (or good Russian) and bad Nazi. There are American films about the Second World War, Russian films about the Second World War, Polish films about the Second World War, Swedish, Finnish, Danish, and Czech films about the Second World War. In one of these — a Russian one, it appears — a man goes back to Germany to revisit the town where he first became a man. As a young soldier he invaded this town, fell in love there, and first knew the terrible dichotomy between love and war. His German *Mädchen* still awaits him, now become a stout blonde matron of forty, widowed by her good German burgher (formerly a captain in the SS).

They whirl on the dance floor, and the bombed-out town regrows its bricks and beams as though they were shrubs and trees. Time stops. The couple freezes on the dance floor. Their youth and the Second World War are one. Man's need to plunder and woman's need to cling are embodied in this myth of the Second World War, and so on it goes, eternally played on the screens of our retinas. When will this war be over? The "good war," the war of my parents' generation, has an independent existence, independent of history itself. We keep it alive because it is needed, because we need a myth of good battling evil and triumphing. Our generation has no such myth. Our generation knows that when evil battles good, it's often no contest — or a draw. Or else life is too complicated to be characterized in those terms. That's the tragedy of our generation — we haven't even *got* a myth of good battling evil. We are mythed out. Except for Shakespeare. And who reads Shakespeare anymore but actors and poets?

Ah, little girls at private schools in New York read Shakespeare. My ten-year-old Antonia has already memorized a few sonnets, having inherited her mother's memory for lines of verse. I cannot think of my daughter without pain — though I know she is well taken care of, physically if not emotionally. An only daughter is a needle in the heart, some fluent Irishman once said. And it is true.

In the dreamlike, womblike screening room, I think of her and ache; she is with me always.

Nor is my longing for my daughter diminished by the films themselves, for the other great myth enshrined in the films I see is the myth of childhood — childhood innocence, to be precise. In one Russian film, two adolescents keep traversing a frozen lake, looking for a sunken cathedral. When they find its golden onion dome, frozen in snow and ice, they remember childhood summers when they used to dive in this very lake, swim into the tower of this submerged cathedral, and pull on the bell cord underwater, creating an eerie symphony of underwater chimes. Through frame after frame, the girl holds one ear to the ice, listening for this summer symphony. (The girl is about Antonia's age and indeed looks like her — copper hair, freckled nose, a little girl's lanky yet pot-bellied body.) Again and again the filmmaker cuts to the boy, swimming like a merman underwater, pulling the bell cord. Childhood, like a bell, calls us back again and again. "Ding-dong bell," says Shakespeare. Full fathom five thy childhood lies, of its bones are coral made.

There are wonderful moments, wonderful images, in all these films, but in general the level is mediocre to low. So many have labored so long and so hard to produce films that don't quite work. The colossal effort of it all! I know that making a film, even a bad one, is like orchestrating an entire world war. The script has to be written and rewritten, the money raised, the cast found, the locations scouted, and thousands of logistical arrangements fulfilled. Through it all, hundreds upon hundreds of egos have to be stroked (or bullied) lest the whole enterprise collapse. You have to be a great general to be a film director, as well as a great visionary. Today, Napoleon would be a film director, and Custer, and Robert E. Lee. And yet all this effort, all this cajoling, caterwauling, casting, and casting about for completion bonds and last-minute infusions of cash can easily come to naught if the essential theme is too paltry, too unworthy of all this effort. Great films need great subjects and there are few enough minds that can conceive of great subjects in these small times. Björn is one. And Björn always goes back to the classics. Mozart and Shakespeare — these are his muses. He knows that

27

in a spiritually bankrupt time, an artist should at least know enough to go back to the classics.

Another day's screenings over, the jury yawns, stretches, thinks of food. We trudge back to our rooms at the Excelsior, dodging photographers, trying to remember what we have seen. Dozens of phone messages are jammed under our doors, along with schedules of the next day's cocktail receptions for directors. Björn Persson and Lilli have still not appeared. The international press speculates on the meaning of this. One of Björn's films is due to be screened the next day and the director's whereabouts are unknown.

This is pretty much how the beginning of the festival felt. The badness of the films, combined with my nine-hour jet lag, created in me the sensation of being trapped in a nightmare — and not even an exciting nightmare, but an extremely boring and repetitious one. We got up at eight-thirty, attended films all day and all night, then returned to our suites exhausted. Except I've neglected to mention that as the days passed, and Grigory Krylov escorted me to the screenings and back home to the hotel again, it started to appear in the press that we were lovers. At least, pictures of us together kept cropping up in the papers and little innuendoes in the gossip columns created the illusion that we shared a bed as well as a flashbulb.

This didn't bother me particularly since, as an actress, my whole life is illusion, and *I* knew I was not Grigory's lover. Besides, when I was younger and a sex symbol, I'd had the experience of perfect (or imperfect) strangers coming up to me on the streets of New York or even London or Paris and saying in the appropriate language: "You are disgusting — whore!" and spitting at me. I never knew then whether my roles were at fault (for a while I played prostitutes in my American films) or whether the very fact of a woman being a public personage, an artist, an earner of money, created this reaction in certain frustrated souls. Needless to say, it had unnerved me when I was younger, but now that I was older (and presumably wiser) I had a healthy disregard for the causal connection between my actual behavior and what was publicly reported of me. So I gave little thought to my increasing involvement with Grigory in the public prints. At this rate, we should be married by festival's end — a horrifying prospect.

On the fifth night of the festival, Björn's film of *Don Giovanni* (in which Mozart and his father both appear as characters in a sort of framing tale for the opera) was due to be presented, and still Björn and Lilli had not arrived. I began to worry. The press was reaching a fever pitch of speculation regarding Björn's mental health, I was being pelted with telephone messages (which anyway I had no time to answer because I was always in screenings), and Grigory was becoming a gigantic pain in the ass about our newsprint love affair.

"Jessichka," he'd say as he escorted me back to the hotel from the last screening, "since anyway we are lovers in the eyes of the world, do you not think it is our fate to consummate this passion? It could be kismet, *La Forza del Destino* — no?"

"No." I'd laugh. "A newsprint love affair can never break my heart, but a real one is another matter. . . . I'm afraid I'll fall in love with you and all will be lost."

So I said to salve his ego, but in reality I was not only through with love but through with sex. Life was so much simpler without it. My head was so much clearer. And I could concentrate on my work. At night I went to bed with volumes of Shakespeare ranged around my pillow and no lover to jealously kick them onto the floor. I cherished my solitude, my books, my maidenly envelope of cool, clean sheets, my guardian white roses. What could Grigory Krylov offer me but thorns?

I had not come to this delight in solitude and chastity easily, as you might imagine. I had lived much of my life for love — with results as predictable as they are common: heartbreak, yearning, drinking too much, and stoical decisions never to love again, no sooner made than broken. But this time I was not merely determined but indifferent. Love was my addiction and I was weaning myself away from it one day at a time. Oh, it was safe enough to sleep with Shakespeare — or so I thought at the beginning of my stay in Venice.

*

29

The night Björn's *Don Giovanni* was to be presented (with or without Björn) was the night of the Red Cross Gala, when *Le Tout Venise* came across the lagoon dressed in their best glitter — the ladies in Valentinos, Krizias, Givenchys, Yves St. Laurents; the gentlemen perfectly dressed by those elderly private tailors who still can be found (if not in great abundance) in Italy.

I had bought a black Zandra Rhodes ball gown in London, with great leg-of-mutton Victorian sleeves (Princess Di's virgin wedding and Victorian wedding gown had inaugurated a whole new Victorian age — it seemed), and I was looking forward to wearing it to the gala. It was being lovingly pressed by a sweet little laundress at the hotel who had seen my films and who even kindly offered to resew some of the fallen paillettes and black pearls "in honor of my art," she said — a term that sounds less soppy in Italian. *Onore dell'arte* — a thing still known in Italy, though less and less as the American tyranny of the bottom line takes over even here.

The last afternoon screening had finished rather earlier than usual that day, and the Red Cross Gala was due to begin only at eight-thirty or nine. So while my glorious Zandra Rhodes was being pressed, I betook myself to the bar to order a cappuccino in a quiet corner — an act of courage, really, since I might be besieged there.

I found a little round table in a sort of nook that overlooked the sea, and positioned myself so that I faced away from the bar and toward a plate-glass window that gave out on a *terrazzo* usually teeming with *paparazzi* and autograph-collecting *bambini*, but at this moment empty because of the odd hour. Everyone was either eating or getting sloshed at private happy hours in bars, press suites, or hotel room rendezvous.

I sipped my cappuccino contentedly, savoring the sweet foam. If only we could live for the little moments that linger only fleetingly on the taste buds, I thought, life could be so fulfilling. The trouble is: we want too much. Grand passions, great historical movements, the need to possess things, people, houses. Sometimes, I think that I have always been happiest in transit — in rented houses, or while flying from one place to another. I know that I have been happiest between marriages — when all was possibility untapped and nothing was nailed down, when tomorrow the prince of princes, the poet of poets, the lover of all time, might walk through the door and lift my life to paradise.

With this thought, I laughed aloud at myself over my cappuccino. Imagine having such a romantic notion while claiming to be the arch antiromantic of all time. And yet the two are very close, aren't they? Romanticism and antiromanticism, flip sides of the same coin? Though I had been married and married, my heart always leapt in assent when Gloria Steinem said she had never married because she "couldn't mate in captivity." Marriage seemed to be like castling in chess — a useless move that saved neither the king's life nor the game.

"May I?" came a voice.

I looked up to see a young man with brown and luminous spaniel eyes, shaggy brown hair, an aggressively badly cut tweed jacket such as German intellectuals wear in München or Berlin (to show their contempt for frippery), and a pleading mouth. I recognized him as one of the German delegation, a young man who wrote films for — or coproduced with, or fetched schnapps for — one of the great German directors here to receive a prize, but whether this young man was called Rainer or Karl or Wolfgang, I swear I could not remember.

"Wolfgang Schnabel," he offered, refreshing my recollection. "May I?"

"Of course," I said, sighing.

"But, I interrupt your thoughts?"

"No, no," I said. (What woman has thoughts that cannot be interrupted by a man?)

"So," he said. "Your first film festival?"

"And last," said I. "It's too much work, and the films aren't good enough to merit all this time — except, of course, the ones out of competition, like your director's."

"Of course," said he. "But we come for other reasons. To meet our *Kollegen* — colleagues — to raise money for future films, to be inspired by beauty. . . ."

Here he looked deep into my eyes.

"And I do not mean — how say you — celluloid beauty but the real beauty, the *Modell* for beauty, Venus herself or Aphrodite. . . ."

(He pronounced it "Afro-ditty.")

"Ich meine — Dich. I mean you. . . ."

I grew embarrassed by this German blarney. Was it just a pass, or was it the real German schmaltz, a yearning, young Goethe besotted with poetry and art? For Wolfgang looked to be about twenty-eight or twenty-nine, the prime age for hungering young men who fall in love with cinema queens. Don't be a cynical pill, Jessica, I said to myself. Maybe this young Werther is really aching for you — *Schatzi.* They do that aching thing so well in Germany. But I also wanted to giggle. Love, *Liebe, amour, amore* — it was all a trap to make you crazy, to make you obsessed. I knew where it led: cock above art. Yearning for that special, sweet rod that would make the world go away. Well, I liked the world — with its cappuccino, its candy-chandeliered hotel suites, its *motoscafi,* its screening rooms, its temporal amusements while we waited for eternity to begin. Down with love if it meant annihilating all of that.

While I mused, Wolfgang burned his eyes into my own.

"I have no words," he said. "You are the wonder of this festival."

"No," I said. "You are too kind."

"Not kind at all," he said, "or, as your poet says, 'a little more than kin and less than kind.' "

Shakespeare again. Why did Shakespeare seem to be everywhere in the air? Was I drawing him to me with my thoughts of him? For I believed in such magic. I knew an artist was a sort of witch and I had had other proofs of my witchiness in the past. Well, if I were a witch, I was a *good* witch, *una fata* — not *una strega,* or bad witch, as the Italians say. What a civilized language Italian is to have such distinctions!

Wolfgang persisted: "Your eyes are astounding — never from your photographs could I have guessed. Not even your films do them justice. . . ."

"Thank you," I said, blazing my eyes at him the harder, trying to make time melt and Wolfgang become my Shakespeare, if only for a moment. For it is part of my craft to make every swain fall in love with me. I do it for sport, for craftsmanship, on a bet, on a dare. My heart fills, my thighs ache; my silk panties moisten; the sense memories of love make me feel that I feel love though I love not — or only love my art — ah, my first acting teacher, Arnold Feibleman, would be proud of me! As would dear feisty Vivian Lovecraft, my mentor. To make someone believe you are in love when you are not — this is my craft, my witchery. For, as I gaze into Wolfgang's eyes, I fall in love with the image of my beloved self that I see there. Oscar Wilde was right: an actress is a little more than a woman, an actor a little less than a man. I cannot help myself, I am in love with the Jessica that Wolfgang is in love with! I am besotted with my craft, like a witch who turns a mouse into a lizard only to prove she *can*. Poor mouse, poor lizard, what do *they* know? Acted on as they are by the powers that be, what do *they* feel when time stops and the fur turns scale? Poor creatures. *Poveretti*. We witches, we actresses, are as wanton boys to flies; we kill them for our sport —

Stop it! I think.

Stop it. You'll mislead this boy and then you'll be sorry. You'll have to pay in bed. And then he'll make *you* pay. You'll start out blithe and end in bondage. *Basta*.

But no. He looks at me with those deep and burning eyes and says again, "You are the wonder of this place. Do not leave this night unless you leave with me."

He touches my hand. For a moment, I am stirred. I could easily (so deep is the power even of suggested love) go to my suite with him, make love, and even be moved by it. Surely I have done it often enough in the past — though whether I was in love with sex, with the man, or with my own witchy power is not clear.

But I resist. And the battle is not a difficult one — no Lepanto this, no Waterloo, just a simple decision not to succumb. As I invoked this poet, so can I also banish him. Besides, he is speaking in a foreign tongue, his words of love half translated from another language.

"Your eyes," he says again. "You have the most extraordinary eyes." He is still burning, not yet realizing that I have turned the fire off as simply as one turns off the jets in one of those L.A. fireplaces. I run my finger along the hairy back of his hand, stand up, clasp my bag, and say, "I must go and change now. Thank you for all your kind words." It is how I would close the response to a fan letter.

"May I escort you to your room?"

Persistent bugger, isn't he? Well, men go through the world led by their cocks, plunging here, plunging there, while women are finally mothers or else deniers of maternity. Hundreds of years of feminism and that's where we still are. It's all so simple and human. Both sexes have their griefs, their pains — equally as sharp. I pity them both.

"No, I must go alone," I say.

And so I must, even though traversing the lobby will be, as usual, a trial.

I walk briskly to the elevator, looking down, avoiding the eyes upon me — including Wolfgang's long, lingering stare, which burns holes in my back.

Up in my suite again, I find my ball gown carefully hung in the armoire, the paillettes and pearls all carefully restored. And turning around, I suddenly see another gigantic bunch of white roses, to replace the rather wilting ones of five days past.

Again there is the parchment envelope, with JESSICA on the outside, and within, again in beautiful calligraphy, another sonnet.

> Being your slave, what should I do but tend
> Upon the hours and times of your desire?
> I have no precious time at all to spend,
> Nor services to do, till you require.
> Nor dare I chide the world-without-end hour
> Whilst I, my sovereign, watch the clock for you,
> Nor think the bitterness of absence sour
> When you have bid your servant once adieu.
> Nor dare I question with my jealous thought
> Where you may be, or your affairs suppose,

But, like a sad slave, stay and think of naught
Save, where you are, how happy you make those.
So true a fool is love that in your will,
Though you do anything, he thinks no ill.

I read the sonnet and it gives me chills.

3

White Rose, Red Cross

THE WHOLE PALAZZO DEL CINEMA is ablaze with lights the night of the Red Cross Gala. And the ladies are arriving, dressed in their Krizias and Valentinos, their St. Laurents and Givenchys. The men — well-brought-up aristocrats (or pseudoaristocrats) that they are — all know how to kiss a lady's hand by bringing the fingers not quite to their lips and kissing the air that eddies above the flesh. As they do this, they bring their heels together in a sort of Prussian salute. It is all terribly decadent and nineteenth century — a little *Anna Karenina* in the midst of the punk Lido of the eighties, where teenagers with spiky orange hair, or shaven heads sporting one long, black braid, roar around on immense, phallic motorcycles.

I am wearing my black Zandra Rhodes Victorian fantasy (and underneath it, a red-trimmed black Merry Widow that dangles red satin garters). I am staggering about on four-inch heels from Susan Bennis/Warren Edwards, having forsaken my comfortable Maud Frizons for this occasion. That the black Merry Widow makes me look like the heroine of a de Sade novel is known only to me — nonetheless, it gives me special secret pleasure as I cling to Grigory's arm, entering the Palazzo del Cinema, and the photographers' flash attack begins.

Grigory is wearing a very un-Soviet Savile Row tux, with red silk bow tie and red silk cummerbund ("in honor of the Party, Comrade Jessichka"). He strokes my cheek, cuddles my bare shoulder, squeezes my hand — all for the benefit of the press. I am starting to feel a little miffed by these constant displays of bogus passion, but also curiously resigned. The press will pair me with *someone* — so why not Grigory, who, after all, is photogenic and makes good copy? I feel as if my pseudobiography is being created even as I live my actual life. Who would believe that I sleep with Shakespeare? Who would believe that on my bedside table is a tall bottle of San Pellegrino and on my pillow the same volumes of sonnets, comedies, tragedies I went to bed with as a book-mad adolescent girl?

Grigory and I are seated in the special section reserved for the jury. We are in the second row, right behind Walter Wildhonig *und Frau*, Benjamin Gabriel Gimpel and wife, and Leonardo da Leone and *fidanzata*. The other members of the jury are ranged around us. Sitting right in front of us is an ancient woman whom I do not recognize. She continually fondles a silver-headed cane, and from time to time she turns to stare at me intensely as if she were about to speak. I notice that her right eye is much larger than her left and both her eyes glitter like dark crystals. A musty odor of mothballs and garlic issues from her clothes. The sight of her makes me uneasy — as if she were spying on me.

The air is stiflingly hot. I feel the stays of my corset pressing into my flesh, almost as if I were an Elizabethan lady. My books on Shakespeare have made me particularly aware of feminine costume and its effect on women's lives. Just as I have gazed at the famous Chandos portrait of W.S. and felt that I knew and loved the man behind those luminous brown eyes, those eyes of genius and lust, of tenderness and resignation to the cruelties and follies of the world, so too have I gazed at portraits of his queen and marveled at her attire. To be a woman of will and determination, seduction and guile, in an age that demanded tightly laced corsets, immense ruffs that rose to the back of the neck in great gauze wings, and, under all, a wheel farthingale — which made one's very skirt into a kind of pup tent to be maneuvered through doors, into coaches, onto litters — why, what discipline this *alone* required! Nor did Elizabeth shrink from it. Tough as any man, tender as any woman, she was fast becoming my heroine. The more I read of Elizabethan England, the more I submerged the present into Shakespeare's past, the more I realized that all the last four hundred years had been a falling away from the feminism that Elizabeth herself embodied. Not for her the confusion between dressing like a man and thinking like a monarch. She *was* a monarch, but she was also a woman. And what was her strength, above all? Never marrying. Never tying her fortunes to one man. In this particular alone, she outshone (and outlasted) her cousin Mary who lost her head, and lost her head — the classic plight of woman.

It is the custom of the film festival to introduce the director and the principal actors for each film before the film is shown, but the actors have long since arrived and still Björn is not here. They wait expectantly, empty seats in their midst. There is the lovely sweet young thing who plays Donna Anna (and Constanze Mozart), the young actor who plays Don Giovanni (and Mozart), the handsome middle-aged actor who plays the Commendatore (and Leopold Mozart), and last but not least the homely middle-aged actor who plays Leporello (and Salieri).

Grigory and I have arrived late, at the very tail end of the introductions and speeches concerning the Red Cross Gala, the funds raised and by whom, the fulsome congratulatory speeches to rich matrons before whom *Le Tout Venise* grovels. This is the main difference between dogs and men (as Mark Twain might have said): dogs will not grovel before money. One lady, a certain Contessa Venier, is the chairperson of the gala. Immensely fat, with a jaundiced tinge to her freckled, oozing flesh, she is helped to the lectern by two toadies in tuxes. She herself is stuffed into an unbecoming pear-shaped sack of shocking pink chiffon, festooned with iridescent pink sequins; sinking pink satin boats support her swollen feet. She staggers to the lectern, lifts to her dim eyes a bejeweled hand bearing a bejeweled lorgnette, and reads a list of acknowledgments and thanks. This goes on for a while, delaying the commencement of the film, but still Björn and Lilli do not arrive. It's clear that the actors are extremely anxious awaiting their director. Contessa Venier drones on.

"She was a cabaret singer in Tunis," Grigory says in a stage whisper, "when Count Venier found her. At that time, *he* was married to the first Contessa Venier, whom some say she poisoned. A true story of capitalist decadence — eh, Jessichka? . . ."

I shoot Grigory a look that says: You Soviets have decadence, too — but he is so self-satisfied that he doesn't get it. All at once, the whole room seems to turn around: Björn and Lilli are entering from the rear of the mezzanine. The actors buzz among themselves. The jury turns to stare, and there is Björn, pale, blue-gray-eyed, balding Björn in an inky tux and white silk turtleneck, a long, white silk aviator scarf thrown about his neck. Sailing into the room at his side, in battleship gray moiré, is Lilli, her silver hair ballooning about her ears like a Gibson girl's, her eyes blazing green to her husband's misty blue ones — and dark with determination.

Lilli helps a rather distrait Björn down the steps of the center aisle of the mezzanine and into the section where the actors sit. The Perssons take their places while the Contessa Venier drones on, unaware of their arrival. Soon another toady in a tux is dispatched onto the stage to inform her that Björn has arrived. She looks up, sees him in the mezzanine, and begins winding up her fulsome acknowledgments. When she finally shuffles offstage, using the flunkies as crutches, the lights dim and the president of the Biennale, his face blanched moon-white by a single spotlight, comes out to introduce Björn and the leading actors in the film.

"*Si presenta in sala il maestro Björn Persson,*" says *il direttore*. And the applause is deafening. The whole orchestra section stands, almost in unison, and turns toward the mezzanine to applaud Björn, who merely nods his head and waves his hand diffidently, then indicates his actors. It is Lilli who seems to acknowledge the applause most regally, Lilli the maestro's wife, a part she was evidently born for.

"*Salute al maestro,*" *il direttore* says again. And again and again comes the deafening applause. Oh, I know the Italian habit of promoting *signore* to *dottore*, *dottore* to *professore* (even hotel directors here are called *professori* if they have been in the profession long enough and are loved and feared), but never have I heard the word *maestro* uttered with such surpassing respect.

Even when the applause abates a little and the actors are introduced, the tumult in the room is still so great that we can hardly
hear their names. The maestro is here; the maestro is triumphant.

Presently, the houselights dim and Mozart's overture to *Don Giovanni* thunders forth, full of pathos, full of the terror and wonder of
lust. This marriage of the cold north and warm south, this hybrid
of Teutonic discipline and Latin *dolce far niente* — Mozart's music
perhaps even more than Byron's poetry, or Browning's — embod-
ies the vitality that results when north falls passionately in love and
mates with south. And where more perfectly are these elements
meshed than in *Don Giovanni*, the story of a cruel, perfidious, empty
lover softened only by the prayerful playfulness of Mozart's music?
Mozart, like Shakespeare, has the ability to make even his villains
human, softening their edges with song.

A small, provincial opera company in Germany is rehearsing *Don
Giovanni*. The director of the company is in love with the soprano,
but so is his son, a charming, roguish ne'er-do-well, who is the rehearsal pianist for the company. The son is a bit mad, and in his
madness imagines himself to be Wolfgang Amadeus Mozart and his
father to be Leopold Mozart. As the opera is rehearsed he falls more
and more into a fantasy of himself as Mozart, wooing the soprano
with music he claims to have composed especially for her. All his
inadequacies as a man, an artist, a lover, are assuaged by his passionate identification with Mozart.

We cut back and forth between the rehearsals for the opera and
the offstage life that goes on among this curious love triangle. This
part of the film is in black and white: the rehearsals, the backstage
maneuvering, the introduction to the story. Then suddenly it is the
opening night of *Don Giovanni* and the film bursts out in full color.
The curtain rises and the opera begins with its thundering chords.
We see the members of the orchestra fiddling, blowing, pounding
their drums. We see the conductor's face, a mirror of the complex
beauty held captive within the music. The incomparable overture
blends into the opening scene, and suddenly we are with Leporello
as he paces before Donna Anna's house.

The opera reduces us; the opera masters us; and we are off into

its world, now identifying with Leporello as he bemoans his fate, now watching Donna Anna pursue Don Giovanni, now caught in the mortal struggle between the Commendatore and Don Giovanni, now feeling Don Giovanni's impenitence as he boasts of having raped the daughter and murdered the father.

We settle into the opera with a sense of perfect familiarity, knowing the moves to come, knowing that each of our own feelings will be uncannily embodied in a main character. In Don Giovanni, impenitent evil; in Leporello, doubt and cynicism toward a master coupled with grudging admiration; in Donna Anna, grief and outraged innocence; in Donna Elvira, bitterness and rage. We are borne along on this current of familiar feeling and on the complementary current of Mozart's music. The whole theater seems to relax. The audience is in the familiar, the traditional, a crisis whose outcome is totally known.

Björn, master magician that he is, knows all this. He allows us to wallow in the opera as far as Leporello's famous aria *Madamina, il catalogo è questo*, but just as it is coming to a close, he blasts our sense of the familiar by taking us backstage where the rehearsal pianist, the son of the director, has gone entirely mad and is claiming himself to be Wolfgang Amadeus Mozart. He insists that he has rewritten the opera in such a way that Don Giovanni does *not* go to hell at the end but instead becomes a saint and goes to heaven, and he demands that the singers perform it *his* way.

There is a palpable feeling of unrest when Björn cracks open the opera like this, but what the audience does not yet realize is that another phenomenon has been occurring simultaneously. All the empty seats and the standing room places have been filling up with punk teenagers from the Lido, who have infiltrated the theater (Have they bribed the guards? Have they overpowered them?) in a frenzy to see the mad maestro about whom there has been such speculation in the press. They are waiting in the aisles, faces cool beneath their spiky orange hair, each of them a gun cocked and ready to go off.

Have I been the only member of the jury to see the kids creep into the theater? I can feel their heat and unrest as they breathe all around us. I can feel their desire to disrupt the proceedings and rout their elegant elders.

Why have the proper matrons in their Valentinos said nothing about this? Why do people say nothing when they sit in a theater and smell smoke? Herd instinct? Fear of being the first trouble-maker? Some deep reversion to childhood that overtakes us as members of an audience in a darkened room?

The film goes on. The Mozart figure begins raving about the unfairness of Don Giovanni's final punishment and how *his* happy ending to the opera is really more just, more true, more fair. In front of me, the witchy woman with the large right eye begins to cackle, then turns and catches me in her glittering gaze. "Beware, Jessica," she mutters, or do her lips merely form the words?

It is my very own Grigory who starts the riot.

"Decadent capitalist rubbish!" he thunders, standing and turning to storm ostentatiously out of the theater. "Free the film festival!" he shouts. And, as if on cue, a chorus of teenagers repeats: "Free the film festival!" (Only some, of course, heighten it to "Fuck the film festival!") Whereupon masses of them, letting out war whoops and whistles, begin to leap over the seats and storm the mezzanine where Björn, Lilli, the actors, and the rest of the jury sit quivering with fear. The insanity in the film has suddenly become real.

Whatever Grigory's reasons for making the protest (to appease the ancient politicos in the Kremlin at home, to ensure his next trip abroad, to silence those naysayers who claim he has lost his political nerve), the punk kids have surely been waiting for just such a signal to go wild. They scream and throw things, jostle the panicky parental figures in the audience, light joints, drop matches, and run whooping and whistling through the aisles.

The passive audience turns into a stampeding mob! Countesses in their glitter, counts in their "smokings," actors and actresses in their tuxes and sequins, all scramble and try to flee the theater as if the *ancien régime* were newly overtaken by the *sans-culottes*. But the side doors are sealed, and the kids, emboldened by Grigory's apparent support — for the moment he is their hero and he seems once again the young revolutionary he never really was — storm the mezzanine as if to kidnap Björn. (What they wish to do with him is not clear.) All the while Mozart's music keeps pouring forth. Lilli takes charge of a very shaky Björn and begins to escort him to the rear of the mezzanine. Leonardo da Leone follows, trying at the same time to restrain Grigory's outbursts and to protect Björn.

I experience a moment of sheer terror when I realize we could all be crushed or killed or burned in this melee. But then I use my old stratagem of impersonating a brave character I myself have played. What would Lady Macbeth do? Would she succumb to fear? What would Rosalind or Portia do? Dress up in men's clothes and solve the crisis! Well, then, I shall do no less — even in spike heels, a Merry Widow, and a Victorian gown!

Fortunately, the side doors are opened and the panicky counts and countesses, players and playboys, can escape into the moonlight. Grigory makes his way through the crowd, pursued by screaming kids; Björn, Lilli, and Leonardo stagger bravely on, flanked by punk youngsters chanting, "We want Björn! We want Björn! We want Björn!" as if in a parody of something they have seen in an American movie.

I rush to Björn's side, take his other arm despite Lilli's obvious disapproval, and whisper to Leonardo that he must summon the security guards at once.

"How are you?" I ask Björn, who makes his gentle way like a bemused Hamlet, his elegance somehow untouched despite the frenzy all about him.

" 'In sooth I know not why I am so sad,' " he says, quoting the first line of *The Merchant of Venice*.

" 'Your mind is tossing on the ocean,' " I say. " 'There where your argosies with portly sail / Like signiors and rich burghers on the flood, / Or as it were the pageants of the sea, / Do overpeer the petty traffickers / That curtsy to them, do them reverence, / As they fly by them with their woven wings. . . .' "

"Exactly," says Björn, but his face looks ravaged.

"Think of the next film, Björn — our film, *Serenissima*. And think of what all this publicity will do for *this* film. It will make you rich!"

"Björn never wanted to be rich," says Lilli. "He wanted to be respected."

I laugh. "So did we all," I say. "But this is *show* business!"

45

The security guards arrive and officiously take charge of Björn and Lilli. I am pushed out of the way. The air is thick with the resinous, sweet smoke of pot and hash. A fire under these circumstances would be disastrous.

For a moment I am locked within the grip of the crowd, pushed forward and back will-lessly by stampeding bodies. Then all at once a wave takes me, as if from the depths of the sea, and I am borne forward on it toward the door, down the teeming stairs where I clutch at the banister wildly, trying to keep my balance in my spike heels. Carlos Armada is behind me and he gallantly seizes my shoulders, steadying me on the stairs.

"Where is your Soviet escort?" he shouts.

"Ah, politics is his true love," I say. "He is off somewhere making love to her."

I toss this off as a joke, not knowing for the moment how terribly true it is.

Carlos says, "I survived the Civil War in Spain, Jessica, and I shall also survive the War of the Lido and the Biennale."

Arm in arm, we allow ourselves to be pushed down toward the exit. All dignity is lost in the squirming, screaming mass of bodies. At last we reach the bottom of the stairs, and the doors of the theater are in view. At last we are pushed through them along with the whooping masses of kids. As we burst out into the street and the sea air hits us, I truly feel reborn.

There's a full moon over the Lido and the breeze from the Adriatic is fresh. Motorcycles roar by, but even they cannot spoil the sense of relief I have at being free.

For the first time we have a real event at the film festival, a real crisis, and the photographers are nowhere in sight. Where *are* they? Crowds of people are pouring out of the Palazzo del Cinema (later, I even hear that some people have been stampeded in the crowd and badly hurt), but there are no *paparazzi* at all to be seen now — only curiosity seekers and fans with little instant cameras snapping away at the fleeing countesses and celebrities.

"Jessica — to the beach!" says Carlos Armada. "Take the beach!"

My crusty old Spanish Civil War veteran indicates an alley leading to the water and pulls me by the hand, out of sight of the fans.

"Your shoes . . . take off those ridiculous shoes," he says.

I obey, stopping to hitch up my gown and unbuckle the ankle straps of my come-fuck-me sandals. Carlos again steadies me.

"The Battle of the Biennale will never be won in such shoes," says Carlos. *"Come!"*

He shoves my shoes, one by one, into the side pockets of his tux and grabs me by the hand, making me run in my stocking feet all the way to the beach. My stockings are soon in tatters from the abrasiveness of the cement, but I am exhilarated by the adventure. Holding my voluminous skirt with one hand and Carlos's hand with the other, I run, laughing madly, to the beach. What a pleasure it is to be out of that stifling hall, out of that incipient riot, out of the tension of that last film.

"Come, come," says Carlos, as we reach the beach, "how about a swim?"

"Not in *this*," I say, thinking of the three thousand pounds I paid for the Zandra Rhodes — and that was two years ago, when the pound was still relatively firm.

"No, no, never part a lady from her gown — except with her consent. But look here . . ." He indicates one of the white cabanas belonging to the Excelsior — and even produces the key. "How do you think I have survived this festival — except by bathing all these films away!"

He opens the cabana and gestures for me to go first. "There's a bathing suit in there for you if you wish."

The cabana is quite civilized. There's a large wooden hanger for my gown, a mirror, a white Lastex bathing suit (his girlfriend's, I guess), a hotel bathrobe, some towels. The old exhibitionist in me considers, then dismisses, the possibility of prancing about on the beach in that fabulous black Merry Widow — but no, it would be just my luck to meet a *paparazzo* — or a shark attracted to the glitter of my garters. (I have never quite gotten over the movie *Jaws*.)

When I emerge, Carlos takes over the cabana and changes into his suit. He has a good body despite the natural softening produced by eight decades of gravity, eight decades of war, eight decades of poetry. But poetry proves to be a great preservative. Carlos has the vitality of those few chosen artists on whom the Muses smile; like Picasso, like Henry Miller, he has the *joie de vivre* of a young man. Art keeps one young, I think, because it keeps one perpetually a beginner, perpetually a child.

Carlos runs to the water, bidding me follow — and dives precipitously into the waves.

The sight of this hardy octogenarian plunging into the Adriatic (where Byron used to swim) quiets my fears both of pollution and of sharks — and I follow.

The water is amazingly clean, and the moonlight makes the swim eerily beautiful. The moon is looking out for me, I think, and I remember to thank her for my life, for my curious gift. Spared again. Once more the White Goddess, my muse, is looking out for me. But what of Björn? And what of Grigory? Well, that I shall know soon enough. Meanwhile — swim, Jessica, swim.

As I reach my arms out in the inky, moon-splashed water, I think again of Antonia, whom I taught to swim when she was only two, at a "waterbabies" class at the 92nd Street "Y" in Manhattan. Whatever I am doing — swimming, watching a movie, dreaming, acting — I think of her, and my fingertips ache.

Carlos walks out of the water looking for all the world like an ancient satyr. I follow. He is beaming at me.

"You know, Jessica," he says, "even at eighty, you want to be alive!"

"I believe it," I say.

He puts a wet hand on my shoulder and walks me to the cabana. For a moment our eyes meet and we contemplate carnality. He runs his index finger along my lower lip, caressing its curve as if he were touching those other, lower lips. We kiss. His kiss is very young for one so old and we are both stirred by it. So much so that we draw back, in surprise, from the intensity.

"My mistress would be very cross," he says, looking hungrily at my breasts, "not to mention my wife, my comrade in arms. . . . Better not."

"Better not," I say, drawing a deep breath and deciding not to complicate my life with passion. "But you certainly are an old lion."

I kiss him fondly on the cheek, then look up at the moon, my mother, who approves.

A little while later I slip back into the hotel, wearing a CIGA toweling robe, a towel around my head, big black sunglasses (belonging to Carlos), and cradling my folded gown in my arms like a baby. I run up the stairs unrecognized despite the crush of people. With hidden hair, with face bare of make-up, no one seems to know me.

Something exciting is afoot in the press suites I pass on the second floor, but I cannot tell what it is. I see huge banks of lights and hear the murmur of hundreds of voices. A great number of people are milling about outside the double doors. Whatever the event is, it is apparently S.R.O. One voice is amplified above all the others. Do I detect Grigory's slithery Russian syllables?

Afraid to linger and be unmasked, I continue up to my suite, lay my precious Zandra Rhodes out on the bed, and take a shower to wash off the moonlit Adriatic. Then I carefully make up my face, change into an elegant Missoni knit dress, slip on another pair of come-fuck-me pumps (purple glove-leather Maud Frizons, these), and head downstairs again.

By now, the crowd on the second floor has dissipated and technicians are carrying away lights. Whatever has occurred there is now ended.

Some press people look as if they are about to accost me for interviews so I tuck my chin under, lower my eyes, and hurry down to the dining room. "Miss Pruitt, Miss Pruitt," one calls. I pretend not to hear. If nothing else, I can eat. All this excitement has made me ravenous.

Grigory is holding forth at a round table in the corner of the dining room. He is surrounded by some other members of the jury — Leonardo da Leone, Walter Wildhonig, and Pierre de Houbigant, with his beauteous, sphinxlike Oriental wife.

Grigory makes a place for me at his side. He is glowing, animated, ebullient. He looks like a man who has just made wild and passionate love to his mistress and is now about to savor a hearty meal.

"My friend," he is saying to bristling, mustachioed Walter Wildhonig, "would I dispute *your* right to criticize a film because *you* found it fascist?" (Walter is a famous antifascist.) "No, of course not. I would *never* interfere —"

"But *Don Giovanni* is hardly an example of *ein faschistisches Film*," says Walter, *"gar nicht. . . ."* (Although Walter speaks English well enough, he lapses into German when he wishes to be emphatic.)

"Besides," says Leonardo, twitching madly, "as a member of the jury you have no right to make political pronouncements before the judging is over. No right whatsoever."

"I have the right to represent my government," says Grigory self-righteously, "the right to represent the noble pursuit of art for which we have been elected. Am I not a poet? Am I not a filmmaker? Am I not a critic of all the arts? My dear colleagues, why invite me here if you would muzzle me? Doesn't the West believe in its famed freedom of speech?"

"Well," says Leonardo, "we must have one thing above all clear: you will not make any statements to the press until the jury has met and deliberated. Is that agreed?"

Grigory smiles like the Cheshire cat. The rules of these petty bureaucrats do not apply to him. "Do you not trust me, my friends? You know my art. You know my ardor. . . . Why such cynicism? Why such mistrust? Am I not still your beloved Grisha, your poet? Would you muzzle spokespersons for culture as you accuse the Kremlin of doing?" His eyes twinkle wickedly.

Pierre seems to be nodding off during these verbal pyrotechnics, but he wakes up long enough to say: "My dear chap, I think you were quite unfair to Björn. The poor fellow is so sensitive to criticism anyway. Who knows where he has fled now —"

"Where *is* Björn?" I interject.

"Fled," says Leonardo. "And *Dio* alone knows where. He and Lilli called a *motoscafo e sono fuggiti* — but not before he had a mini-nervous breakdown and withdrew *Don Giovanni* from competition. That was *his* protest. I wanted to call a special meeting of the jury to offer Björn an official apology, but he would have none of it. He withdrew the film, and — poof — disappeared."

"And what of my film? What of *Serenissima?* Does anyone know?" I asked.

Leonardo shakes his head and gives a mighty vertical twitch. "*Chi sa?* Who knows?" he says. "Björn has been known to vanish for months at a time in less dramatic circumstances. Do you remember when the Swedish tax authorities found a minor discrepancy in his film company's records? He was hospitalized for 'nervous collapse' that time. Who knows what will happen to him now? You are very wicked, Grisha," he says, waggling a twitchy finger at Grigory. "You know your customer. Björn is a sensitive plant. That outburst was truly unkind."

"Kind, unkind, is not the question, my dear Leonardo," says Grigory. "Sometimes I must be cruel in order to be kind. You Westerners are very good at muzzling your Soviet friends in the name of free speech. But then, you are completely free to criticize *us*, to claim that we silence *our* writers. Such baloney." (He pronounces it with a very Russian "nyeh" sound so that it comes out halfway between "baloneigh" and "balonyeh.") I am glum. What will become of *Serenissima* now? It was my hope, my treat, my reward for a year of doing two abominable television miniseries and one violent quasi–science fiction film to earn my bread. (I tried always to have my projects spread, like good investments: one for art, one for money, one for exposure and publicity. Well, there goes art for this year, I think. I do not even want to contemplate what this will do to my career.)

"Besides, Grigory, comrade *mio*," Leonardo is saying, "if you really wanted *Don Giovanni* to sink without a trace, you would not have made any protest at all. Your outburst will only en*sure* its success —"

"Then let it succeed!" says Grigory. "I am not the man to muzzle the great maestro Björn Persson! But also let me speak. I was invited here to speak, not to be silent. Björn should pay me a percentage of the gross from dollar first — should he not? Isn't that how you capitalists do it? *Publicitas vincit omnia — n'est-ce pas?*"

I laugh dutifully, my career for this year "in the toilet," as they say in my adopted Land of LaLa. A charming phrase, which betrays what American moviemakers think of their industry. That it is all shit. If I ever sink so low that I am driven to write a book about Hollywood, I'll call it *In This Business* and subtitle it *In and Out the*

Toilet Bowl like some deranged disciple of Fritz Perls. The Land of LaLa is famous for the speed with which it condemns people to the toilet bowl — only to fish them out six or seven years later in a gaudy comeback, usually accompanied by glossy magazine confessions of drug dependence, broken love affairs, and marriages gone badder than bad. Come back little Starface, all is forgiven, the collective culture seems to say. But first you have to check into Rancho Mirage, give up "substance abuse" (at least for a *while*), shed your current spouse, reconcile with your kids (who are also about to graduate from a trendy rehab — in Hawaii, say), and then confess it all to *People* magazine in the most lurid terms. All you sacrifice for this comeback is your privacy and your dignity. A small price to pay if you had none to start with. Ah, Grisha is right: *Publicitas vincit omnia* — though I know he has his own twisted reasons for saying so.

"Come," says Grisha to Leonardo, "let us make peace. Let us order some champagne — the most decadent French champagne, Roederer Cristal, let us say — and let us make peace. We have no disputes between us. We are all artists here."

"Only if you will solemnly promise not to give any interviews before the final judging," says Leonardo. "Will you promise?"

"Will I promise? Will I promise to be muzzled? Is that the price of peace in the West? Well, then, my dear Leonardo, let us toast. I can drink to that!"

Roederer Cristal is called for — two bottles of it — and chilled champagne flutes are brought.

Grigory will not allow the waiter to open the bottles but ostentatiously opens them himself and pours the champagne most ebulliently. With a flourish he hands each member of the table a glass, then prances up on his chair to offer a toast that the whole dining room can hear. The members of the table rise as if bewitched.

Grigory holds up his glass ceremoniously, admires the pale ashen gold of the champagne while he thinks of an appropriate toast.

"Aha," he says. "A favorite line from your greatest poet, Shakespeare — from his most moon-drenched, lunatickal play, such as is suitable for nights like these." He indicates, with one long-fingered Slavic hand, the full moon over the ocean.

" 'I'll speak in a monstrous little voice . . .' *Midsummer Night's Dream*, Act One."

The members of the jury pause, wondering whether or not to drink to this peculiar toast. A small voice — whether monstrous or not — has never been Grigory's problem. What on earth is he covering up? I wonder. He is concealing with his words rather than revealing — a true Russian politician.

"Let me counter with a line from *The Winter's Tale*," I say. " 'There was speech in their dumbness, language in their very gesture. . . .' "

We all raise our glasses and drink, not knowing what on earth, or in heaven, we are drinking to.

Grigory has bamboozled the jury somehow — but how he has done it is not yet clear. We get a little buzzed on champagne, order supper, and consume it along with six more bottles of Cristal — Grigory's treat.

By the meal's end, everyone at the table is cockeyed from champagne. My head is pounding and I am in despair about *Serenissima*. I know Björn, and knowing him, I am worried. He is not so much unstable as terribly stubborn, and he uses his stubbornness craftily. An event like this could become the pretext for six months of seclusion on his part. Let the new film fall around his ears — he won't care. One reason he has endured so long as an artist in a business that has made a fine art of crushing artists is that he knows when to turn off and say to the moneymen: "It's your problem — solve it." Then he plays the prima donna and stomps off, leaving *them* the dilemma of wooing him back. "I don't want to make the film, anyway," he has said many times, within my hearing. "I just want to write. If you want me to work on your bloody film, seduce *me*." This master stroke of reverse psychology works every time. Björn is sensitive but he is also crafty. Which is why he has survived to make so many films.

But I am not crafty enough, especially when I am depressed by a major setback. This must be why tonight, after so many previous protests and so much fine, cunning resistance, I allow Grigory not only to take me as far as my suite but to enter it.

"Ah, Jessichka, I knew you would succumb eventually," says Grigory, lunging for me cave-man style. He attacks my neck, slobbering over it, nipping and nibbling with bites and kisses.

Why on earth am I doing this? I ask myself. Lust? Hardly. Love? Are you kidding? This is merely despair, which sometimes (think of *Don Giovanni*!) masquerades as lust.

I allow him to take off my knit dress, to run his hands down my lavender lace teddy, to kiss the skin that peeks between my lavender silk stocking tops and my long, lavender satin garters. (Am I doing this just to share my *underwear* with an appreciative man?) But no, it's been a long time since I've gone to bed with *anyone*, and Grigory's kisses on my neck, my breasts, my thighs, begin to stir me.

He slips off the top of my teddy and uncovers my breasts.

"They are like wild berries of the woods, my Jessichka," he says, "such sweet cloudberries, rosy raspberries, California strawberries. . . ." He sucks on my nipples and I begin to warm toward him in spite of myself. My thighs spread, my clitoris begins to throb, my mouth finds his. Though he reeks of alcohol and cigarette smoke, I am aroused — and so, apparently, is he. He seems mad to lick me, bite me, hug me, rip my clothes off, but after a while it becomes clear that the appendage necessary to consummate all this frenzy is not in the appropriate state to achieve that end. Dutifully I bend my head, unzip him, and try to encourage it with my lips, my tongue, my fingers. I suck and suck, lick and lick, run practiced fingers from stem to stern — but nothing rouses it. Ah, alcohol has increased the desire but taken away the performance, just as Will predicted — Will Shakespeare, who said just about everything there was to say about lust, perhaps because it was also a synonym for his name. ("Whoever hath her wish, thou hast thy Will, and Will to boot, and Will in overplus.") Not so with Grisha. A great strapping giant of a Siberian poet and no will to speak of, or none that *I* can speak of at any rate. What do I feel about this? Mostly relief.

"Darling, let's sleep," I say.

Grigory groans in assent, banishing the last lingering vestiges of my tumescence. With my help, he struggles out of his clothes and climbs under the covers with me. I have neglected to draw the blinds and I just lie there for a while, wishing I were rude enough to throw him out. (Alas, I am not.) But presently I catch sight of the moon twinkling spookily at me. "It's all in my plan," she seems to say, "which will be revealed in due course."

Good night, moon, I think.

Good night, she seems to wink.

4

Publicitas Vincit Omnia

FOR SOME REASON I sleep later than usual the next morning —
despite the open blinds and the sunlight streaming in from the sea.

The first moment I open my eyes I am not quite sure where I
am. Not that this is unusual for me. I have lived in so many hotel
rooms, in so many cities, that many mornings I awaken unsure of
where I am. Often I wake up half wishing, half believing, that I am
in my old bedroom on Seventy-third and Park — the nursery, we
called it, though it was my room alone. Connected to my brother
Pip's by one of those New York bathrooms with two doors, my
room had a kind of Audubon-print wallpaper that covered even the
ceiling, so I would open my eyes and see arbors with birds above
my head in the arborless midst of Manhattan. I loved that room and
that wallpaper (someday someone should do a book on the effect of
wallpaper on childhood memory), but I loved my room in the country house even better. It faced a lagoon you could sail straight through
to Long Island Sound, and though it was in dusty, musty Darien —
which my mother derisively called "dreary end" — it was softened
by birds and church bells and the sound of rushing water. Sometimes I awaken thinking myself back *there*, and six years old again,
with my whole life about to begin. If only I could return and start
over, getting it right this time. If only!

Being an actor is certainly a blessing — how else would we endure the pain of life except by turning it into a play? But of course
it is also a curse because it necessitates a kind of constant exile. If I

57

feel the history of the Jews in my blood (I have lately been reading about the Jews of Venice for my part as Jessica, a part that now I may never play), perhaps it is because the Jew is the quintessential exile, like the artist. No matter how entrenched, how rich, how established, how necessary to the regime, how seemingly tolerated, there was *never* a time when they could not be expelled at a moment's notice. The Jews of Venice were a perfect example of this. Their moneylending was the lifeblood of the Serenissima, the very basis of its maritime wealth, and yet they were reviled for doing what kept the republic alive. Time and again in history one found the Jews in this appalling double bind, viciously attacked for doing exactly what preserved the society in which they found themselves. No wonder neuroticism was in their very blood. They could never be right. Like poets, like actors, the world needed them — but also needed to disclaim its need for them.

The phone rings, shattering my reverie. Too dopey and dreamy to think straight, I pick it up.

"Signor Krylov, *per piacere*," comes a voice.

"*Un attimo*," I say unthinkingly, and pass the receiver to a very sleepy Grigory.

"*Pronto?*" he says.

Click. The snooper at the other end hangs up the phone, now knowing beyond doubt what he needs to know.

I leap out of bed in a fury at myself. How stupid of me! How could I have done that? I grab my robe and head for the shower, cursing my own idiocy.

By the time I am showered, Grisha has ordered breakfast, and when it comes he opens the door just wide enough so that a phalanx of waiting photographers can snap us together in our bathrobes.

I slam the door in a rage.

"You bastard!" I scream. "All you want is to ruin my reputation!" (What have I said? What reputation have I left to lose?)

Grisha laughs. "You know the old proverb, Jessichka — if your reputation is ruined, might as well have fun!"

"Some fun!" I say, sitting down to breakfast.

Grisha has called for all the Italian papers as well as the Paris

Herald Trib, Le Monde, and *The Times* of London. Now I see why. The judging is not yet complete, and Grisha has already given his personal press conference.

In *Corriere della Sera, La Stampa, La Repubblica,* and *Il Giornale,* he has glommed front page headlines.

POETA SOVIETICO CONDANNA LA MOSTRA DEL CINEMA it says in *Corriere.* MOSTRA DEL CINEMA: IL CASO GRIGORY KRYLOV E BJORN PERSSON shouts *La Stampa.* KRYLOV E PERSSON E MOZART says *La Repubblica. Il Giornale* heads the piece: IL POETA SOVIETICO E IL CASO DON GIOVANNI. The Italian papers have all put him smack in the middle of page one. Even the *Trib* says: SOVIET POET BLASTS FILM FESTIVAL. And *Le Monde* has a circumspect but clearly important column debating the pros and cons of his protest.

Grisha is absolutely delighted. With all the glee of a naughty child, he is reading his clippings and comparing his pictures in the various papers.

"I like the one in *Corriere* best — eh, Jessichka? A very brooding, handsome Heathcliff image." He proudly shows me a picture of himself two columns wide.

"But this one" — he indicates *La Stampa* — "is not flattering at all."

"You pig!" I say. "You were very busy while we were all trying to escape being trampled. How could you *do* this and then lie to Leonardo that you would not give a press conference before the judging was complete? How could you *be* such a snake?"

"My dzear Jessichka," Grisha says, sitting back and sipping his cappuccino, "I did not lie to Leonardo at all. I merely toasted my colleagues with fine champagne. If Leonardo chose to assume that was a solemn promise to be silent, then he is more of a fool than he seems to be." (Here Grisha does a wicked imitation of Leonardo's twitch, which makes me laugh in spite of myself.) "Besides, I will *not* give any more press conferences in the future — that much was quite true."

"Well, why didn't you tell him you had *already* given one while everyone was worried sick about Björn?"

"He did not *ask,*" says Grisha, smiling devilishly. "Why should I volunteer information? Even we stupid bumbling Russians know never to volunteer information if it is not demanded of us. Ah, you are not much of a political animal, are you, Jessichka?"

"Compared to you, I'm a beginner," say I. "I'm totally outclassed. Would you consider being my press agent? You're incredible. I'd rather have you on my side than against me."

"A rare compliment coming from you, my dzear, but alas, I am already engaged. Like Leporello, my work is difficult and the hours are long, but I serve a master who will not be disobeyed."

"And who, pray tell, is your master, Grisha?"

"Truth, Jessichka, truth above all. Ah, yes, that and free speech — the things you Westerners love so dzearly."

I laugh again. "I'd just as soon not be there when Leonardo reads the papers."

"And you need not be," says Grisha, "nor need *I* be, either. Because you know what day is today?"

"No — what day is it?"

"Regatta Day in Venezia, Jessichka, and all the screenings are postponed except for one tonight — *your* film, *Women in Hell*. But until then we are free as birds, free as *lastochkiy*, free as *uccellini!*" Grisha prances up on the double bed and does an arm-flapping, birdlike little dance in his bathrobe and underwear. "And I am going to take you — how do you say? — out on the town. We shall attend several receivements —"

"Receptions," I correct him.

Grisha blithely goes on. "The first, a very grand one given by Contessa Venier in her *incredibile* palazzo. The second, a very Bohemian one frequented by poets and artists. And the third, a very perverse one where everyone shall appear to be of another sex than the one they truly are. And many elderly, rich men shall appear with beautiful young 'nephews' — the famed *settembrini* of Venice, if you understand my meaning. If we do all this, we shall not see Leonardo until this evening, and by then he shall be over his rage."

Grisha gives another drastic mimetic twitch and again jumps up and down on the bed like a small boy. "Will you be so kind as to accompany me?"

"I'd do anything to be away from here when the storm breaks. But how do we get out? And then back by tonight? Unfortunately, I have to be presented when my film is shown."

"I know just the way," says Grisha, prancing down off the bed and gathering up his precious newspapers.

"I shall cut these later," he says solemnly. "Meanwhile, where to hide them? Oh, yes . . ."

He piles them neatly on the floor of my armoire. "I would not want the maid to throw them out," he says, "such beautiful pictures of the angry, impassioned Grisha."

I look at him mockingly. "You're in big trouble, baby," I say, "when you start talking about yourself in the third person. This I know for a fact. Look what happened to Salvador Dali."

"What do you mean?" Grisha asks like a rebuked child.

"Once he started saying 'Dali like this, Dali don't like that,' his art deteriorated. Mark my words, Grisha, it's a bad sign."

"You are crazy, Jessichka. Crazy American cunt. You think too much. Russian women don't think so much. Makes them sexier. You *pretend* to be sexy, but you don't know how to treat a man — too aggressive, that's why we shall never fuck like bunnies." (He pronounced it "bunn-yees.") "Too — how you say? — castrating."

I have been en route to the bathroom to make up my face, but now I freeze in my tracks and glare at him. "What exactly are you saying, Grigory? I challenge you to say it again really *slowly.*"

He begins. "You don't know how to treat a man —"

"Listen, buster," I say, "if I hadn't been so damned well brought up, I'd have thrown you out on your limp dick last night and let all the *paparazzi* outside the door *photograph* it. Then I'd have called a press conference — the way you did — and announced to the world just what a bust you were as a lover. But I went to the Chapin School, and I grew up in a family where knowing which fork to use was considered *much* more important than truth, justice, honesty, and free speech. And you're damned lucky I did, because otherwise *you'd* be the sacrificial lamb in those precious papers today — not Björn Persson."

Ah, I am beginning to warm to this monologue. I am really beginning to enjoy it. What a part! Outraged innocence is my middle name! Some actors believe — my old acting teacher Arnold used to say this often, in fact — that anger is the easiest of all emotions to play. Perhaps this is true, but it certainly is cathartic! And Grisha is not the subtlest of actors himself. He fills football fields when he reads his poems. In his own country, he is more like a movie star or soccer hero than a poet.

Propelled by my own mock fury, I go on. "You *bastard*. You have single-handedly trashed my next film, humiliated one of the world's great directors, and destroyed my own credibility at this festival — and now you have the utter gall to imply that *my* behavior, and not your boozing and your limp cock, are to blame for the fact that we didn't fuck last night. I'm *glad* we didn't fuck last night — even though the whole world will think we did, thanks to you. But when you have the nerve to call me 'castrating,' I draw the line. You damned well know I should have thrown you out last night. The only reason I didn't is my goddam breeding, my decadent, capitalistic manners — which you are such a *putz* you don't even know to be *grateful* for!"

By the time I finish this monologue I am screaming, and Grisha, who has been standing there with his mouth hanging open, promptly falls to his knees.

"What may I do to atone, Jessichka? I am truly sorry."

"I doubt it," I say. "But if you can get me out of this god-awful hotel suite and to the regatta without a million reporters following, I just may forgive you."

Let it be known that Grisha did redeem himself, at least for the moment. He hired a private *motoscafo* and had it meet us not at the Excelsior, where the press lay in wait for us everywhere, but at the back of a private villa down the road (whither he drove us by motorcycle!). Ah, yes, I embarked on my travels that Regatta Day wearing a Thierry Mugler jump suit (a futuristic silver one absolutely festooned with zippers), silver cowboy boots, a silver motorcycle helmet, and silver goggles with reflective lenses. Punk for a day! There was nowhere I couldn't go in Venice in that outfit.

*

And so we are off — off to the Contessa Venier's for starters, and then who knows? We shall wend our way through the city of Venice, stopping here, stopping there, like the strolling players which in fact we are.

The Contessa Venier's emporium on the Grand Canal — Palazzo Venier-Grimani, it is called — is our first stop. We enter on the water side, met by a butler in eighteenth-century livery who takes my silver helmet and silver goggles as if they were a feathered tricorn and gilded walking stick. He bows ceremoniously and directs us up a stone stair, plushly carpeted with red.

On the cavernous first floor of the palazzo are several ancient gondolas and sedan chairs. One gondola above all is polished to a fare-thee-well and stands upon its own special rack. It is an old gondola, complete with *felse*, or cabin-covering — the sort of gondola perfect for romantic assignations or political spying (two activities that often require the same equipment).

"It belonged to Doge Andrea Venier," says Grisha pompously, "the one who died of plague."

"Impossible," I whisper. "First of all, it was Doge Andrea *Vendramin* who died of plague in 1478. And secondly, if it *were* that doge's gondola, it would have long since rotted away because wooden boats don't last that long." (I have been reading and I know my Venetian history and boat lore by now.) "Get your doges straight, pal," I add.

Grisha says, "Not sexy to know more history than your man, Jessichka."

"Well, then, that proves it — you're not my man."

"Shall we go up?" asks Grisha, bowing in mock humility.

"Indeed," I say.

We climb the stairs to the next floor and then continue on up to the *piano nobile*, where a glittering reception is in progress.

"First, you must meet the countess," says Grisha, leading me by the hand past warty duchesses, celebrities of stage and screen and soccer field, anonymous millionaires, showy pseudomillionaires, and well-dressed paupers masquerading as millionaires. There are hairdressers and fashion designers, gossip columnists and fashion journalists, true believers and miscreants of every persuasion. All the languages of the jet set are being spoken, often simultaneously or even as part of the same sentence. For these people are the fashionable of the world who can utter the same clichés in Italian, French, German, English, and make small talk about restaurants and resorts in all these tongues, but are never called upon to plumb more difficult subjects. Indeed, they might be at a loss for words if asked to.

The Contessa Venier is sitting in a golden chair ("the barge she sat in, like a burnish'd throne / Burn'd on the water; the poop was beaten gold . . ."), but no Cleopatra she. She oozes in her chair, all flab and diamonds, and raises a yellowed hand, covered with freckles, warts, and rings, for me to kiss. For a moment her piggley brown eyes meet mine, but then, seeing my unconventional costume, she begins to look about the room for others more eminent.

Grisha, my appointed press agent, notes this subtle shift of eyes and all at once bursts out, "Contessa, this my dzear friend, the great American qveen of the cinema, Jessica Pruitt."

Whereupon the contessa whips her head around and focuses upon me once more, now assured that I am important enough to be worth another millisecond of her attention.

"*Enchantée*," she says.

"*Piacere*," I respond, knowing the rules of the international set: never engage in a conversational exchange in less than two languages — preferably neither of them your own.

Grisha now bows to the contessa (a *most* un-Bolshevik bow, a Romanov bow, in fact), and seizes my arm to take me on a tour of the palazzo.

Arm in arm, we promenade past petronian displays of food — pyramids of glazed ducks, breads braided like the Titian hair of ancient *cortigiane*, pink prosciutto curled about open, amber figs, sculptures of the Palazzo del Cinema in sugar candy, marzipan gondolas and gondoliers. The food is so gorgeous, it hardly seems decent to eat it, but none of the other guests appear intimidated. In the crowd I spot various darlings of the international set, people one always meets in Venice, Cap d'Antibes, the Marbella Club at Dragon Bay, or else the Pelicano at Porto Ercole. I recognize several familiar faces whose names have been mysteriously detached from them and, mingling in the crowd as well, I spot Paloma P., Prince Alfonso Von H., the Maharanee of J., Tina C., Jackie O., Arianna S., Iris L., and Gloria V. Hubert de G. is there (he's so splendidly tall you cannot miss him), and the incomparable Gore V. is holding court, making everybody laugh at his legendary aphorisms. (He emerged from the pool at the Cipriani the other day, I have been told, looked around at all the British octogenarians, and said, "By God — Lourdes.") The only International Darling occasionally wittier than he (I mean Princess Margaret, who uttered the deathless line "The trouble with Gore is: he wants my sister's job") is not in evidence. But Grisha will not let me stop and greet my special favorites in this throng because he wants to show me something more important.

"Come, Jessichka," he says. "To the chapel."

He leads me through rooms hung with huge, tarnished mirrors, rooms hung with immense, twinkling floriform chandeliers. He leads me through rooms full of Titians and Tintorettos, Giorgiones and Bellinis, Carpaccios and Veroneses, Guardis and Canalettos, Longhis and Luinis. He leads me under Tiepolo ceilings, past beds hung with ruby red damask, past beds hung with sapphire blue damask, past beds hung with emerald green damask. He leads me past the central courtyard and stair where, in the pit below, the no-longer-used Venetian wellhead can be seen growing moss and flowers in a damp, stony courtyard filled with classical bric-a-brac: the torso of a Graeco-Roman Venus, the head of a Hellenistic Zeus, the sarcophagus of an unnamed Roman patrician.

At last we arrive at what appears to be the grandest master bedroom suite of the palazzo: an immense, altarlike canopied bed supported by writhing columns made of some dark walnuty wood; a Tiepolo ceiling resplendent with androgynous angels and heavy-thighed mythological matrons recumbent on *schlag*like clouds, ascending above a pink candy sunset; a many-branched chandelier big enough to light a ballroom; and portraits of sixteenth-century Venetians hung about the room, ancestral witnesses to the pleasures, or the purgatories, of the bed.

Adjacent to this bedroom is a smallish antechamber or vestibule leading to a tiny chapel. The chapel has a Crivelli Madonna (apple-cheeked baby Christ, apple-breasted Virgin Mary in an archway hung with pears and apples). On the altar are golden candles and behind it, a red damask curtain.

"Look, Jessichka," says Grisha, whereupon he pulls the curtain, revealing a window and beyond it a whole cavernous church below. "Voilà — they could sin *and* confess without ever leaving the bedchamber," Grisha exclaims. "Shall we do the same?"

I am marveling at the convenience of the arrangement, and my mind is racing ahead to plots for films, mysteries, historical epics, that would hinge upon this proximity between bed, chapel, and church. But even as I dream of future plots, Grisha is aroused beyond anything my mere flesh could inspire by this odd combination of sensuality and piety — a combination evidently crucial to his sexual demons.

"Kneel, Jessichka — kneel!" he commands, pushing me down on my knees at the altar and pressing his now very turgid cock against my rear.

I swing around, laughing, only to see him unzipping and preparing to thrust his Soviet specimen into my mouth.

"Oh, Grisha — I didn't realize you were so religious!" I say, and then fall apart in gales of laughter. But Grisha is determined to have me, if not wickedly on the altar then at least decently on the bed. He drags me to it and begins clawing at me in what seems like a rape pantomime drawn from a B movie. I have played this scene before myself. And I know it has only three possible scenarios: the girl gets raped, the girl gets killed, the girl gets killed and raped. Rewrite the script! I command myself. That is your whole life's task, after all, to rewrite these hackneyed scripts and make them real, true, authentically heroic. Grisha is pinning me to the bed, but, like most bullies, Grisha is weak. He is big, but not agile. He has bulk, but he does not have the subtler martial arts at his command. I do.

A quick knee to the groin amazingly loosens his grip. A few well-placed kicks and I am already getting up and smoothing my silver jump suit, when a veritable parade of Beautiful People, led by Gore himself, enters the bedchamber.

"Is this the position of poets in the USSR? On their backs?" asks our waggish freedom fighter.

"It is better than being on their knees before the balance sheet like bourgeois capitalist writers," says Grisha, leaping off the bed and zipping his pants.

But I am already gone. I have taken off at a sprint down the labyrinthine corridors of the palazzo, under the Tiepolo ceilings, past the damask-draped beds, past the walls of great paintings, the gorgeous table of food, down the steps, past the liveried footmen, and out via a side door that gives onto a narrow *calle* leading to the Grand Canal.

At the end of the *calle* I can see the gondolas, *sandali*, *topi*, all the reproductions of historical craft — the great *Bucintoro* among them — already bobbing on the waters for the Regata Storica, which is about to begin.

Damn! I've forgotten the silver helmet and goggles, but there's little chance of my being recognized in this throng. I have an extra pair of sunglasses in one of the zipper pockets of my jump suit, so my incognita is prepared. Anyway, the *calli* are teeming with Venetians, some of them costumed for the various historical reenactments. I see young men in doublets and hose, their wigs slightly askew, young women dressed in sixteenth-century bodices and farthingales, their skirts hitched up as they run along the cobblestones.

Intermingled with them are kids in punk attire and matrons in polyester dresses, so that two epochs (or more) seem to be merging in the streets of Venice. It is the same on the Grand Canal, where boats from every era of Venetian history bob on the waters, awaiting their turn to race. Out on the streets are the hoi polloi, while the Beautiful People overlook the tumult below from their balconies, just as in Tiepolo's or Veronese's frescoes. Sometimes, one is thrown even further back in time, and the scene seems painted by Carpaccio, with gorgeously liveried gondoliers and fluffy little dogs (or big mangy ones) perched upon the prows to cheer their masters as they skim the waters.

One with the crowd now, having forfeited my perch above the Grand Canal among the worthies of the fashionable world, I am pressed into the *calle* with the screaming throng. Nobody recognizes me here. They are all intent upon struggling to the water's edge to have a better view of the regatta.

Jostled, elbowed, shoved, I am pushed almost to the end of the *calle*. There I stop, find a place to lean against the cool stone wall of a palazzo, and catch my breath.

Suddenly the face of a beautiful young man swims into my view. His hair is golden and hangs over his shoulders like a pretty girl's. His eyes are clear bright blue, his mouth red, his brow high, arched, imperious. He cannot be more than eighteen or nineteen, and he wears (or can I be imagining it?) the garb of a patrician Elizabethan: a lace collar with blackwork that rises at the back as if it had not quite made up its mind whether or not to become a ruff; a peasecod doublet; full, loose breeches of the sort the English called "venetians"; flesh-colored hose; and shoes of a pale natural color.

"Milady, you are welcome hither," he says. "Shall we attend my friend?"

Startled, and yet not startled at all (it is only as if I have gone from the twentieth-century wings onto the Elizabethan stage and begun speaking Shakespearean English), I answer, "And who, pray, is your friend, Sirrah?"

"Why, Master Shake-scene, the upstart crow, the great — or soon to be great — Will Shakespeare. A wanton lad who prizes wenches but slights not lads. Like many a player, he hath the morals of a monkey, the lust of a lion, and the appetite of a tiger. . . ."

"Doth he not have the heart of a lion as well?" I ask, astonished not to be more astonished.

"Ah, Milady, that remains to be seen. Come, will you meet my friend? He would fain meet you."

"I have met your friend," I say.

"In word but not in flesh," says the young man. " 'Tis very like reading about this watery city of sin and sensuality, yet never having been here. We, too, dreamed of Venice. But now that we are here, we find it quite familiar yet altogether strange — like unto the unicorn, which is almost a horse, almost a goat, and yet is compact'd of magic and of poetry in a strange, new way no mere mortal could guess at. For it is touched with the breath — and the brush — of the Muses. Do you not agree?"

I nod my head and stare into the young man's eyes, not quite sure whether in a moment he will not turn into a mere bit player in my life — a tourist disguised for a Regatta Day party, or the son of an old friend playing dress-up and picking me out of the crowd to tease me (for in Venice, on Regatta Day, one meets everyone!). But no, he seems quite the real thing — though who can tell in this city of mirrors and reflections, this city where past and present mingle most incredibly, where even our best contemporary chronicler of the place — I mean, of course, Jan Morris — has changed not only names but genders like some astounding present-day Orlando. Ah, Venice has that effect upon all sensitive souls: we change shapes, epochs, even sexes — bewitched by that *fata* (or is it *strega?*) manifest within the labyrinthine ways and byways of the city.

"Jessichka! Jessichka!" comes the echo down the *calle*. I whirl around to see Grisha Krylov waving furiously at me above the crowd, and then I whirl around again to find my fine Elizabethan dandy gone. Vanished into thick air. And I alone again, with Krylov in pursuit.

I am determined to flee him, determined to find my Elizabethan friend again — but it is no easy task negotiating the streets of Venice on Regatta Day. Every *calle* is packed with people, and it requires great agility, and no small amount of pushing and shoving, to elude a great, thundering, would-be rapist of a Soviet poet who is waving his arms madly and blowing consolatory kisses. But elude him I do, for Venice belongs to the Venetians on Regatta Day, to the working people of the city, and one can get lost in their ample collective bosom. The Beautiful People on the balconies are just so much window-dressing — the *glitterati* irrelevantly glittering — but it is the common people of Venice who love the regatta most, who know the names of all the *regatanti* and *regatante*, who cheer for the Regata delle donne (their mothers and sisters), the Regati degli Alberoni, the Regata di Pellestrina, the Regata dei Traghetti, the Regata dei S.S. Giovanni e Paolo, the Regata di Mestre, di Burano, di Murano, and so on. This is their *festa*, a day on which even Grisha

Krylov might be swallowed up by a crowd, a day on which all Venice belongs to the beautiful, muscular gondoliers (and even their ugly brothers).

As the boats begin to race on the Grand Canal, it becomes apparent that Venice is not at all the city of glittering, famous foreigners it often seems to be (at least in the summer season) but a city of cheering shopkeepers, boatmen, cooks, waiters, dustmen, fishermen, maids. *This* Venice — the Venice that belongs to the Venetians, the Venice that belongs to the flourishing bourgeois of this most bourgeois of cities (despite its patrician past, and reputation) is, in fact, the true Venice (if there is such a thing as one true Venice). They are people with whom Shakespeare — if indeed he *were* here — would be very much at home, for he knew their like in London. They were his audience, his kinsmen, his friends.

I wander through the *calli*, along the *fondamenta*, through the *campi* of this city with the true Venetians on this their day of days, but nowhere do I find the young Earl of Southampton again (for that is who I presume he is). At one point I turn a corner into a *rio terrá*, a little filled-in street, and I think I see him, but it proves after all to be a slim, young American girl with long, blonde hair, an embroidered peasant blouse from Yugoslavia, loose black velour pantaloons, and pale tan ballerina flats on her slender feet. Perhaps it was she all along and I was merely hallucinating.

For I am not much more certain of my own sanity these days than I am of Björn's. I am feverishly suggestible in the best of times, and all these hallucinatory movies, my nightly immersion in Shakespearean studies, the anniversary of my mother's death, missing Antonia, these crazy crowds, these press conferences — not to mention the hot pursuit of Grisha Krylov — may have addled my already exhausted brain. Anyway, whenever I have been pressed to the breaking point in my life, I have generally retreated into the past. At Chapin I fell in love with ancient Greece and Shakespeare's sonnets, in college with Shakespeare's heroines. At the worst of times in California, when the frenzied high school competitiveness (I have a better car than yours, a better house than yours, a better body than yours) of the film industry began to get to me, I would take off somewhere, anywhere, and play Shakespeare. One gig, no matter how obscure or badly paid, with a real company of actors who all loved word-drunk Will as much as I did, and I would feel sane again, centered again. For I would know that it was the work that mattered, the word that mattered, and not who had the best deal, the best agent, the best car, the best house, the best body. So he had been my salvation many a time, and if ever I met him (even in a dream), I would want to repay that debt. Somehow.

The *regatanti* and *regatante* race on the Grand Canal (or Cana-lozzo, as the Venetians call it in their curious dialect), and I am tossed about the city on the tide of the crowd. At one point I find myself in a certain *campo*, crisscrossed by screaming Venetians, and there who should I run into but a passel of my fellow jurists — Carlos Armada and his girlfriend; Leonardo da Leone and his; Benjamin Gabriel Gimpel and his wife; Gaetano Manuzio; his wife, Elisabetta; and his mistress, Barbara. (Elisabetta and Barbara are walking arm in arm, one pondering the paving stones, the other examining the sky.)

"*Ciao*, Jessica!" waves Gaetano gaily.

Leonardo just scowls.

"I'm very cross with you, Signorina Pruitt," he says formally.

Now, whenever anyone says they are cross with me, I cringe — as if I were still in kindergarten. In fact, I seem to fall forty years back through the rabbit hole of time and find myself *in* kindergarten again, with no escape in sight.

"Why cross with me?" I ask.

"Because of your Soviet friend and his shenanigans," says Leonardo.

"But I had nothing to do with *that*," I say. "In fact, I strenuously disapproved. I lobbied for sanity and restraint — but, alas, too late. He had already rallied the press around him."

Carlos springs to my defense. "It's true," he says, "*verissimo*. Jessica was not consulted in this *folie*, this I know. It was a solitary folly, not a *folie à deux*."

"And how do *you* know?" asks his girlfriend suspiciously.

"Because, *tesoro*, I am a poet. Poets know everything."

She seems unconvinced, as does Leonardo.

"There is an old Italian proverb," says Leonardo, "two who sleep together conspire even in their dreams."

Gaetano scoffs: "I never heard of such a proverb. You invent it, *amico mio.*"

Leonardo shrugs, twitches, then puts his arm around my shoulders. "Well, Jessica, what do you say? Benefit of doubt? I will give you that."

"Thanks," I say, my blood boiling. I want to shout: But the bastard is *not* my lover! You insult my taste! However, I seem to have forfeited that right. Discretion is the better part of valor, I think, biting my tongue; and Leonardo, now forgiving, leads me toward another party in another palazzo.

This palazzo (whose name I am not told) has been gutted inside and redone in the starkest modern style. A pure white staircase — banisterless, and reminiscent of the inside of a nautilus shell — leads upstairs from the flowering courtyard to the *piano nobile*, which is pure white, hung with glassy black Venetian lamps in odd mushrooming shapes, has black leather furniture, white marble floors, and walls covered with white linen. The window shades are huge white linen sails, like the sails of Venetian galleys, and the paintings hung about the room represent a fortune spent at Sothebys: Picassos, Braques, Miros, Rousseaus, even a few Monets and Manets, Renoirs and Matisses. This palazzo is, in short, the modern equivalent of Contessa Venier's.

"It is done by Scarpa," says Leonardo, knowingly.

"Beautiful," I say, absorbing the fact that the owners, whoever they are, are very rich and very chic. They are also partial to the same Picassos that move me most — the saltimbanques and strolling players — those acrobats about whom Rilke wrote:

> But tell me, who *are* then, these wanderers, even more
> transient than we ourselves, who from their earliest days
> are savagely wrung out
> by a never-satisfied will (for *whose* sake)? Yet it wrings
>   them,

bends them, twists them, swings them and flings them
and catches them again; and falling as if through oiled
slippery air, they land
on the threadbare carpet, worn constantly thinner
by their perpetual leaping, this carpet that is lost
in infinite space . . .

Of course, they move me because they are myself. I, too, am a strolling player, wandering through time, a vagabond, a saltimbanque of sorts. But the people at the party are also strolling players, the same strolling players as those at the *other* party. Wandering out to the balcony where the races can still be seen along the Canalozzo, I turn and see, mingling in the crowded salon, Jackie, Paloma, Arianna, Gore, Tina, and company. Can Grisha be far behind? The party has merely moved from one palazzo to another. And again the Beautiful People are somehow cut off from the common folk of Venice whose *festa* this is. They might as well be painted figures on the wall, or masqueraders dressed for a costume ball. They inhabit one Venice, the street people another.

"Jessichka! Jessichka!" comes the call of Grisha Krylov, and at once I start to flee down the shell-shaped stair. But Leonardo sees him too, and before a word is spoken flings a slim, octagonal flute of *prosecco* in his face.

"Pig! *Cochon! Tiy sveenya!*" Grisha screams, punching poor Leonardo in the nose. Down he goes for the count, and I take off, making good my escape.

More headlines for tomorrow, I think — or maybe not. At any rate, I'm safer in the streets than with the glitterati among the Picassos. Funny, I think, how all these starving painters' paintings are now the ultimate status symbols, conferring greater proof of wealth than gold, emeralds, private islands, or ocean-going yachts. It is the artists who make the true value of the world, though at times they may have to starve to do it. They are like earthworms, turning up the soil so things can grow, eating dirt so that the rest of us may eat green shoots.

Off I go again through the streets of Venice, suddenly finding myself lost in a *sestiere* I do not know, with only shadows, angles, and byways before me. For the moment, there seem to be no people. Laughter comes through an open window. A mother cat nurses her kittens in a packing box in a filthy alley. The sounds of cat-scratching and cat-mewing reverberate in the *calle*. The water sounds of a back canal (the slap of water against mossy stone, the muffled tapping of boat hulls against half-rotted wooden poles) can be heard, though the canal cannot be seen. Smells rise around me as if in Satanic prayer. This is the incense of the devil: offal of the streets, banana peel, dog shit, filthy candy and gum wrappers, dead maggoty birds kicked into the corners. There is a grated door to a thirteenth-century house before me, and within, a narrow staircase leading God knows where.

Suddenly I look up, and in a window on the second floor an auburn-haired man with an earring glinting in one ear is kissing the same blond courtier I saw before. It is a kiss of such lingering passion and longing that I can almost feel it here on the street where I stand.

The blond looks down, sees me, laughs derisively, and slams the window shutters hard. Laughter reverberates in the alleyway, and I am left not knowing what I saw or did not see, whether it was the same American girl as before, or the Elizabethan courtier, or whether, in fact, they are one and the same person.

If I were to climb that stair right now, I think, and enter that shadowy, thirteenth-century house — over whose door there is a mocking stone face, a death's head with a gaping toothless mouth, stained by centuries of rainwater — would I encounter Will Shakespeare and his beautiful boy lover or merely an Italian punk Romeo and his American bimbo? In my heart I know it is the poet, locked in that window frame, longing for his lover, possibly forever.

> Eternity was in our lips and eyes,
> Bliss in our brows' bent.

So he wrote, years later, in *Antony and Cleopatra*. That he knew love, longing, passion, unrequited love, and love festering into resentment, fury, murder, self-murder, is unmistakable from the plays, from the sonnets, from the lines of poetry themselves. Whoever he was, whoever he is, he knew those mortal things; and the goddess he worshipped at all times — whether in England or in Italy, whether in time or out of it — was the muse, the Mother of all living, the White Goddess whose kiss is at once spider bite on the sleeping cheek and lingering tongue kiss on the tip of the waking genitals, where she leaves her mark: crystal tears, *lachrymae dei*, the white stain of eternity, its milk.

5

Harry and Will

HOW I GOT BACK to the Lido, I do not know; who won the regatta, I do not know; who won the fistfight between Grisha and Leonardo, I do not know; where Björn and Lilli fled, I do not know. I only know that by sunset I am back in my suite at the Excelsior, stripping off the silver jump suit, my face burning with fever, thinking, thinking only that I must dress and go, dress and go to my première of *Women in Hell*.

But I am will-less. My head aches, my cheeks burn, my heart pounds. I tell myself I shall lie down on the bed for a little while, only a little while, and I do. I stretch out on the cool linen sheets, half dressed and half undressed, sweating, frightened, immobilized by lethargy and weakness.

I must have drifted off.

It is plague time in Venice. My groin, my armpits, my neck, are swollen with buboes. I lie alone in a sweat in the same narrow house with the rain-stained death's head above the door, and I wait, I wait for someone to come and find me, whether to tend me or to cart away my body, I am not sure.

And suddenly I am out of my body. I have left it behind and I am rising now, hovering above it near the ceiling and looking down at Jessica, who lies there on the carved walnut bed, caged by writhing columns. What a beautiful young woman, I think, to die so soon. Her hair is chestnut brown with titian red-gold streaks; her eyes are brown, flickering to gold. She wears the garb of a wealthy young Jewess in the ghetto and she is all alone.

77

But not quite alone; for as I watch, two men appear, one carrying on a silver salver poultices and beverages in golden goblets, a jar of leeches, a bleeding bowl, a straight razor; the other is empty-handed. They are the two Elizabethans again — one auburn-haired with large spaniel eyes, one blond and blue-eyed and aristocratic with a pouting girl's mouth.

The first one speaks. "We are poor physicians, Harry, to minister thus to the wench. For shame —"

"Hush, Will," says the other, "don't be a frightened puppy. This is Venice. All fevers and contagions breed here."

He lifts the woman's heavy head, brings a golden goblet to her lips, and bids her drink. She does. A few gulps go down, but the remainder stains the front of her bodice.

"*Un goccino, per piacere,*" says the blond courtier, his Italian as precise and perfect as his English. She drinks again, whereupon he hands the goblet to his friend. Then he lifts her skirts, pulls down her undergarments, and bends his sweet girl-lips to her nether ones, saying, "O here are the charged chambers, the velvet leaves, the cunnus, the quim, the tropic country for which we are homesick always. . . . Come, let me suck the fever out of thee."

As he brings his lips to her feverish, purple nether lips, I myself feel the soft sweetness of his tongue, the riotous excitement of the friend looking on, the heightened confusion of my fever. I begin to come, tumultuously, as one sometimes does in dreams or in illness, and as I do, Will falls upon Harry and pulls him off Jessica's body, raining blows upon his blond head. The phone shrills. I stab my arm out at it, knock it to the floor, crawl across the sweat-soaked sheets, drop my feverish head over the edge of the bed (where it hangs like a throbbing, overripe melon), and grab the receiver.

"*Pronto?*" I mumble, the dream courtiers fleeing and I longing to make them stay, for now I lust for them both. My reverie is pierced by the voice of one of the young secretaries of the film festival, a certain Oriana Ruzzini, whose words are hushed with her reverence for me, for I am her idol — obviously she does not know my dreams!

"Signorina Pruitt," she says, "your film is about to begin. They are about to present the actors in the Sala Grande."

"My God," I say. "I'm so sorry. I felt ill. I shall be there at once."

"Do you need help?" says Oriana. "A doctor? Anything?"

"No. Just make them wait."

"Certainly," says Oriana.

In a fog I get out of bed, throw cold water on my face, make up, and dress. I must really have a fever, I think, for my cheeks burn and my armpits ache, and my throat throbs as if with swollen glands. Whatever my temperature is, I don't want to know it — for it is a point of pride with me never to miss a gig no matter how ill I am. I have played whole performances much sicker than this, I tell myself, much sicker. I'll make it. I know I will.

Dressed in a black satin "smoking" — last year's St. Laurent — low, black satin pumps by Andrea Pfister, and a silk top hat from the Astaire era that I picked up in a vintage clothing store in Tribeca, I am ready to go. I may have chosen the low-heeled pumps because I could not walk in higher ones, but I dare not tell myself this. I'm fine, I say to myself, applying the finishing touch: a black veil, dotted with tiny rhinestones, which I drape over the top hat, pinning it so that it just covers my eyes and nose. I race out of my room to the lobby.

My plan is to run all the way to the Palazzo del Cinema, but I have not counted on how sick I am. In the lobby, I collide with the *portiere*, who says, "Miss Pruitt, may I help you?"

"A taxi, please," I mumble.

It is late, the screening should have begun (it must be nine already), so there are a few vacant taxis at the door. I get in one of them and tell the astonished driver that I want to go the two or three blocks to the Palazzo del Cinema. He's not at all happy about this until I press 50,000 lire into his hand.

I just about make it out of the cab and up the slippery marble steps of the Palazzo del Cinema before another wave of weakness hits me and I have to lean against a wall to gather my strength. I take a deep breath, concentrate all my powers (as Vivian Lovecraft taught me to do), and open the double doors to the mezzanine. They seem like lead, the very gates of hell, and the burst of maniacal applause that greets me as I enter the mezzanine does not diminish that illusion. I am picked out by a single spotlight as I descend the stairs to my seat among the actors. Blinded by the spot, terrified that I am going to stumble and fall, I overhear these words: "Some grand entrance," says an unknown woman near the aisle. "What a prima donna." That seems somehow to be the last straw.

I take my seat among my fellow actors from *Women in Hell* — Hanna Schygulla, Catherine Deneuve, Liv Ullmann (who have all just flown in for the screening). I squeeze Liv's hand. Hanna blows me a kiss. Catherine waves. My director, Gian-Pietro Robusti, nods hello. Then it is time for the presentation. I barely make it to my feet to take my bow before I sink back in my chair, exhausted.

"Are you okay?" Liv asks, her beautiful round blue eyes moist with empathy as ever.

"Oh, Liv, you are the kindest person I have ever known," I say. "I'm fine."

In fact I am as close to unconscious as one can be without actually being in a coma. The film begins. Thank god for that. Now I can sleep. I am hoping to reenter my Elizabethan dream with my two gentlemen of Venice, but alas it does not come. Instead I find myself back in the old apartment on Park and Seventy-third, with the birds on my bedroom ceiling, and Mummy sipping sherry on the chaise longue in her bedroom down the hall. It is night, I have had a bad dream, so I toddle into Mummy's room and find her passed out on the chaise, a bottle of sherry on the floor beside her, a sticky empty glass beside it, and a Steuben ashtray overflowing with fuchsia-lipsticked burnt-out ends of Dunhill cigarettes (intermingled with Pall Malls — for my mother had this theory that smoking could not hurt you if you alternated two brands), and the terrifying feeling that this time, something is hideously different.

I grab her hand. It is limp and cold. Mummy's dead, I think, Mummy's dead. And then I tell myself: *be calm*. You're the mother now. And then Antonia, my daughter, is suddenly there (though she cannot have been born yet), and she is a baby of nine months or so crawling around on the carpet and I am crawling after her. She seems to be putting funny things in her mouth. She has found these pink and green capsules of Mummy's with some odd markings on them — Greek letters, it appears — and she is grabbing them and

80

shoving them into her mouth. I have to stop her, *I have to stop her*. And now I am crawling along the rug, feeling for the pink and green capsules that are lost in the deep shag. I brush the wool this way and that, searching for them, and suddenly they have turned from capsules into segmented bugs, those little crustaceans one finds under rotten logs, and with a panicky feeling I am creeping after the baby to keep her from eating *those!*

My mouth feels crawly with insects as if I have eaten the bugs myself — and my cheeks still burn. Wake up, I say sharply to myself, this is a nightmare. Wake up! And when I do wake up I am in my suite at the Excelsior in broad daylight, with flowers all around, and Liv is still holding my hand.

"You were very ill," she says. "A strep throat, with swollen glands, and your fever is still high. Try to sleep again."

"What happened?" I ask. "What about . . . the film festival?"

"It ends tonight," Liv says with her lovely Norwegian brogue, "but you're much too sick to get out of bed. Just rest. I will take your place at the awards ceremony. I've arranged to stay another night to do it. Now rest."

I sink back on my pillows. The room looks like my hospital room when I gave birth to Antonia — there are roses and lilies in profusion everywhere. The funereal odor of the lilies unfortunately overpowers the scent of the roses.

"Thank you, Liv," I say weakly.

"What are friends for?" she asks, getting up and quietly walking out of the room.

I try to get up but I cannot.

From where I lie in bed, I can see three large vertical rectangles of light bounded at the bottoms by little stone balconies that overlook the Adriatic. The empty wine glass from several days ago is still there. But I cannot see the sea itself, or the beach, without getting out of bed. Above me is the spun-sugar chandelier with its whorls and twists of light held captive in glass — that unique Venetian invention: light imprisoned (imprismed?) in molten sand and woven into a lucent braid. I know that if I rise and walk to the window, however wobbly, I shall presently see the white tents of the Excelsior beach club and the fat *bambini* gallivanting on the sand — or shall I? Perhaps the whole present tense has been abolished and I am back at the Lido as it must have existed in Shakespeare's time (for it did even in Byron's): a sandy strip of beach to gallop across on the back of your Arab steed.

Are my two Elizabethan courtiers then racing along the strand? I can almost see them, urging each other on with cries and calls, bets and dares, as the hoofbeats of their horses drum on the wet, hard-packed sand at the edge of the water or sink with muffled thumps into the drier sand farther from the sea.

Or are they damned ghosts that I have seen? For Venice's very air is full of ghosts — just as the clouds that flit across the sky are camel-backed, weasellike, whalelike. If there ever were a place to see a ghost, have discourse or intercourse with a ghost, Venice would be that place.

I must get up, I think, and go to the window to judge for myself whether I am in the present or the past. Are the tents of the Excelsior there, or is it a bare beach with two Elizabethans galloping along the strand? I am no longer sure! They fool me to the top of my bent — or else my fever fools me.

The very air in this room existed in Shakespeare's time, in Byron's, in Browning's. Where does the air go? I wonder. Why, where *can* it go? Is history all a matter of changes in the air? For it lingers from one century to the next, and in its bright strands souls are captured, souls who have some business here below because they are not yet at peace. Shakespeare knew such souls; he wrote about them obsessively; clearly he believed in them. And the Earl of Southampton surely was such a soul — with his love of poetry, his pederasty, his eventual treachery, and his improbable pardon (when all his coconspirators were dead). But was Shakespeare also one of these restless souls? Dead at fifty-three, the cause unknown — one Shakespearologist even claims he was murdered — a gentleman, a property owner, but still with some words unsaid? That I would like to know. That I intend to know.

I get up and in my delirium stagger to the window. There is the sea, with the white arabesque tents of the Excelsior huddled before it, and the *bambini* trading autographs on the sand.

Deeply disappointed, I turn away from the window. Still in the present tense, I think, still here not there, still trapped in this bubble of time called 1984, which was cursed by a mere writer, who, because he called into being a terrifying fantasy about that year, was able to bewitch that actual year when it occurred, decades later. Oh, the raising of visions is a dangerous thing — as Shakespeare also knew.

Still, since I'm up, I might as well have a look at the cards attaching to all these riotous bouquets of flowers.

I start to peek at them: day lilies from my agent, Lance Robbins; yellow roses from Liv; calla lilies from Grisha (does he wish me dead with this funereal display of flowers?); a mixed bouquet of red and pink roses from the venerable communist Carlos Armada; an enormous potted palm from the managing director of the hotel; a low bowl of mixed anemones and tiger lilies from Leonardo; mums and gladioli from Per Erlanger; and then, behind the other floral displays, as if in hiding, two dozen more white roses in a tall, clear glass vase, with this sonnet affixed:

> Th'expense of spirit in a waste of shame
> Is lust in action; and, till action, lust
> Is perjured, murd'rous, bloody, full of blame,
> Savage, extreme, rude, cruel, not to trust;
> Enjoyed no sooner but despised straight;
> Past reason hunted, and no sooner had,
> Past reason hated as a swallowed bait.
> On purpose laid to make the taker mad;
> Mad in pursuit, and in possession so;
> Had, having, and in quest to have, extreme;
> A bliss in proof, and proved, a very woe;
> Before, a joy proposed; behind, a dream.
>   All this the world well knows, yet none knows well
>   To shun the heaven that leads men to this hell.

I read the sonnet slowly aloud to myself and then fall back on my bed, exhausted.

*

I toss and turn in my fever, soak the sheets, ring for the maid to change them, soak them anew. Where I am I do not really know, unless I am in that realm called fever, speaking that timeless language called fever.

I think of all the artists who have died in Venice and conclude I am done for. If Titian was felled here by the plague, if Dante died of a fever caught on a journey here, if Wagner and Browning both breathed their last above the Grand Canal (not to mention Diaghilev, Stravinsky, Ezra Pound, even poor Baron Corvo), why should I be spared? This is it, I think. I expire amid the contagions of this lagoon, hallowed by history, hallowed by the deaths of poets. Alone in Venice with only two dream courtiers to attend me — this will be my Aschenbach-like fate.

And then my thoughts shift to Shakespeare and particularly to his sonnets, that curious sequence in which he surely bared his heart. If you read the sonnets carefully, the pain is unmistakable. This was a man who loved and was betrayed. This was a man who was hurt to his heart's very quick. Whoever the "straying youth" he loved, there is no question that he loved an arrogant narcissist and that he himself was the unrequited lover, not the beloved. The ache is *in* the sonnets. It is palpable. It is most palpable, in fact, when the poet most tries to rationalize himself out of it, as in the sonnet that describes the young man's seduction of the poet's woman.

> That thou hast her, it is not all my grief,
> And yet it may be said I loved her dearly;
> That she hath thee is of my wailing chief,
> A loss in love that touches me more nearly.
> Loving offenders, thus I will excuse ye:
> Thou dost love her, because thou know'st I love her,
> And for my sake even so doth she abuse me,
> Suff'ring my friend for my sake to approve her.
> If I lose thee, my loss is my love's gain,
> And losing her, my friend hath found that loss:
> Both find each other, and I lose both twain,
> And both for my sake lay on me this cross.
> > But here's the joy: my friend and I are one;
> > Sweet flattery! Then she loves but me alone.

Was ever a lover so self-deceiving and so undeceived both at the same time?

Harry and Will, Will and Harry. Have I met them or only imagined them? And who is the Dark Lady? Can she in fact be me?

I am dark now, with auburn lights, but my hair has always been changeable, running the gamut from gold to sable. The changes of my hair have reflected the changes of my life. And as I have fretted over my life, I have always fretted over my hair.

"Titian gold" my mother called it, when I was fifteen, but then it darkened to auburn, then to sable with reddish highlights. I have read that Shakespeare had the same color hair — that his hair was russet or auburn before he went rather bald, poor chap.

Of course, I have never liked my hair. (What woman has?) When I was a child, people raved about its color (it was silky, long, and reddish gold like my daughter's is now). It got curlier and darker as I got older, so that by adolescence it was tarnished gold, forming a curly, cuprous aureole around my head, and by the time I reached college it was positively Pre-Raphaelite. I see myself in pictures from that period (Sarah Lawrence, I mean) looking for all the world like a Burne-Jones angel. Still, that didn't mean I ever *felt* beautiful. On the contrary, I felt ugly. Nor was curly hair the vogue in the late fifties, early sixties, when hair was the most important thing in my life (besides dieting, finding — or avoiding — sex, and ampheta-mines). I did everything to flatten my curls: "wrapping" my hair, having it "pressed," "relaxed," or stretched on giant rollers (we even *slept* in them in those days). The point was to achieve the opposite of what you had: lank, flat hair if you were born with curly; curly hair if you were born with straight.

Ah, adolescence — I do not miss it! Even fever is better. Even fever has its own inner logic. Hair and fever bring me back to Shakespeare who knew both, knew them intimately. And suffered.

Why does the White Goddess make her devotees suffer so? Why are her priests and priestesses so cursed? Is it because she requires the deep cut of pain to release the poem? Or is it because her poets must fall in love harder than their muses so as to make them more open to the Goddess's silver darts? Has She bred a whole race of martians whose main purpose on earth is to love, feel pain, write poems, and die? Yes, I think in my delirium. This is the logic of it, and I am here in Venice to die and rejoin that cursed/blest company of poets. Perhaps when I do, my soul will fly out of my body and rejoin the Dark Lady, Jessica, Shylock's daughter, or whoever I was in that sixteenth-century life I keep trying to remember.

Madness, I think. All this is madness. No, not madness, only fever, which is a kind of madness, a kind of earthquake in the brain and in the body. "Some say the earth was feverous and did shake." Well, my body is feverish and doth shake, and what other earth have I but this body?

In my fever, I remember things I would rather forget: how my baby brother, Pip, and Antonia's father, Lincoln — since he was named for the great emancipator, he felt free to play the jailer whenever possible — organized the lawyers and accountants who managed Mother's trust against me, so that I became dependent entirely upon the dubious beneficence of LaLa Land and its curious laws. If not for their treachery, I might have my daughter still, and also the emoluments of Mother's money. Not that I care so very much about money for its own sake, but in my profession it can buy a certain freedom, a certain immunity from the cruel caprices of filmdom. And then there is the question of my grandfather's will. . . . In my delirium I am obsessed by wills of all sorts!

My grandfather's will was at the root of many of my mother's troubles — though I doubt that he intended it to be. It was simply that my grandfather was the sort of man who thought more about keeping a fortune than a family intact. In homage to that he had designed and built for him (by one of those posh New York law firms with twenty partners on the creamy, copper-plate-engraved letterhead — including some who had been dead for decades) an ironclad monument to his cupidity, his appreciation of money above life. This will created what is known as a layered trust, ensuring that his millions (hundreds of millions, actually) would pass through the generations as much united as possible and as undiluted by taxes as the law allowed. None of the children or grandchildren was ever to get her (or his) hands on the capital, but to receive only a stream of income directed, or misdirected, by the trustees and executors.

Wills are always troublesome (think of the "second-best bed"), but a will such as my grandfather's is more troublesome than most. The trouble is, of course, that the maker has to die (although the nature of the document is such that it appears intended to *deny* the reality of death). And when he does, other living, breathing, fallible creatures — lawyers — must carry out what they presume to be his wishes. And more than likely they stand to gain plenty from their role as "sprinklers" of the estate's balm.

My poor mother had all the disadvantages of being an heiress — a sapping of strength and ambition, a tendency to attract the lowest sort of fortune-hunting rogues, a profound disbelief in her own lovability — and none of the advantages. She could not thumb her nose at the whole male-dominated world as a powerful female dispenser of inherited money might, for she was ever in the thrall of lawyers and investment bankers, who dispensed the bounty — or the curse — of grandfather's money as a sort of commentary upon her values and aspirations.

The money never seemed to bring anyone any pleasure — and it gave a lot of people pain. My grandfather, in the first place, was guilty about it, because it had been made chiefly through selling poison gas to the government in World War I. My grandfather — Wardell Benjamin Bostwicke III was his name — had been, in his youth, a cellist and a lover of Mozart. He was also a man with one of those great and deeply felt classical educations that Southern gentlemen of the old school used to receive at the University of Virginia, and you can bet the irony of fiddling while the world choked in the trenches was not lost on him. He tried to kill himself with his shotgun, in fact, though the family always declared it an accident, but he missed. And when I knew him, he was an ancient man with a still suppurating, schrapnellike wound in his forehead, out of which pieces of metal were rumored to have fallen during rides in the car (a Delahaye), during dinner, or at tea.

My grandfather Bostwicke did one good thing with his money, however; he set up an arts foundation that was supposed to enshrine his love for the classics — Mozart, Shakespeare, the study of Latin and Greek. Unfortunately, upon his demise, his ever-vigilant trustees and executors had found a way to divert much of the money for this foundation into their own pockets, so his intentions had not been carried out. But the potential for putting at least some of the Bostwicke booty to good use was there — if one were prepared to do battle with the successor trustees and find the proper legal minds to help.

My mother had been too embroiled in her own marital woes to undertake this, nor had she truly cared. She was of that lost generation of women, born in the twenties, too young to be flappers or suffragettes, and too old to be liberated superwomen of the sixties-turned-seventies (though whether or not my generation is truly liberated is certainly the mootest of moot points). When I came to inherit at twenty-one, I was of the fuck-you-I'll-do-it-myself school of heiresses. I thumbed my nose at my inheritance — as any true, idealistic child of the sixties would have done. The result was that my baby brother, Pip, and Antonia's father (both of whom were lawyers) managed to quietly usurp every vestige of my control. I had never cared to fight them on it. Now I was beginning to wonder if that had been so wise.

Here comes the doctor, at last. I almost expect him to be wearing one of those long-nosed masks like the plague doctors of the sixteenth century, but he is not. Rather, he is a silver-haired, suntanned Italian bachelor in his sixties who looks more gigolo than medic.

"How are you today, Signorina Pruitt?" he asks me.

"Feverish," I say, sitting up in bed. (Have you ever noticed how the mere arrival of the doctor makes you feel better, lowers your fever, makes you feel safe? I note all this with amusement, since any doctor can kill you, but in Italy your chances of dying from the medic, not the disease, are infinitely higher.)

Dr. Dazzi (for that is the doctor's improbable name) is the doctor they always call for suffering foreigners in Venice, since he speaks four languages (all of them badly).

"Would you like penicillin or erythromycin?" he asks, as if he were requesting my preference in *gelato* flavors.

"What do you think?" I ask the doctor.

"Is up to you," says Dazzi. "What you like? You like a shot, or through the mouth?"

"What will get me *well* faster?"

The doctor shrugs. "Mah!" he says, as if this were an existential question, too complex to be determined except perhaps by God, Jean-Paul Sartre, or lottery. My attempts to make him into the authority figure I require in my delirium are failing totally.

"If you take a shot of penicillin," says Dazzi, "you will get better in seven days. If you don't take it, you will get better in a week. What do you like?"

Torn between my feverish panic and my desire to rejoin the Elizabethans as soon as possible, I opt for penicillin by mouth.

"Good decision," says the doctor. "I will order."

He sits on my bed and calls the pharmacy, a really touristy one near San Marco, which dispenses the same penicillin as any other pharmacy at twice the price.

Wearied from this much exertion, I fall back on my pillows again.

"I shall come tomorrow," says Dr. Dazzi.

"Good," I say, not really sure I will be there at all. Perhaps by then I will have figured out how to get back to Harry and Will.

As soon as the doctor leaves, Grisha bursts in with piles of fresh newspapers. His fistfight was a great success! It generated more column inches even than his protest against Björn.

"And your illness, Jessichka, was a journalistic coup. Brilliant publicity — I could not have thought of it myself." He shows me some Italian newspapers in which I have made front page news for being sick and fainting dead away at my own film. One paper speculates about whether or not Robusti will demand an apology. Or will he realize that my fainting was no comment on the film?

"That's the silliest thing I ever heard of," I say to Grisha. "Why should I protest my own film?"

"Publicity, my dzear girl, publicity. . . . If you learn Grisha's

89

lesson well, you already know this. Well, I must go and dress for the closing ceremonies. May I take my newspapers now?"

"Does this mean good-by?" I ask warily, knowing the answer already.

"Of course not," says Grisha. But I know he lies. If he exits with those newspapers, he exits my life forever.

Am I happy about this? You bet. But it does seem rather the end of an era. There goes détente, such as it is, I think. As Grisha Krylov waves and shuts the door, clutching his beloved newspapers, the cold war recommences with a fury.

I am lying in bed, cooling my heels while my brow burns and mad fantasies of dead Elizabethans flit through it. They are closing the film festival without me, and soon all the jurors and journalists will disperse, leaving Venice to the Venetians. What's to become of me? Do I wait to see whether Björn turns up? Do I head for Pacific Palisades again? Someone had better send word soon. Until then I shall just lie here slipping in and out of time, waiting to see which century will claim me, whether I love a dead man or a living, whether I myself am dead or alive, mad or sane, Jessica or . . . Jessica.

6

In War with Time

THE FILM FESTIVAL is over, the jurors are beginning to disperse; but I am still lying in bed too sick to move. That doesn't mean, however, that my bed is a quiet retreat from the world. On the contrary, it seems to be the center of the universe. The phone shrills constantly and visitors come in and out bearing newspapers, bearing flowers, bearing tidings both good and ill.

The morning papers bring the news that *Women in Hell* has won no awards whatsoever (perhaps in part because of my "protest"); the Golden Lion has instead been won by an obscure Indian film about peasants herding pigs across the Ganges; and the best actress award has gone to an amateur player in a Filipino documentary that worthily recounts labor troubles in that country. Best actor has gone to a broken-down drunk of an American cowboy of the Reagan era who had the guts (or the sheer gall) to appear in a Polish film about the Second World War, directed by a Russian. Even the two best supporting awards have gone to virtual unknowns. As usual, the Venice Film Festival has gone out of its way to put perversity above excellence, and its choices for the major awards are as far out of the mainstream as possible.

Grisha has fled — but not without making further protests about the awards, protests that will certainly ensure the Kremlin's sending him abroad again as soon as possible. And Björn has still not been heard from, at least by me. I am in despair. *Women in Hell* is neither a critical nor a commercial success, and *Serenissima* may now never happen. What do I do? I'm forty-three years old, deathly ill, and washed up. Even my agent, Lance Robbins (né Lou Rabinowitz), has called to "commiserate" with me over the mess at the festival and tell me that maybe he can still get me a part as an aging tart in Aaron Spelling's hot new miniseries if only I will come to my senses and come home. (Lance Robbins, of Malibu, California, is a beach boy of fifty with silver-gray hair, a perfectly muscled chest, a voice that sounds like olive oil on velvet, and absolutely no inkling of why I would want to wait around in Venice for Björn Persson when I could be taping a miniseries called *Vegas II* — *Vegas I* has already made Neilson history — with Joan Collins and Suzanne Sommers. But then, Lance Robbins only dates twenty-five-year-old starlets with implants, and probably thinks Will Shakespeare is a hot, new restaurant on Melrose opened by Wolfgang Puck. He adores me in his heartless William Morris Agent way, but he also thinks I'm *meshugga*.)

"*Meshugga*," he says across six thousand miles and nine time zones. "Why sit around for a picture that may never happen when you've got a real deal here with a project that's a definite go. This is a terrific part, Jessica, with real meat in it. You play this hooker in Las Vegas who figures out a system to beat the house odds in roulette and gets pursued by the mob. It's dynamite writing, not your usual schlock. Really top writers — Susan and Herman Blotnik — and a director you can trust: Herbie Plotkin. Blotnik and Plotkin — if you can't trust them, who can you trust in this business? You've got script approval, and believe me I can build all kinds of other sweeteners into the deal. It's not exactly as if you're getting younger, Sweetie. I mean all this high art stuff is very noble, but —"

"Let me think about it, Lance."

"Well, think about it, but don't think about it for more than a day or so because there are plenty of other actresses dying for the part. Elizabeth is thin again and looks great, and even Raquel is willing to do a miniseries now. It's not slumming like it used to be. And the exposure is incredible. It could turn your whole career around."

"It's that bad, huh? One film festival and I'm finished?"

"Of course I don't mean *that*, Sweetie," Lance says, "but Björn

Persson, even when he's *not* being temperamental, doesn't get you the exposure we're talking here. . . . Let's face it. Swedish art movies are not network television."

"That's why I want to do it."

"Be reasonable, Jessica, you could knock yourself right out of place in line. Rocky, Elizabeth, Joan — they're all working in television now. Well, get better, kid. Watch out for *Death in Venice*."

"Thanks, Lance," I say, putting down the phone.

It's only nine A.M. in Venice, which means it must be midnight in Malibu, the moonstruck night before.

I can just visualize Lance in his house on the Pacific Coast Highway, with the Jaguar XJ6 and the Mercedes SLC parked outside. He could be calling me from the hot tub on the redwood deck overlooking the ocean while his main tootsie, Elena, a calculating little number with flaxen hair and tits that don't move at all, rubs his back and tokes on a joint, thinking of how she can talk Lance out of making her sign an antenuptial agreement *should* he marry her. Not that he is about to. She does drugs too much, and works too little, and Lance thinks he may be able to do better. Even marriage in the Land of LaLa is subject to high-powered deal-making. And as for drugs, Lance doesn't do much dope anymore — except before sex — because it makes you too mellow, man, and he needs all his greed and graspingness intact for the work he does.

I shut my eyes and astrally transport myself to Carbon Beach. The same moon that shines on the Adriatic here is shining on the Pacific there — and I love the Pacific, no matter how many William Morris agents line its shores. But it seems a greater feat of time travel and space warp to go from Venice to Malibu than from 1984 to 1592. Harry and Will still seem more real to me than Lance Robbins and his Elena in their glass-and-redwood house above the Pacific. William Shakespeare still calls to me more persistently than William Morris.

The phone rings again. It's Per Erlanger, my would-be Shylock.

"Per? How are you?"

"Yessica," says Per in his rhythmic, Swedish singsong, "may I come to your suite? It's very important."

"How can I ever resist someone who calls me 'Yessica'?" I say, referring to an old joke between us. Per laughs appreciatively. I go on, "But will you forgive me if I look like hell?"

"Don't be silly, Yessica. Don't forget that I've seen you in all kinds of hells."

"True," I say, remembering some I'd rather forget.

I throw cold water on my ghostly face, brush my hair, my teeth, put on a clean robe, and brush my cheeks with blusher. I contemplate my enormous array of costly cosmetics, set out on the dresser top, but decide I haven't even the energy to do my face. The pots of paint in their glistening bottles and jars must languish while I regain my strength. I still look like death warmed over, but it's true that Per knows me. We are an old story to each other.

A few minutes later he knocks, and I stagger up to greet him.

"Thanks for the flowers," I say. "They're lovely."

"Oh, it's nothing," says Per, a big man, stooping, gray, grizzled, diffident in his guilty, Swedish Socialist fashion about being thanked. The years have not been good to him. He drinks too much. Worthy roles and worthy political views have not saved his life. When we had our affair a decade ago in Stockholm, he looked better. So, probably, did I.

"Sit down," I say. "Can I order you some tea? Some coffee?"

"No, I just ate. God — you look pale. Isn't anyone looking after you?"

"Only Shakespeare," I say. "I keep getting these curious bouquets of white roses signed 'W.S.,' with sonnets enclosed. At first I thought they were from Björn, but now I don't know. It could be a prank, or maybe not. . . ."

Per shrugs, then changes the subject. Mysterious roses and sonnets are not his thing. He is a political animal, not a poetic one. "Listen, Yessica, I have not heard from Björn directly, but Lilli *has* communicated with me. She and Björn are in Lugano, staying with Anthony and Liana Burgess. They are in hiding, so to say. Björn is trying to get the financing for *Serenissima* back on track. When Grisha made his big scene and Björn fled the festival, the RAI — the Italian state TV — pulled out. I think they would look for any excuse to do so anyway because of the usual political crisis here, but Björn also lost his German financing at the same time and suddenly there was no film. . . . But now, Lilli says that if we wait, she and Björn may just get the Germans back, this time with a French company coproducing. She pleaded with us not to leave, not to give up."

"What are you going to do?"

"I intend to stay. *Serenissima* will be a great film — that I know. And I trust Björn to get it back together. The Mozart film was splendid, but this one will be even better. And Lilli sounded so resolute. I know she is strong and can do it."

"Where are you going to stay?"

"Well — I shall move to the Gritti, if I can, as soon as possible. I called my old friend Nico and he was very kind as always. The tourists begin to clear out of Venice after the regatta, after the Campiello, after the film festival, and it becomes another city. . . . I intend to wait. But you — you are too sick to go home anyway. I should stay here and look after you till you get well. You *need* someone, dear Yessica. You are too much alone. You need a bodyguard, what the Mafia call a walkaround man. You are too vulnerable by yourself. I could see the way Grisha Krylov forced himself on you — and you were too weak to resist. That, by the way, was a pure KGB maneuver. They *want* him to seduce Western celebrity women, as many as possible, so that he has an excuse to visit them abroad. It's classic."

I was suddenly alarmed that Per would move in with me, banishing the Elizabethans. I wanted my solitude now, more than ever.

"Per, that's a good idea — move to the Gritti. I will join you there in a week or so, when I'm better."

"Meanwhile, what will you do? Who will look after you?"

"The doctor, Dottore Dazzi."

"That crank? I'm a better doctor than he is."

"Anyone is." I laugh. "But I'm on penicillin now. In a day or two I should be better. Call me and check on me. That will be enough, I promise."

Per shakes his head and pulls at his curly gray beard. "Am I too much of a Jewish mama?" (He pronounces it "Ewe-ish mamá," as even the most expertly English-speaking Swede would.)

"I need a Jewish mama — you're right. All orphans do. But you can mother me by phone. . . . Go. I give you permission."

Per kisses me gently on the cheek, clasps my hand. I wonder (I often wonder when meeting my former lovers or husbands) how on earth I ever could have been attracted to him? He seems a nice man — worried, soulful, sensitive, self-punishing, and a bit of a drunk, but not the least attraction for him stirs either in my gut or my quim — as Mummy always called it. (She said it was a shame that one of the most beautiful things in all of nature did not have an equally beautiful name, and quim got her vote for such a name. "Vagina," she claimed, was clinical; "cunt" and "twat" were both beneath contempt. In retrospect, I feel immensely grateful to have had a mother who mused about such things!)

Per, however, no longer causes any tumult in that secret place. I wonder why. Do the stars govern these things? The planets? Are people attracted because their zodiacs are in a certain alignment at a certain period of their lives? Would Romeo and Juliet, ten years later, walk by each other with never a flicker? Jessica and Lorenzo? Portia and Bassanio? Desdemona and Othello? Shakespeare and his Dark Lady? Is it all a question of interlocking zodiacal tracks that hold us as if spellbound, and carry us back, back, back to childhood obsessions? How often I have been in love, and how empty all those loves seem today! It seems to me now that I will never be in love again — unless it is with someone I invent, or someone centuries dead.

After Per goes, I am alone again with my flowers and my thoughts. I get up and look at the white roses once more, stare into them searching for some clue, reread the sonnet about "lust in action," and examine my little crystal ball for some sign of my two Elizabethans. Perhaps they will peer out at me and tell me where to find them. But no. The crystal ball is clear. It reflects only the room, the sky, the ocean, the lucent braids of the great chandelier. Suddenly, on a sort of inner dare, a wild hunch, I opened the little silver casket Vivian Lovecraft gave me. It has always been empty, containing only Vivian's good wishes for me, her white magick, her craft. Not so now.

My heart nearly stops beating when I see that now it contains a little parchment scroll. And on that scroll, lettered in the same perfect calligraphy I have come to know from the proferred sonnets, these words: "Who chooseth me must give and hazard all he hath."

I am dumbfounded. This is the line from *The Merchant of Venice* around which the whole play revolves. These are the words that constitute a test for Portia's suitors. These are the words devised by her dead father to test her future groom. And it is only when Bassanio has the wit to choose lead above gold or silver, and hazard above surety, that he gets the girl — and her fortune as well. Risk alone is sure, Shakespeare seems to be saying. In life there is no safety, except by risking all for love.

Damn, I mutter to myself. There is no question of going back to the Land of LaLa now. I stay in Venice till I solve this mystery. But how? At the moment I have no idea.

The phone shrills. I let it ring, too tired to answer it. When it stops, I call the front desk, ask them to hold my calls, and I doze. I am hoping that somehow in my dreams I will solve the riddle, as sometimes I have solved the problems in certain roles by merely going to sleep and letting my unconscious take over. This time it does not work. I toss on my feverish bed thinking of my dead mother, my living daughter, my dead father, my dead grandfather, whose will confounded generations of lawyers and executors and ensured that the remaining family members would claw each other to death for decades after his demise.

It is still early — only nine-thirty or so in the morning, and in New York, the wee small hours are just dawning. Antonia sleeps, her copper lashes shading her freckled cheeks, her masses of red-gold hair tousled on her pillow, the back of her neck moist with the dew of her preadolescent dreams — in which, I hope, I at least figure as a fairy godmother. That I cannot call her and wake her at this hour is, in a way, a blessing, since when I reach her at her father's house she is always somewhat torn — wanting to talk to me, yet holding something in reserve, in part because she does not want to alienate her father by loving me too loudly, and in part because she must keep her turbulent longing for me in check in order to accept her life.

I know all this, and as her mother the last thing I want to do is cause her pain, so I telephone her sparingly, always at times when I calculate Lincoln will not be there. We were nearly inseparable until she was five, when her father remarried and instantly began plotting to take her from me. How naive I was about those plots! I thought a man as boring as Lincoln Devendish Fuller II had not such duplicity in him, except when it came to leveraged buy-outs, but I was wrong. He began innocently enough — suggesting that Antonia stay with him one fall and go to kindergarten in New York while I was making a movie in Morocco.

It was to be temporary and I had no reason to see harm in it. Our divorce had been perfectly amicable — though I'm now inclined to believe that an amicable divorce is a contradiction in terms. Previous to that, he had visited the child as often as he wished and she had suffered remarkably little as a result of my easy, open attitude toward his involvement in her life. But once he had Antonia in his clutches, he moved swiftly. Unbeknownst to me, he had hired a detective to document my sexual life for the past two years. Not that it was lurid by LaLa Land standards — three leading men, one Texas oil billionaire, one exercise instructor in his twenties — but it was enough to *look* like depravity to a bribed judge. Lincoln sued for custody on the grounds of my "promiscuous lifestyle" and the fact that I traveled a lot for my work. And he got it, whereupon he began making it harder and harder for me to see Antonia at all, treating her like the princess in the tower for, supposedly, her own good. Enough said. What the world does *not* need now is another story of a bitter divorce. Still, you can imagine my sense of betrayal at having had my openness and trust abused. All that had happened five years ago, but the wounds would always be fresh — like that mythic wound in my grandfather's head.

I sleep fitfully for a few hours and when I awaken, it is to the sound of a note being pushed under my door. Shaky, with a dry mouth and a pounding head, I get up and retrieve it. The envelope is one of the standard hotel ones marked EXCELSIOR LIDO, VENEZIA — but inside is a note typed on buff-colored parchment with no letterhead. It reads:

Liebe Jessica,

I shall assume you have not received any of my messages, for certainly you are too kind to ignore them totally. Please forgive my bad English and my breaking heart. I cannot leave this place without seeing you again. May I come to you, if only in a dream?

Ich Liebe Dich
Wolfgang Schnabel

It is impossible to describe the devastating effect this note has upon me — especially in my delirium and fever. I have totally forgotten the German swain who romanced me in the bar before the Red Cross Gala, and it has certainly never occurred to me that his initials were W.S.!

I feel as if all comfort, all succor, all hope for the future, have been taken away and I am doomed to return to Pacific Palisades to endlessly play tarts in miniseries set in Las Vegas, in which I am flanked by other aging actresses and pursued by mobsters who were once my leading men. I refuse to spend what's left of my life, my gift, my voice, my heart, playing characters even Lance Robbins would not recognize as human. *Meshugga* I may be (what actress is not?), but I would rather die in Venice than wither away in Pacific Palisades, my heart (not to mention my head) shrunken by the roles left to me. I refuse! I rebel! I take Wolfgang Schnabel's note, carefully tear it into little pieces, and throw it, like confetti, down to the beach. The pieces flutter. The *bambini* look up, hoping for autographs. I slam the windows and take to my bed.

So I stayed. I stayed at the Excelsior while I recovered from my fever, and after that I stayed at the Gritti, having mournful drinking bouts with Per in the dark little bar on the first floor. I stayed while Venice emptied of tourists; while the Japanese tour groups (who glide down the Grand Canal to the strains of Neopolitan music in gondolas ranged six abreast) departed again for Tokyo, Nagoya, Kyoto. I stayed while the Cipriani pool grew colder and colder and the English octogenarians fled to London, Oxford, Henley, Uxbridge, Staines, Brighton, Bath; while the *settembrini* ceased their cruising and went home to New York, London, Paris, Key West, San Francisco, East Hampton; while the hardy German hikers took their rucksacks and went back to *Universität* in München, Berlin, Frankfurt, Heidelberg; while the honeymooners (of all nationalities) went home to face Real Life in Cleveland, Sydney, Stuttgart, Sofia, or Stratford; while the Venetians reclaimed Venice.

It grew cold. It was in fact the coldest autumn in a hundred years. Snow came from the Alps and settled. Canals froze. The jollity of Venice in summer — all red-ribboned straw hats and *gelato* in a rainbow of flavors — was banished as Venice became a city where bitter wind whipped through gray and frozen *calli*, and getting warm and dry became life's major quest.

After the Gritti, I moved (to save money) to the Fenice; after the Fenice to a funny little house in Dorsoduro that belonged to a friend of my dear friend Lorelei, the honey-curled Viennese painter who has lived and worked in Venice for twenty-five years. Lorelei was going through a bitter divorce, which occupied much of her energy, but nonetheless, with her characteristic generosity she had found for me a crooked little house on a back canal where the rooms were filled with a variety of odd antiques and Mexican folk art, as well as Braque, Chagall, and Miró drawings, some small Picassos and Dalis, and even a Diego Rivera drawing. The owner was a very old, very beautiful Greek woman painter named Demetra, who flickered in and out of madness (and lived, these days, in a cave in Crete, worshipping the Mother Goddess); and the works of art had been given her by the painters themselves, who were all, at one time or another, her lovers. The house had a haunted feeling about it, and I was glad to move in with my volumes of Shakespeare, my books on Venice, my clothes, my notebooks. I was determined to continue my study of *The Merchant of Venice* and not to lose hope. Having had my fill of hotel life, I was pleased to shop at the Rialto, trudge through the *calli* in the bitter cold (carrying in one hand my string bag full of groceries and in the other my witchy black umbrella).

Lance Robbins had long since given up on me. Phone lines to Venice are bad enough in the best of climes, but with the weather so horrid they were positively impossible. I assumed that Raquel or Elizabeth or *someone* had my part. Who cared? It was all unreal to me. I read neither the trades, nor the news magazines, nor the Paris *Herald Trib*, nor the indispensable *New York Times*, nor even my beloved Liz Smith.

"Read not the Times, read the Eternities," said Thoreau, who knew a thing or two. And really it was quite easy for me to tune out both New York and Los Angeles as if they had never existed (nor did they, in 1592). Being in a time or place is merely a question of accepting its givens, of subscribing to its world view or participating in its *Zeitgeist*. If you feel your career is washed up because you will not play a hooker in *Vegas II*, then it is. But if you don't give a damn because you believe you are in the sixteenth century, then it isn't. It's all that depressingly simple. Actresses kill themselves in LaLa Land because they are trapped in a world view that pronounces them finished, over the hill, washed up, just when they are beginning to command their powers. "She took a taxi," they say, meaning that the lady in question died — or her career did. But if you reject all that, you can live on, saying: "Reports of my death are greatly exaggerated." I was determined to do no less.

I saw Per from time to time, just to get the latest news from Björn and Lilli. But Per's drinking depressed me, so I avoided him more and more. The less I drank, the more I could smell the liquor emanating from him, the more I could hear him repeat himself again and again, the more I could see him stagger when he stood up to walk. He thought liquor made him cheerful; I could see that it made him morose. But I was not about to reform him. I had tried that ten years ago, and it had brought our relationship lurching to an end. Per did not want to stop committing suicide slowly — as alcohol enabled him to do. Some deep guilt convinced him he deserved to die, and alcohol was his gradual poison.

Lorelei, despite her beastly divorce, continued to give the best parties in Venice: little soirees where descendants of Borgias and Grittis, Dandolos and Sforzas, Vendramins and Loredans, mingled with Greek and Brazilian millionaires, English and American expatriates, and the odd Eastern European artists who had had the luck (or the political cunning) to make their way to Venice. I felt at home with the flotsam of the world. I always do. Something in my blood tells me that I shall wind up in a Venetian *sestiere*, a Tuscan hill town, or on one of those rocky beaches in the south of France where shady people seek sunny places in their twilight years. I am comfortable with those conversations that switch from Italian to French to English to a smattering of Russian, Czech, Hungarian; with those people who, like me, cannot go home because they have burnt their bridges (if they ever knew where home was, anyway).

"I want to die here," said an elegant lady at Lorelei's party one freezing night in November, "and so I know I want to live here. The place where you want to die is the place where you want to live." She was one of those beautifully groomed, blonde ladies of indeterminate age, the widow of a rich Brazilian, and she had the well-preserved look that only money — lots of it — provides. Her clothes were by Valentino, her skin courtesy of La Prairie and Dr. Niehans, and her glow came from a numbered bank account in Zurich, daily massages, two facials a week, and her own yoga teacher (in that order, I believe). She was so rich she never thought about money (or carried it), and having said how much she loved Venice in the autumn, she was departing the next morning for her house in Rio and perhaps another little nip and tuck with Dr. Pitanguy. The other guests were equally elegiac about Venice (though many of them were also leaving soon for warmer climes), and the conversation turned on the Ball to Repopulate Venice — the brainchild of another Venetian artist and designer who had decided that since Venice's population was declining, it would be appropriate to give a benefit with that theme. She designed and had printed these wicked invitations in which a huge blackamoor in a turban was hefting the Campanile in place of his immense, erect penis, and the Venetian authorities, having seen these, were now determined to cancel her ball.

"What a pity," said Lorelei, shaking her honey-colored curls. "Venice needs something that's really fun, really outrageous. Even the Carnival is finished. It's become a punk nightmare."

Everyone nodded in agreement and drank more *prosecco* and Pinot Grigio. They would all be back for Carnival, they agreed. Would I?

"I have no intention of leaving Venice," I said. This was greeted by oohs and ahhs of admiration by the departing guests.

Venice is a city that has only passionate lovers or vehement detractors; no one is indifferent to her. I was more lover than tourist, but lovers are, of course, the most passionate tourists. I wandered through the Scuola di San Rocco, squinting at the Tintorettos in the bad light. I took the *vaporetto* to San Michele and dutifully stood by the graves of Stravinsky, Diaghilev, Pound. But even more than the famous dead I loved the obscure dead, particularly the foreigners who had died in this feverish lagoon city. I would sometimes stand in the Protestant corner of the cemetery and read their tombstones, imagining their faces and inventing stories about them to myself, pretending that I knew them, weeping as if I were a bereaved relative. Some of them — Germans, English, Dutch, French — had died in the nineteenth century, but still I could weep for them, couldn't I? For what was time but a convention, a habit of mind, a custom of dress? Anyone whose fate I could imagine might be my brother, my sister, myself. And what is an actress, anyway, but someone who can put on other modes of being as a model puts on clothes? Sometimes I slipped in and out of so many modes of being that I truly forgot who I was.

Anywhere one lives for a period of time, a sort of life accretes around one. No matter how you prize your solitude, you must commune with *some*one — the vegetable man, the cleaning woman, the bag lady who feeds the stray cats in the corner of the *campo*. The joy of Venice is that it is in fact a village; you see the same people over and over, and even if you don't know their names, you come to nod and smile at their faces. Life is very much as it was centuries ago. Life revolves around procuring food, cooking it, eating it, disposing of waste. Nourishment, garbage, excrement — the eternal circle. Take sex, art, and poetry away, and that is basically what life is. Human beings are tubes. Food goes in one end. Shit comes out the other. Without love, without poetry, without the longing for the divine, we are no more than that. The wonder is that so many people seem so contented with so little. How *can* they be? Or are they really discontented, numbing their discontent with alcohol, dope, television, compulsive shopping?

A puzzlement. I had nothing to numb me. I was open to the elements — open and raw.

I kept running into the same cast of characters over and over in my crisscrossing of the city in the freezing rain. There was the ancient silent-film actress called Arlecchina, whose heyday had been in the twenties, and who these days claimed to be a witch. She certainly looked like one — with that larger right eye, her bent-over posture, the evil glitter of her gaze, and the jagged sparks of her laugh. I had not known who she was when I saw her lurking about the film festival in August (she had even tried to talk to me at one of the screenings), but unlike the others, she had not gone home. Arlecchina lived near the Accademia, on the garret floor of a palazzo, attended by one remaining retainer, whom some said was her lover, or her familiar — a pleasant, plump blond man, about thirty years her junior and with no front teeth. It was said in Venice that she had knocked his teeth out in a quarrel, or bewitched them out. But Venice thrives on gossip, and half of what you hear cannot be believed. It is the labyrinthine nature of the place that often causes even one's own stories to come back to one, as original, with certain particular details heightened or changed.

It was said that Arlecchina made love philtres and poisons; it was said that she could cause *acqua alta* or banish it. It was said that she was heiress to the old alchemical formulae for which the ghetto of Venice was famous in centuries past. It was said that she had the power to raise spirits and interrogate them. Who knew?

I only know that I would meet her again and again on my ramblings through the city — she was always trailed at six paces by her toothless retainer — and she would croak to me, in English, "I *know* you!" And then she would wave her silver-headed walking stick at me, cackle maniacally, and move on.

There was also a Bulgarian painter with an exophthalmic gaze whom I met again and again on my shopping excursions. I had been introduced to him at one of Lorelei's soirees, and I knew he wanted to pay me court, but I was indifferent to him. I understood that he was married and in search of a convenient Venetian liaison. Besides, I didn't fancy him. Sometimes I thought I had become sexually numb, except in my dreams — I who in the past had lived great portions of my life only for love, or was it lust? How could I be so uninterested in sex? I wondered. I scarcely missed it.

I found I was drawn again and again to the ghetto: those curious, tall, narrow buildings where the Jews of Venice lived in centuries past, pursuing their traditional occupations of old-clothes dealing, alchemy, astrology, medicine, the teaching of music and dance, maritime trade . . . for the Jews of Venice were not all moneylenders, as aficionados of Shakespeare might imagine. They pursued a wide variety of occupations even under the multitude of restrictions that the Serenissima imposed upon them. As in all of Venice, gambling flourished even in the ghetto — except in times of plague, when the rabbinical warnings against it were heeded because the people suddenly feared the wrath of God. And the Jews of Venice were famous for astrology, alchemy, medicine, as well as music and theater — those other alchemical pursuits.

Stolen things, lost things, bartered things, things gambled away, tended to turn up in the ghetto too. Paintings, plate, jewelry, tapestries, cloth of gold. Scarcely a sixteenth-century traveler left Venice without a trip to the ghetto — either for curiosity's sake, or to acquire some item, or else to hear its famous orators, or to see its plays, its women players, its astoundingly beautiful women.

In limbo between two worlds, I wandered daily in the ghetto in the freezing rain — hoping, I suppose, to meet with my two Elizabethans, but I did not encounter them. Occasionally I had the mad notion of going to Arlecchina, and asking her help, when a most unexpected occurrence suddenly changed my plan.

7

Jessica . . . Jessica

LORELEI'S HUSBAND died. They had been feuding bitterly over a divorce (even to the point of constructing a wall across their fifteenth-century house, dividing it in two), when suddenly he had the good manners, the courtesy, the *gentilezza*, to drop dead. For he literally dropped dead, on the front steps of the Fenice Theater, after a concert, in midsentence. (He was inviting a young woman out for drinks.) A hale and dapper yachtsman of sixty or so who had never worked a day in his life, he had looked rather like Claus von Bülow — as Venetians can sometimes look like Danes, having their complement of Celtic blood. (Many Venetians are blond and blue-eyed, with tawny skin.) Alvise Rattazzi — for that was the dead man's name — died as if on cue, becoming more of a gentleman in death than he ever was in life.

His funeral was one of those wonderfully somber Venetian affairs, with a gilded four-postered barge embellished by gilded lions, rowed by four lugubrious, elderly gondoliers in tattered livery, and a train of mourners in smaller gondolas, holding black umbrellas aloft. The weather was chill and damp, with fierce interludes of icy rain. Little rain squalls painted the sky above San Michele with washes of gray and black, and the cypress tops whipped frantically about in the wind.

Most of the expatriates had left Venice by now, so only the diehards were present in that train of gondolas that followed the funeral barge as baby ducklings follow a big mother duck. In one of the gondolas were Arlecchina and her loyal toothless retainer.

Hunched under her umbrella (held for her by the toothless one), Arlecchina smiled as if she loved funerals. I guess certain very old people reach an age where every funeral becomes some sort of insane confirmation of strength, rather than of vulnerability, as it is when we are in our thirties or forties and our friends die.

"I *know* you!" she called to me, as she always did, when our gondolas came abreast at the landing of the *cimitero*. "Jessica," she said, looking into my eyes with her uneven, witchy gaze. "But which Jessica *are* you?" And then she cackled wildly like a cartoon witch.

Presently, she pulled off long black gloves (that looked to be of some strange fur — cat fur, could it be?) and she drew a gold ring off a gnarled finger. She handed it to me across the arm's length of freezing water.

"Wear it," she said. "And if you go to the synagogue and wish on it there, so much the better."

Thunderstruck, I took the ring, put it on — it fit perfectly — and looked at it.

Did I imagine this or did it really scald my finger as if it were heated in some flame? (Or was the flame in Arlecchina's flesh?) The ring had a transparent crystal enclosing an elaborate knot of auburn hair. It was the sort of ring they used to give away at funerals centuries ago, distributing the deceased's hair (and thus his magic) among his loyal friends. Around the bezel were inscribed some letters, nearly rubbed out of the gold by time, but what they were I could not make out. Or even which language. Was it Latin, English, Italian? The letters were so faint that I could not tell.

"The synagogue," said Arlecchina again, cackling. Then our gondolas drifted apart and I was left with the ring burning through my finger, and a feeling of unreality about what had occurred.

I put my hands in my pockets, as if the very sight of the ring could blind me, and I tried to put the disturbing event out of my mind.

Later, at the graveside, I asked Lorelei how it happened that Arlecchina knew English.

"Oh, didn't you know?" Lorelei said. "She's American, though she's lived here since the twenties." Lorelei shuddered. *"Una strega,"* she said. "I do not like her. Do you?"

I shrugged. I did not tell Lorelei about the ring.

If Lorelei's problems were solved by the funeral, mine were only just beginning. I kept trying to find the strength to go to the synagogue, but my courage failed me.

This was the real thing, I thought, the showdown, the witchy transport back in time I craved. Or perhaps it was nothing. Perhaps Arlecchina was mad. Perhaps the ring was bogus — a bit of clichéd stagecraft, gothic crapula, the magic ring to the magic kingdom, the magic ringdom of all my desires. . . .

It was finally on a cold and gray Friday afternoon in early December that I made my way to the Spanish synagogue, the Scuola Spagnuola, in the ghetto (for I assumed it was that synagogue she meant). Venice once possessed a fully functioning synagogue for each nationality, but these days that was no longer the case. The other synagogues, or *scuole*, in the ghetto — the Luzzato, the Levantina, the Scuola Grande Tedesca, the Scuola Canton — are, in particular, either no longer open for regular worship or only opened at certain times for tour groups. (The German synagogue is part of the museum of the Jewish community and has those maddeningly minimal hours that so tantalize and infuriate expatriates in Italy.) The population of Jews in Venice has dwindled, just as the population of Christians has. Venice is no longer the center of the commercial world; New York is. But I was drawn back to a time when Venice was as frantic, competitive, and cutthroat as today's New York.

It was not yet Chanukah, but it was the Sabbath, and nightfall comes early in Venice in December. Of course, the Jews of Venice no longer all live in the ghetto. Some have ornate palazzi on the Grand Canal, some starkly modern ones, some villas on the Lido, and some cramped little apartments here and there about the city, but those who worship in the ghetto all seem to know each other and many are kissing cousins. It is a small and closely knit community — and a jolly one. The outside of the Spanish synagogue is simple, almost austere. A plaque commemorating the Venetian Jews deported in 1943–44 is a somber reminder that the persecutions of the Jews have accelerated, not diminished, throughout history, but inside the Spanish synagogue the mood is far from somber. It is more Italian than Jewish (though Italian and Jewish often seem identical to someone who is heir to WASP family melancholia of the alcoholic, suicidal sort *my* crazy family knew). Boisterous, noisy, full of the sounds of laughter, children, music, the Spanish synagogue is, above all, cheery. (Oh, I knew that Jews were neurotic, but what wouldn't I have given to have *their* neuroses rather than my own.) My sense of intruding upon alien mysteries was counterbalanced by the curious informality of this jovial place.

Although there is a latticed women's gallery upstairs, it has fallen into desuetude and the men and women sit facing one another in separate galleries on the main floor. Even so, one doesn't have the feeling of abrupt division of sexes thanks to the celebratory atmosphere and the omnipresence of children. Sometimes a little boy sits on his mother's lap in the women's section, and there is much waving and greeting and chatter back and forth across the dividing aisle with its inlaid marble floor, its red carpet.

I found the synagogue extraordinarily beautiful, with its dazzling brass chandelier at the center, brass wall sconces between the windows and red window hangings, and tall brass candlesticks before the altar. Sitting, in the dark walnut pews, among the women, even a WASP can experience a feeling of homecoming.

I sat taking in the jollity and warmth of the synagogue while the rabbi began the services, while the cantor sang, while the children fidgeted and the mothers scolded, while time stopped as it sometimes does in holy places. I felt, as I have often felt in my life (felt with that nostalgia for belonging, which is the fate of orphans), that being a Jew would be so *cozy*. They seemed to have more blood, more poetry, more sensuality than my people — whoever my people were. And then I suddenly realized how lost Shakespeare's Jessica was — how lost, self-hating, and finally anti-Semitic — to pawn her mother's ring for a monkey, to betray her father for a foppish young man who never quite treated her like an equal because she was a Jew. "A wilderness of monkeys," Shylock said after her elopement. And that was Jessica's legacy, wasn't it? A wilderness of Christian monkeys and, finally, no home to go to. Exile was the worst punishment one could think of. Exile was worse than death.

I stared at the ring. The knot of auburn hair might have been Shakespeare's. Or mine. And the letters around the bezel appeared, in this light, to be runic. I knew no runic prayer so I chose Hebrew — as strange to me as runic. *Baruch atoh adonai*, I thought, not knowing what it meant but liking the sound — as I also liked the sound of the cantor's voice, the warm golden lights, the red and gold of this antique synagogue (which was quite new in Shakespeare's day). *"Baruch atoh adonai,"* I muttered to the ring.

Were these words witchy enough? I wondered. Or was there some incantation for shape-shifting (through wishing on rings) that I should know? Shakespeare had written reams about rings, magic rings, rings that symbolized bonds, that conveyed magical powers. In *The Merchant of Venice*, which I continued to study in the hope of Björn's return, many central lines are devoted to rings — as when Bassanio says to Portia:

> If you did know to whom I gave the ring,
> If you did know for whom I gave the ring,
> And would conceive for what I gave the ring,
> And how unwillingly I left the ring
> When naught would be accepted but the ring,
> You would abate the strength of your displeasure. . . .

But would these serve as magical incantations? Surely something stronger was needed. Some ferocious formula from an Elizabethan grimoire, or perhaps some Ovidian verses that might have inspired Shakespeare, who loved Ovid, to attempt metamorphoses with his verse.

This was absurd, I thought. I should have gone to Arlecchina and requested a spell from her. But was a spell really needed? "Wish on the ring," she had said. The strong force of wishing could do much in life, that I knew. In fact, it was best not to wish for something unless you were sure you earnestly desired it, for wishing could make things happen — strange things, terrible things, things you could not later control.

I wished. I wished with all my might. I squeezed my hands together, shut my eyes, clenched my bowels, and held my breath. I thought of my mother and remembered how I could summon her, despite the number of years she had been dead, just by inhaling her perfume, Joy; calling up the odor of her cigarette butts in her Steuben ashtrays; or looking at her old-fashioned diamond rings, which she had left me and which I uselessly kept in a vault at the Morgan Bank in New York. It was only, finally, a question of missing her enough — for strong force of longing could bring back the dead.

So I wished, knowing that all time was eternally present and that we can, any of us, slip into other times, other modes of being, just by wanting to badly enough, just by believing that they are still there, lingering in the air.

And then I opened my eyes. The twentieth-century rabbi still stood before me. The twentieth-century cantor was still singing. And the twentieth-century Jews of Venice were still around me in their twentieth-century costumes. The magick had failed. Devastated (yet oddly relieved), I did not wait for the end of the service, but got up, excused myself, and left the synagogue. As I made my way down the white marble steps, past the wrought-iron gates that stand open at their bottom and out into the dark Campiello delle Scuole, I felt desperate. Perhaps it was, in fact, time to go home to Pacific Palisades and resume my life, such as it was. Perhaps it was time to contact my daughter, Antonia, whom I deliberately stayed away from these days because she was in her father's custody (living on Park Avenue with a wicked stepmother, attending Chapin as I had), and I sensed that my visits made her feel even more torn, more pained — though they comforted *me*. She was the dearest thing in life to me, but I deprived myself of her company for *her* sake, knowing somehow that when she was old enough she would come back of her own sweet will, and we would talk of many things, of cabbages and kings, and if the sea is boiling hot and whether pigs have wings. . . .

I stood in the darkness of the Campiello delle Scuole and looked about me. The paving stones were shiny wet, the cold rain came drizzling down. I made an abrupt turn at the corner of the *campiello* in search of the *fondamenta* and, eventually, a *vaporetto*, but I found myself instead going deeper into the Ghetto Vecchio.

Panic seized me. Suddenly I felt lost, even though I knew that in Venice you are never lost but only a few echoing footsteps and deft turnings from your intended destination. I turned back and found myself in the Calle del Forno — the street of the great oven where, to this day, matzohs are baked. Then I turned again and ran along this *calle* until it rejoined the Fondamenta di Cannaregio, the street that runs along the Canale di Cannaregio, which presently feeds into the Canal Grande. I looked, and then I looked again.

Something felt different, but I couldn't figure out exactly what it was. Something was a little off. Fog was rising from the canal before me, giving me the sense that all boundaries were permeable and perishable — even the boundary of time. I thought I would walk a bit, find a *vaporetto*, and go back to Lorelei's. I was cold and lonely, and Lorelei always had a glass of wine for me, a funny story, and some cheer. I looked for a *vaporetto* in the familiar yet unfamiliar scene — but there was no *vaporetto* in sight, not even a light piercing the fog. Not only were there no *vaporetti*, no *motoscafi*, but the misty Canalozzo seemed now to be filled with *gondole*, *sandali*, *topi*, little wherries of every description — many of which I had seen in the regatta but many of which I had never seen at all.

Humble working people were rowing home; magnificently dressed aristocrats were venturing forth for a night of dancing, gaming, whoring. The aspect of the *fondamenta* was otherwise not so different than it had been before: paving stones glistering with misty rain — the tall, tottering houses of the ghetto, their shutters closed to the night. But suddenly I looked up and saw the telltale sign, the final proof: no TV antennae among the chimney pots on the tilting tile roofs! Could it be? Or was this just another Venetian mirage?

I turned and ran back into the Campiello delle Scuole — arriving not a moment too soon, for all the doors of the synagogues were just now opening and Jews were pouring out of the Friday night services. Yellow-turbaned Levantine Jews were coming down from the

Scuola Levantina. The Scuola Meshullanim and the Scuola Co-hanim (both destroyed at least a century ago) were, to my astonish-ment, disgorging worshippers: men in their distinctive red hats (the hated sign of the Jew in the sixteenth century) and women in their magnificent Sabbath finery. Even the Scuola Spagnuola, where I had recently been and which I had found so homey and simple, was now opening its doors to fill the streets with splendidly dressed mar-rano refugees, clean shaven, wearing the goffered ruffs and velvet Venetian breeches of sixteenth-century men of fashion, but above it all, the distinctive scarlet hats of the Venetian Jews.

This was a movie I was in, wasn't it? Presently the extras, the "ambiance," would disperse and we would all find ourselves back in our trailers, drinking wine, kidding around with the crew and with each other in that quasifamilial way people fall into on movie sets, the young and foolish ones smoking a few joints, snorting some toot. But this crowd of extras seemed oddly earnest about their work. The red-hatted Jews didn't seem to *know* they were extras, nor did the Christians. For there were Christians in the crowd as well, and yellow-hatted Jews from the Papal States. Nor could you tell a Christian from a Jew except by the hat — that desperate mark of humiliation forced on a people who otherwise would thrive and prosper too well.

At once exhilarated and terrified, I tried to run (terribly impeded by the high clogs I wore — *zoccoli* — against the *acqua alta* so prev-alent in the Venetian winters). My feathered fan flapped against my waist (to which it was chained in the Venetian fashion), my tight bodice — long, pointed, and padded in the front, and high and laced in back — and my trailing brocaded skirts all made running diffi-cult. I wrapped my cloak about me, covering my half-naked breasts upon which my enormous pearls from the Orient tossed heavily with every step. I could feel the stiff ruff, which rose like one large ornamental wing at the back of my neck, and putting my hand to my hair, I could feel my forelocks divided into two hennaed horns in the persistent fashion of Venetian ladies. All this I had seen in old prints — and now I had entered one!

With no thought but to get home, home to Dorsoduro and my

strange little house, or back to Lorelei's so that I could tell her of these marvels, I hobbled along down the Ghetto Vecchio toward the locked and gated Ponte di Ghetto Vecchio, hearing the clatter of my own clogs, fearing the slippery stones and my footing. Suddenly a guard shouted at me from a passing gondola patrolling the waters.

"Ho! Who goes there? The ghetto has been closed since sundown!"

The face of the man is fierce beneath his scarlet hat, and his bare sword promises mischief.

" 'Tis time all *signorine* should be homeward bound!" shouts his confrere, more gently.

I turn back and walk sadly along the Ghetto Vecchio, accepting my fate. I know a Jewess cannot venture into Venice by night. Even masked, disguised, and in a secret gondola, she risks nothing less than her life.

Then all at once I see him. He has soft wisps of auburn hair worn loose about his nape and flowing into a wispy auburn beard, which he continually twists into a point. One small gold hoop gleams in his left ear, catching what light there is. Over his pinked, white silk doublet he wears a tattered velvet mandilion that gives but little protection against the wicked night. His velvet breeches, which at one time seem to have been trimmed with braid to match the mandilion, are travel-worn and rubbed. His pale flesh-colored stockings are mud-stained, his pale shoe leather muddy and worn. He appears to be in his late twenties, but who can tell? This man has a sadness and pensiveness well past his years. I know at once who this brave stranger who ventures into the locked ghetto is.

We nearly collide in the narrow *calle*, whereupon he looks up, meets my gaze, and says, all in one gasp:

"Who ever loved, who loved not at first sight?"

My heart pounds. My breath grows short. In an instant I realize that I am drawn to this man and that he will change the course of my life. (One always knows this on first meeting, knows it immediately — however one may try to deny it later.)

"*Signore*," I say, curtsying politely.

"Rosaline," he mutters.

"No," I say. " 'Tis Jessica."

"Rosaline, Jessica, Emilia — what's in a name? A rose by any other name would smell as sweet."

"And you are Will," I say.

He looks amazed. "And you an angel, writing me in her heavenly book — I must be dead of plague, for how else should you know my name?"

"Because I summoned you," I say with the boldness of kindled lust.

"Summoned me? Summoned a poor player that struts and frets his hour upon the stage, a motley to the view, a needy nothing trimmed in jollity that travels here, travels there, bound to a noble lord, a patron upon whose pleasure I attend?"

"All that will be healed and revealed by time. In future, he will be known solely because of you."

Will laughs derisively. "Marry, come up, you jest of scars that never felt a wound."

"Doubt me not," I say, liking this oracular role.

"Where may I find you, come to you, wait upon you?"

"Nowhere, Sirrah, for I am bound as well, but to a father upon whose pleasure I attend. And you are in danger for your very life here in the ghetto after sundown — unless you are a Jew."

"No Jew," says Will, "but one who would fain be one if it would bring me closer to your love."

And at that very moment who should appear — his face a mask of fury beneath his crimson hat, his mantle flying out behind him like a banner in the wind — but my father.

"Jessica," he thunders, "look to your duties. Homeward, my girl. Look to your Sabbath duties. How dare you leave the synagogue 'ere the prayers were done?"

My father takes me firmly by the arm and drags me off.

And now, where does *he* go? For lover that I am already, half my mind goes with him. He bribes a Christian guard to leave the ghetto, whereupon he makes his way tortuously back to the palazzo where he lodges with his noble patron, and finds the young gentlemen gaming. Their faces bear the blank, intent looks of those who are bewitched by dice, knowing that their fortunes rise and fall upon a throw of bones. But Will's head is full of fancies, his heart full of longing. He wonders about this dark lady he has met in the dark *calle*, in the dark and rainy ghetto where he has just been to hear the great rabbi preach. She reminds him of Emilia, the queen's musician who played her way into his poet's heart on the virginals and then betrayed him with his friend — and half of London. Emilia is also a dark Italian beauty, her people coming from this part of the world, he thinks. But she is fiery and unpredictable, unchaste, perhaps even clapt. Or so the burning of his nether regions after their dalliances would indicate. She has more than once sent him to Bath, seeking cure.

He watches the young aristocrats playing at dice. In London, on shipboard, in Venice, they have played at dice as if the world rose and fell upon the game — and, for them, it does. It is a kind of drug, thinks Will, who cannot afford this opiate without growing still more indebted to his patron. But is poetry not also a sort of drug? The scratch of words on a piece of foolscap, the dreamy-eyed state wherein Queen Mab flits through one's brain with her fairy train, and the present world is quite obliterated. . . . Aye — that's his drug! The sound of goose-quill scratching o'er the page, the pages multiplying, one, two, three, four, five, six, seven . . . one hundred, until they lift the weight upon his breast, and by their heaviness in the hand make his head feel light.

The prince of darkness is a gentleman, he thinks, watching these young lordings gaming. The English lord with his flaxen curls and the young Venetians with their sable or auburn ringlets, their gorgeous velvet doublets unbuttoned from neck to belly to let the air in and the mansweat out, all are equally bewitched by the dice. And then there are the whores who attend them, the famous courtesans of Venice with their powdered breasts and painted faces, their reddened curls (reddened, he is told, by sitting on little balconies — *altane* — in the sun and painting their locks with a special caustic mixture). These women look like heaven without, but Will knows they are hell within — for who wants a quim bought with a crown, or a drab bought with however many ducats? Will would rather save his dribbling dart of love for the page, the foolscap whereon it drips imperishable words.

But *are* they so imperishable? Yes, he must tell himself in order to write them — for one thing the world never needs is another poet (or worse, a player-poet!) — but his mind, if the truth be known, is full of doubts. His wife, Anne, mocks him, and his father doubts him. How should scribbling verses feed his three hostages to fortune? Or care for aged parents who have suffered fortune's reverses, fortune's misfortunes, if you will. Will won't think of this, for to think of this is madness. To be here in Italy, a world away, while his kin in Stratford perhaps perish from plague. . . .

Plagues have always shadowed his life, from its very start. The year of his nativity, plague swept Stratford, and he — a mere babe in his cradle, the first of his mother's children to survive — was spared by his stars for a destiny yet unguessed. His mother told him of this often. Little Will saved for some greatness still unproved. "Y'are of Arden blood. And though we have come down in the world," she would always say, glancing at Will's poor father, "we are Ardens still." Just so, he had heard, did Venetian aristocrats pawn their last gold plate, protesting, "We are Vendramins (Veniers, Loredans, Barozzis, Zorzis, Mocenigos, Dandolos, Marcellos, or Pisanis) still!"

"Why so sad, my friend?" says Lord S., suddenly looking bored and restless (because he is losing).

"A lady, Milord. A lady I met in the ghetto."

"Jewess?"

Will nods his head.

His friend laughs. "The exotic drabs amuse you. . . . Come, Will, there are ladies enough here!"

He nods at the courtesans and makes a lewd gesture with his fingers to indicate copulation, country matters, lechery, the business of the bed.

"We'll all three abed," he says, putting his arm around the shoulder of a plump courtesan called Diamante.

"Come, Will — thou belie thy name."

Will knows that this is part of his contract with Harry, to be a player-playmate, to share a woman between the two of them so as to disguise Harry's preference for the double-pricked pleasure of man on man, the passion of a master who is also a mistress, a master-mistress, so to say.

And so they take leave of the damnable whoreson dicers and retire to the bedchamber where, under a ceiling painted by that legendary old man Jacopo Robusti, called Tintoretto (who paints still in Venice), they tangle their six limbs upon a golden bed above which golden cherubim flutter and choir.

Diamante knows her part well. Before the sport begins, she leaves her bodice and her farthingale, her petticoats, her embroidered aprons, her pearls, her silken hose, her high bejeweled *zoccoli* upon a golden chair and draws on instead a pair of Harry's velvet breeches, a padded doublet, even his boots.

And so it appears that we have here three boys playing abed. Diamante begins with Will, who shuts his eyes as she loosens his breech and plays tunes upon his rising flute, his fife, his pipe, his musical pillicock. He groans with pleasure, pretending not to notice when she moves on to Harry and Harry presses his own sweet, red, pouting boy-lips to Will's stiff staff.

What a welter of guilt and confusion is in Will's mind as he pretends not to know what is afoot, acock, abed. For truly, with his eyes shut, he can still pretend that a woman teases him upward to that heaven of choiring cherubim, that a woman squeezes the sweet musical sap out of his tingling flute, that a woman swallows the silver fountain that explodes like fireworks over the Thames on the queen's birthday. And what woman is it, in his fancy? Why, none other than the fleeing beauty he has met in the ghetto, her russet hair feathered with flame in front but for all that not failing to betray its dark and devilish roots.

Now the play turns rough. Lord S. seizes Will by the shoulders and wrestles him to the floor, biting his neck with supposed kisses, drawing little points of blood, but not enough to satisfy his thirst. Thus he draws his poniard from its case and begins to sliver his friend's arm, neck, thigh, with cuts that are less playful than they

119

seem. With a pink and agile tongue, Diamante licks the blood away. Lord S. slashes playfully again, until Will wonders when the jest will grow serious and his lording will kill him wantonly for sport as boys kill flies.

Perhaps to distract Lord S., Diamante now kneels on all fours and urges our young lord to turn his dribbling dart of love toward that dark place that was not made for love. So swift and unmerciful is he that she screams and our poet stops him, strokes her, holds her in his arms. She is sweet and soft to Harry's acrid hairiness, her odor like roses against his musky mansmell, her skin supple and soft.

Now Lord S. is jealous. Now he grasps her in his arms, thrusts his ramrod in her rear again, commanding Will to pierce the other place so that they two can be as twins, of one blood in one woman's body. Obedient, despite his mutinous soul, Will does as his lord commands, turning Diamante to his will, doing the dirty deed from above as Lord S. pierces her from below until they make a three-backed beast that pants and screams and begs for mercy.

Though Will has Diamante in his arms, yet he suspects that the darkness he plumbs belongs to his friend, not to their mutual courtesan; and so it is with reluctance, even horror, that he dies a thunderous death, then slips remorsefully away.

Now it is Harry's turn to spit white into the poet's face, covering it with a stiff mask of seed that stings like fiery rain.

When both men have spent their silver coin of passion for each other, they attend to the pleasure of their pagan paramour, paddling in her peculiar river, tipping her purple velvet flower until Diamante groans with an "Oh" that flies up to the painted angels on the ceiling who are not aghast, having seen more hells in their time than Satan.

What remorse Will feels when the treble act is done! To be a male varlet to a rich patron, a catamite, a Ganymede, a very Patroclus to Achilles, why, neither poetry nor plague justifies this! Sick with regret, he skulks away (leaving Harry and Diamante entangled on the bed beneath the bored and gilded cherubim, the painted angels who never avert their eyes) and goes back to the room where the

Venetian gentlemen — Bassanio and Gratiano — are still gaming. Then he joins their game with a desperate passion, and in a trice has lost more ducats than he can borrow from his lordship without spending more such silver coin of lust for all eternity. He is well and truly captured now, and like Kit Marlowe's Dr. Faustus wants to scream: "Ugly hell, gape not! Come not, Lucifer! / I'll burn my books — Ah Mephistophilis!"

This cycle of lust and sin, passion and poetry, has been going on unabated since first Will fell in with Lord S. and his lovely, lordly ways so much more glittering than Stratford ones. For how should he, a poet, be able to resist the wanton pictures, the music, incense, and sweet burning wood of a noble household, where books gleam in their bindings, players come to put on costly revels, and the queen herself is entertained? A poet must know these things, not linger in homely Stratford, where greasy Joan doth keel the pot. But oh, how he misses homely Stratford, and never more than here in dark Venice, where his Lording Love has grown still more a Lord of Misrule than he was in London.

In debt, in despair, Will now has ample cause to revisit the ghetto on the morrow to beg or borrow money from the Jew, Jessica's father, whose name he does not yet even know.

8

A Mirror of Monsters

I AWAKENED, expecting a world of toaster ovens and telephones, motorbikes and microwaves, Concordes and Explorer satellites, atom bombs and submarines — for present-consciousness doesn't slip away so fast. But when I was indeed awake, it was in a walnut bed with writhing columns, the sound of children running in a courtyard far, far below, water sounds under a queerly boarded- and bricked-up window (open only a sliver on top, as if by chance), and over it the faint ripple of light on a ceiling — *la vecia*, I now remember the Venetians call it. *Fare la vecia:* to squint as the "old woman" squints — that ripply glistening on the ceiling of a room, which one sees in only one city on earth.

Perhaps I have died and gone to heaven, I think, and heaven for me is Venice, that city of the heart; but the actual growling of my stomach convinces me that I am not in heaven, for surely heaven, whatever configuration it takes, has no hunger. (But what about hell? Has hell hunger?)

My maid runs in. She has come to empty the slops and fill the water jug, open wide the shutters on the *campiello*, stoke the fire, and help me dress.

She babbles to me in a curious dialect — part Venetian, part Hebrew, it sounds to my sleepy ears. If Arlecchina has sent me back in time, why has she not given me the language? My head is clogged with the clutter of inventions that have not yet been invented, words not yet shaped to the tongue, the useless impedimenta of the twen-

123

tieth century. Strip all these away, I command myself. Sink or swim. Here I am alone in another time, knowing neither the language, nor the rules, nor my own position, age, history. All I know is that my name remains Jessica. Well, this will have to do.

The girl helps me up. I stagger to my washstand and looking glass, eager to see my face — whether it, too, has changed. It has not.

The same hazel-golden eyes, the same russet curls (though tinged with henna at the front), the same bosom, the same hands, the same feet. Even the hangnail I had some days before — in the twentieth century — is there. What a curious relief!

I allow my maid to help me wash, dress, and do my hair, hoping that with each motion, each garment, I may acclimate to this world in which I find myself. Perhaps even the memories of this past life will flood back to me so that I do not seem like an amnesic but rather like a normal person going about her normal life. Yet it is hard to stay calm in these circumstances. I am transfixed with wonder and terror that Arlecchina's magick has worked.

Then, all at once, a tingle begins in my toes, rises to my knees, my thighs, my quim, my navel, my waist, my breasts, my shoulders, my neck. My face becomes flushed and prickles as if with heat rash. My temples pound. It is as if I am a vessel filling up with the hot liquid of memories, dreams, desires. Every person is not just a physical body but a shadowy, psychic body of accumulated knowledge, longings, reveries. Perhaps the psychic body of Jessica has just, belatedly, caught up with me, and all of a sudden — God knows how — I can speak!

"Signorina Jessica," says the maid, a saucy little number, "your father has gone to his prayers and demands that you come to the synagogue at once. Signor Shalach does not like to wait. He says bad enough that you are a spinster and give him no grandchildren, you could show your face amongst the women in the synagogue so as not to disgrace him utterly."

"Impudent baggage," I mutter, staring imperiously at this maid who dares be so rude to her mistress. I choose a crimson dress over a shift of white lawn and proceed to make my elaborate toilette with the sullen girl's help. This is not so easy. A profusion of pots and paints, pins and brushes, are put before me and I struggle with them, trying not to look like an idiot as I go about this elementary female task of doing my face in another time. But more than the unfamiliarity of the dressing table is the unfamiliarity of the smells. My maid smells rank with sweat. Do I smell the same? The hardest thing to love about the past may be its smell!

Everywhere my nose is assaulted by unfamiliar odors: the smell of fish, the smell of slops, my maid's sweat, my own. I have gone back into a century without deodorants, without abundant baths and showers. Will I ever get used to this? One gets used to everything in time, I tell myself.

Also, it occurs to me that I am friendless here. All my friends are dead — or, rather, they have not yet been born, which perhaps is the same thing. Even Antonia still waits somewhere on a cloud, for me and all her ancestors to be born. That thought fills me with such sadness that a tear comes to the corner of my eye and swells with luminescence, then makes a track down the white paint on my face. I watch in the wavy looking glass while it slides down my cheek. Death is everywhere about me, I think. Even the paint I put on is poisonous with lead. But then the question is, if I have defied death and time by journeying back here, am I still in danger of death from white lead, or plague, or anything? If I die now, shall I have to wait four hundred years to be reborn?

I am alone in this time, I think. But then I remember that I am not quite friendless, for that auburn-haired apparition I met in the ghetto is my friend and I feel I know him. Looking into his sad eyes last night, I felt I knew the depths of his soul. And I have read his poems — even those he thinks he has not yet conceived — and anyone who truly reads another's poems knows his soul.

Staggering on my high *zoccoli*, I am led, leaning on my maid, down into the *campiello*, then up into what seems another, smaller synagogue.

This time I am taken to the latticed women's gallery, where I sit amongst the women while the rabbi preaches in Venetian laced with Hebrew, while the men mutter their prayers below, while I am absorbed into the past.

I look down into the men's section, hoping to spot my father.

Some of the men are clean shaven, some bearded. Many look less Jewish than Venetian, wearing their fashionable doublets and breeches, their goffered ruffs and golden chains.

Suddenly I see the one who commandeered me last night: a bearded old Jew whose face has been twisted by anger, and then has settled into embittered disappointment. He pulls on a reddish beard frosted with gray, and he seems more and more disconsolate as the sermon goes on.

The rabbi, I begin to make out (as I settle into this world, as I begin to understand not only its language but also its gestures and expressions), is preaching against gambling, warning of the plague, predicting that it will surely return if the Jews persist in their god-lessness and game like Christians. He denounces those who ride in gondolas on the Sabbath, who redeem pledges on the Sabbath, who even have Christians in their homes to deal in used things — clothes, jewels, plate — on the Sabbath.

The old red-bearded man coughs and looks discomfited. He mut-ters to himself and shifts in his seat as the rabbi thunders of plague, invoking biblical exempla. The gorgeously dressed women about me shake their heads and give each other ironical looks (as though they know that preaching against these excesses is totally in vain).

Then the rabbi goes on, condemning Jews who watch heathen festivals like regattas and fireworks, who do not keep the faith of their fathers strictly enough. The sermon becomes repetitious, and I observe how, in every age, the mouthpiece of official piety is equally tedious, equally predictable.

All at once, I see him again. He is there in the synagogue, half hidden behind a tall Jew. He is sitting, in fact, not far from my father, taking in the sermon and nodding his head. I can see his thinning auburn hair beneath the black biretta he wears in honor of this holy place. Can he possibly be agreeing with the rabbi? Has he come from a night of sin and depravity, or have I only imagined it? Who can tell?

Later, in my father's private chambers, we meet again. Sabbath or not, my father has a long line of gentiles waiting to redeem pledges, and he has commanded me to come to his aid. I write down each sum in a ledger book and make a careful line through the name of the article redeemed.

What an assemblage of objects has found its way into the ghetto! Small paintings by the great Venetian masters, tapestries, plate, jewels from Constantinople and Cathay, pearls from the Orient, incense from the Levant, holy relics.

My father grumbles as he redeems the pledges. He grumbles that the low rate of interest allowed by the state barely allows him to survive. He grumbles that Jews are nothing to the Serenissima now, walled in the ghetto, bound to a measly five percent of interest — unlike the ten percent of years gone by, when Jews lived freely about the town, had great shops on the Rialto, and were proper Venetians in nearly every respect.

"We are treated like caged-up curs by the city we love and serve," says Shalach, my father. His Hebrew name is Judah, but some call him Leone in the Italian fashion, after the Lion of Judah. He is an embittered man but not, I think, without his reasons. He loves Venice like an unrequited lover, and Venice scorns him for a Jew.

The young Englishman advances with his pledge. He bears a small silver mirror on which the crest of some great English house is engraved. He hands it to my father, who turns it over and over, making shimmery suns on the ceiling of the room. I look up. My eyes meet the Englishman's and my heart begins to race. Every woman knows that a man is a sort of door into the future. Is this man a door into ruin or into freedom? Into life or into death? I cannot tell. Once, in another life, I read of a Jewess flogged in the ghetto for the mere suspicion of her relation to a Christian man. There is grave danger here. I only know that I feel a door is opening on creaky hinges and I am full of longing, and also full of fear.

"How long?" says Shalach.

"Only a little while," says the Englishman. "Then I shall redeem it. How much for it?"

Shalach turns the mirror over and over, now bedazzling the ceiling, now reflecting his own grizzled face.

"My ducats or my daughter?" says Shalach, noting the play of eyes going on between us, the play of eyes connoting future sighs.

"Ah," says the Englishman, "your ducats." But it seems he means "daughter."

"Not more than five," says my father, "and then, of course, the interest, the paltry interest that the great Serenissima permits to those she taxes without mercy, and allows the luxury of these great palazzi. . . ." He indicates with an ironical nod of his head the narrow walls of the ghetto "skyscraper" in which we find ourselves.

"And what's the interest?" asks the Englishman.

"A pound of flesh," jokes the Jew, my father. "A pound of flesh nearest to the heart — *my* heart, of course. But 'tis only a Jew's heart, and so it doth not bleed as doth a Christian's." It is a joke, of course, but a bitter joke under which much truth lurks. "In sum, five percent — not more, not less. I cannot even pay my rent here in the ghetto with five percent, nor clothe this daughter that you find so beauteous, nor gamble like a Christian, buy jewels or plate. . . ." He glances about the room, which is gorgeously appointed with unredeemed pledges, all of them for sale. We live in luxury, amongst things that do not belong to us. Our house is rented. All our richly carved chests full of silk, our tapestries, our paintings in their gilded frames, are but passing through our home on the way to other homes. Yet this is the way of life, is it not? Objects belong to no one. Ducats had as lief be faery gold. They pass from hand to hand, greasing the world but not entering into its essence. And what is its essence? Love.

The Englishman looks at me again. I boldly return his gaze.

"Very well," he says. "Five ducats, with interest." From the way he says this word "interest," it seems he also leaves his heart here in the ghetto.

Shalach dispenses the money.

I take the silver mirror, examine it, look at my own reflection in it, then dip my quill in ink and pause, quill poised to register the object in my ledger.

"What, Signore, shall I name this thing, this pledge of yours?"

" 'Tis the reflection of a noble house of Albion brought low by lechery," says the Englishman.

"Come, sweet Signore, gentle Signore," Shalach says with heavy irony, "we can make do with less philosophy."

"If a Jew can lend five ducats with philosophy, why shall a Christian not *borrow* five ducats with philosophy? Hath not a Christian brains? Hath not a Christian conscience, pain, bitterness, and philosophy as much as any Jew?"

Shalach laughs. "Well said, too. But we do not see many such Christians here. Perhaps in England such wonders abound, though methought 'twas a barbaric land where even the fork is unknown and men eat their meat like curs, with greasy paws."

" 'Tis true," says the Englishman, also laughing. "We bait the bear, eat with our paws, and mate with women who are as scullery maids to the magnificence of your Venetian ladies. I give you good day, Signor Shalach and Signorina Jessica."

"Jessica? You know my daughter's name?" says Shalach suspiciously.

"You might say she made the name breed in my mouth, when my eyes first conceived her," says the Englishman. "What else could she be called but Jessica, which means 'she who looks out' — as out a window opening on faery casements."

My father looks at me with grave and threatening eyes. "In future, look inward, daughter, or your eyes may be blinded by what they see." And to the Englishman he says, "I give you good day, Signore."

In my ledger, I scrawl the words: *"uno specchio d'argento — Inghilterra."*

And then he is gone. He uses up one golden ducat bribing a guard again to leave the ghetto, and then he wanders the city with his four ducats, passing through the Rialto full of bustling shops selling glass and gold, mirrors and tapestries, fresh fish and week-old carrion.

He is thinking of the woman he has met, of her beauty, of his throbbing desire for her, greater even than his desire for that other dark lady who inspired such bitter poems of throttled lust. He is thinking also about money, what people do for money: kill for it, rob consecrated graves, sue without merit, marry those they do not love — thwarting love, thwarting desire. He is thinking also about debt. Debt is not unknown to him. His father in Stratford is a debtor; he himself has known what it is to be a poor supplicant for ducats, pence, pounds; a patron's plaything, a poet, and a player that must eat to play, and play to eat — words being notoriously unnourishing. In his heart there is the rebel thought that somehow he will make his words *pay*, that he will earn enough by words to have a coat of arms, a house, heart's ease for his poor debtor father, and recognition from a mocking wife — Anne, sweet, scolding, bitter Anne — who was once so dark and dirty abed but now has naught but words of money, and the lack thereof.

Love and money. Why do the two go together so insatiably? First comes love, the clinging, the longing, the laggardly mornings abed when nothing matters but the beloved's face, arms, breasts, quim, the wet velvet flower of desire — pure purple. But then comes money — hard, cold, clanking money, like a wall between the lovers. Necessity comes in, and all our necessities are, perforce, different. His necessity is to write. Hers to bear babes, suckle them, and scold him for the folly of being a player and poet. But the throbbing within to strut the boards, to wield the pen, cannot be denied. O reason not the need! Who can judge another's need? Only the muse, or God.

The poet walks the cold, slated streets thinking of love, of money. How will he repay? Gaming? Acting in a show? Or will he borrow from Lord S. again (with what filthy interest he already knows. A Jew's usury is purer). And if he does not repay, what will the Jew do? The joking, bitter Jew that jests of pounds of flesh and is as loath to be a Jew as he to be a player and a poet. Loath, yet also proud — the fate of Jews and poets.

The object wherewith he got the loan, the silver mirror that he stole — nay, not stole, but borrowed — from Harry was a gift from Harry's beauteous mother, the Countess of Southampton, whom Harry so resembles. Curious that a mirror should be surety for the loan. A simple object, yet also an object of great subtlety, an object that gives back the self as money does not, as love does. Love, money, mirrors, loans — all life is loaned to us by God, whose crooked reflections we are. Love alone makes that reflection straight. Love alone gives us back ourselves.

But mirrors are surely subtle and possibly magical things. Will has read of witches who can trap reflections in mirrors and destroy the lives of men. He also has heard of witches who can catch — as in a glass trap — the beloved's image and make her love a chosen one forever. Ah, for one of those, thinks Will, to catch forever the Jew's daughter and win her love!

Mirrors and love, mirrors and players. In London, some years ago, when he first arrived in that astounding metropolis, was published a pamphlet, "A Mirror of Monsters," inveighing against players. The author called them "fiends that are crept into the world by stealth . . . sent from their great captain Satan . . . to deceive the world, to lead the people with enticing shows, to the Devil." And yet this same author, Will Rankins (Will remembers this, for the rogue had his own Christian name), had latterly become a scribe himself, penning plays for Henslowe at the Rose Theatre to be played by Nottingham's men. And not good plays neither! Ah, the ones who inveigh most against the theater are ever thus: poets with broken pens, poor, castrated scribes who scourge the playhouse since they cannot write. Will spits when he thinks of them. And his heart aches when he thinks of London, when he thinks of Stratford. But it aches the more when he thinks of the Jew's daughter, whose eyes beckon like home, golden and glistening: coins whose value is beyond price.

Suddenly he stops in the street, his heart clenched in his chest. There, rooted 'neath one loosened paving stone, sticking up like a pair of grisly scissors made of flesh, are two bare legs — the feet blue with cold, the toenails still growing after death. 'Tis a man buried alive face down! Or what remains of a man. Will halts in his tracks, looks up — for what reason he knows not — at the street sign. The street is curiously called Rio Terrá dei Assassini, but no one seems to care what it is called save he. Dusk is falling early and people rush home, seemingly blind to these legs lately kicking the air above the street, these legs frozen in death's dance, in a posture of surly impenitence.

"Prithee, Sirrah," says the poet to a tradesman hurrying to a wine shop, an *osteria*, "whose legs are these?"

The man shrugs, not understanding his words, not caring for the carrion in the street, not wanting to meddle with the destiny of another unfortunate whose fate might perchance taint his own, or interrupt his drink — or supper.

"*Che cosa è?*" Will asks another tradesman in his rudimentary Italian.

"*La morte,*" says the man, who carries a black broom and a satchel, and has the dirty face of a chimney sweep. "*La morte è la morte.*" And the sweep shrugs in that infinitely philosophical way the Italians have perfected since the days of the Etruscans.

"Yes," says Will, muttering to himself like a madman, a bedlamite abroad. "Death *is* death." That much Italian he understands. Somehow he is sure that this headless man (or what remains of him) died for debt. And Will is colder now than he has been before, and more homesick than ever. He hurries home, the ducats clanking in his pocket like harbingers of doom.

9

The Baptized Babies

WHEN HE RETURNS, his friend is in a fury.

"Who *is* this drab," he storms, "that she makes you venture again and again into the ghetto? And seeking what? And without your lord?"

"Dear my love, I go only to hear the great rabbi who preaches in the ghetto, who calls Christians and Jews from around the globe with his extraordinary eloquence."

Lord S. shrugs. He does not believe his friend.

"Come, Will, I shall take you to a Christian place that shall make you forget all such Jewish drabs. There is a convent on an island hard by Venice, where the daughters of the rich Venetians are put away so that their dowers may be better stolen by their relations. These women, I am told, make such merriment, riot, misrule, and lechery that the very stews of London seem convents by contrast. Come, we'll away by bark, by sea, and spend a night or two amongst these queens and courtesans of love."

"Nay, Harry," says Will. "We've courtesans aplenty here in Venice."

Lord S. laughs derisively. "My simple friend. You are a poet, therefore your true meaning is written in your brow, your eye: you wish to stay in Venice for the Jewess. But you belong with me . . ." (Will thought he almost said *to* me.) ". . . Therefore we venture forth, we two. I shall not stir alone."

"Go, then, with Bassanio and Gratiano, your gaming lords."

"Nay, my friend. They have gone away to Padova — and good for you they have done so, for they made dire threats of what they might do if you do not repay your gambling debt. Their absence buys you time. And I assure you, Will, I shall not pay your debt an you not come with me."

"Pay it not!" Will thunders, with a new determination and rebellion. "I'll pay myself!"

"Hah!" laughs Lord S., his girlish lips opening in a little pink O, slivering at once into a thin pink sickle moon. "And how shall you repay without your lord?"

"I shall," says Will, fingering the ducats in his pocket.

"They say you owe one thousand ducats or even more, and they have buried men for less, drowned men for less, flayed men for less. Fortunately they are not Jews — they charge no interest — except your life. . . ."

Except my life, thinks Will, swallowing his anger for the moment and succumbing to his lord's desire. Except my life, which is but lightly lent, with interest, and may be taken back at any moment. He thinks of the scissored legs of death in the street of the assassins and a shudder takes him, like the approach of death itself.

And so, on the morrow, they sail away into the islands of the lagoon. The weather is cold. The fog, *la nebbia,* the Venetians call it, rises above the basin of St. Mark like a great mythical monster with dissolving wings, a tail that curls into the Grand Canal, and scales of sunlight mixed with mist. Their little boat bobs on black waters like a child's toy in a fountain of some stately home. Will is sad and pensive; his lord is full of gusto for the great adventure.

And he is also brimming with wondrous stories of the other marvels they shall visit after this foray to the convent of the lecherous nuns: Verona, and Giulietta's tomb (the sepulchre of a young maid who died for love); lordly country villas (designed by some fellow called Palladio), which make their greatest English castles seem like hovels; and, finally, a great house in Venice itself where they shall meet with a mysterious Moor who slew a multitude of Turks to become the very toast of the Serenissima. Moors, maidens, villains, villas, nuns, lechery — Will cares for none of these. He dreams only of the Jewess as they sail away from her into the fog.

On an island called Mazzorbo (near Burano, near Murano, where Venetians blow their molten faery glass) stands a solemn convent with an ivy-covered tower, which rises above the sea, amongst weeping cypresses that whip and whimper in the wind.

The boatman moors their bark to a landing that creaks with every surge of the tide as if it would come loose. Should a tempest come up, as the darkening sky seems now to threaten, their bark would be dashed against the rocks and they would never leave the island of the lecherous nuns — or not alive.

Capes swirling about them in the wicked wind, they make their way along a rocky path that leads upward to the convent. Their boatman takes them first along a cloistered walkway lined with the same somber cypresses, then to a slippery marble stair, then to a huge iron gate behind which there is a hewn oaken door, cut, it seems, from one giant tree.

The boatman knocks. A wimpled face looks out from the small grating within the mythic door. 'Tis the pretty face of a very young nun, a novice, not more than twelve or thirteen years. She smiles, then slams the little door within the door, and summons someone inside to open the larger door.

Slowly it swings back on creaky hinges, and the gentlemen enter.

At first it seems a proper enough nunnery: solemn and sober, with little nuns whispering about and tiptoeing from their duties to their prayers. The gentlemen's cloaks, heavy with the splash of the lagoon, are taken by several sisters, who whisper and titter amongst themselves, and soon the gentlemen are led into a narrow passageway, through one door, then another, down a flight of stairs, through another door, up a flight of stairs that twists and turns and turns and twists as it ascends a tower.

The stone is cold and damp, slippery with moss. The first young nun goes before them with a lantern. Presently, as Will's eyes grow accustomed to the dark, he sees imbedded in the brickwork walls of the tower (or *torre*, as they call it here), small, stony plaques with names carved upon them. BERNARDO, GIROLAMO, ELISABETTA, EN-

RICO, MARINO, GIORGIO, BENEDETTA, GIULIANO, ANDREA, ALVISE, MARIA, URSULA, the stones read.

"What mean these names?" asks Will, who is always rapt and raptured when he sees the written (or the carven) word.

"These are the baptized babies," says Lord S. "Their souls have gone to heaven from this tower."

"What?" says Will.

"The babies of the nuns," says Harry, "born, baptized, strangled, with their mother's milk still on their tongues." Harry climbs behind him in the gloom — so Will cannot pause to look and weep.

"Born to die?" asks Will.

"So are we all," says Harry. "The babies are the bastards of these nuns. On earth, they would surely cause dissension and disaster in their families. In heaven, they choir as sweetly as cherubim."

Will shudders again with horror. Venice, he thinks, is a city of horrors, more even than lusty London with its bearbaitings and beheadings, drawings and quarterings, and its dark and muddy streets where a man can be slain at ten of the clock for no more than a watch chain, or a ring with a hair knot. He thinks of his son, Hamnet, his daughters, Judith and Susannah: sturdy enough children now, but when they were small, their little bones spoke to him of imminent disasters — plague, fevers, broken skulls — all the ills the flesh is heir to. Plague rages now in London. Has it reached Stratford yet — Stratford with its plaguy climate, its unhealthful bogs and swamps? What if his only son should die, as innocent in his way (a boy of almost seven now) as these babes? It does not bear thinking of. Many a man is given burthens more than he can bear. And his noble friend, who will not take a wife and remake his own image despite a spate of urging sonnets (penned by Will at the Countess of Southampton's gilded request) — why, what does he know of life, of death? He knows only of lechery and literature, nor wishes to know more.

"Death is cheap, Will," says Lord S.

"Only to those it does not touch," says Will.

They climb higher. More children's names accost their eyes. Each child a soul, each soul a cry to heaven, each cry to heaven a poem, each poem mute.

"Can they keep none of these children?" asks Will.

"None," says Lord S. "What would a nun do with children? But they are safely baptized Christians. They go to heaven straightaway, and are saved. At least, praise God, they are not Jews."

Will continues climbing before his friend, who, from time to time, pokes him in the rear with his gloved hand.

"Onward! Upward!" cries Lord S. "Do not quail in this adventure. 'Tis a poet's business to become a hero!"

Yes, thinks Will, who can justify these travels and adventures only thus: a poet must perforce be an explorer, setting his foot on virgin isles with strange inhabitants only to bring back such exotic fruit as his muse alone transmutes to plays and poems.

At the head of the stair, there is a darkened chamber whose windows are slits the width of rapiers, letting in sabers of light that make a pattern on the stony mossy floor.

Here the gentlemen pause and look about, seeing what seems an empty chamber at the top of this tall, tottering tower, which sways slightly in the wind from the lagoon.

Then suddenly there is laughter and the sound of muffled footsteps above their heads. A wooden trap door opens in the ceiling of the tower and down comes a cunningly carved, small wooden ladder such as is used in the library of a great and stately house to reach the books. On the ladder is a nun, dressed all in white — wimple, habit, even little boots — and where her face should be there is a silvered golden mask, half moon, half sun.

"I am Sister Moon and Sun," she says in English, with a strong Italian flavor. Whereupon she throws her skirts up in the air to reveal a shaven quim, painted all around with a golden sun. "My sun explodes with love!" she coyly says.

Next comes another nun, also in white but with a bird's mask on her face — a strange, fantastical bird, half peahen, half owl, with blue peacock's feathers all around, like another sun. She turns round on the ladder, shows the gentlemen her comely bum, and laughs uproariously, but says nothing.

Next comes another nun, also in white and wearing the mask of a golden lion.

"*Je suis Leone de San Marco,*" she says, half in French, half in Italian, and when she raises her skirt it seems she has woven lavender and rosemary into her quim hairs, for fragrance and remembrance.

More and more they come — nuns in white, masked fantastically as birds, moons, suns, harlequins, clowns, lions, jaguars, rams, unicorns, basilisks, and griffins. A galaxy, a bestiary of nuns! A playhouse and a zoo of nuns! Until the little tower antechamber is full of nuns who now embrace and tease our gentlemen, leading them one by one back up the ladder to the secret room at the turret's very top.

It is larger than it first appeared from the lagoon and cunningly laid out with soft rugs of fur and skin, velvet pillows, little altars of food and wine, and glassy candelabra that give a lovely light.

Diverse nuns lead our two adventurers to pillows on the soft and furry floor, feeding them grapes and oranges (out of season, from the Holy Land), nuts, sweetmeats, marchpane, and some strong amber wine from Bassano called *grappa*.

Will's senses quite succumb to this wine, which burns his tongue, his gullet, fills his head with fancies, and obliterates all remorse, all care. Presently he finds himself entangled with the nun in the sun-moon mask, lifting her skirts to see again her shaven quim, sun-rimmed, then plunging, against his will, into her sun. Love's lance, the cock of every walk, hath a mind of its own, thinks Will as he succumbs to masked love, fueled by the fire in the blood, with this creature of sale.

The deed of darkness is quickly done, quickly repented. But this courtesan and queen of nuns will not let him off so cheaply. Up she teases him again, to die in her lap again. But when she presses for a third and he protests that the fiery fluid they have drunk hath increased the desire but taken away the performance, she brings on other nuns, her sisters, in other masks, to make desire fresh.

'Tis astounding, thinks Will, that a man may die away once, twice, thrice, with the same woman — and be done — but with several, love hath no number and he loses count. Thus doth variety pique the senses and make old ardor new. Oh for a woman, Will dreams, who could be all women in one, whose infinite variety would never cloy and who would make hungry where most she satisfied! He thinks briefly of the Jewess but then slips away even from the vision of her, for the fluid he hath drunk and spent, spent and drunk, hath obliterated all conscience, all remorse, all memory. . . .

A night passes, half a day. Our two adventurers in the turret lie about as sleepy as Circe's swine. The nuns attend their needs, then tiptoe off — except for those few who lie with them as spent with passion as themselves.

Will wakes with a fierce headache and mouth of straw. He feels that black remorse which a man feels after having drunk too much, drained too much (and in which sinks he knows not).

He looks about for Harry, his erstwhile friend, who lies, his mouth open and dribbling spittle, on a velvet pillow near a sleeping nun who is unclothed but for her lion mask, which has slipped back above her head, topping her loosened mane, thus making it appear she has two faces: one woman, one beast.

Will groans, rolls over. His own lady love — is she the one from the night before or another in her place? — loosens an arm from under him and coughs, almost consumptively. He now perceives that this nun's lovely breasts are high, rounded, and swollen, that her nipples are brown as berries, that her belly swells upward with impending birth. Her unicorn mask has fallen back from her sleeping face, which, not more than sixteen summers old, is the face of a babe itself: purplish lids shadowed with jet black lashes, a mouth that curls as sweetly as the furled blossom of a faery flower, and hair so bluish black it makes him think of his late (and now unlamented) love Emilia.

She coughs and stirs, stirs and wakes, sleepily smiling at him with eyes that seem half child's, half woman's.

"You are great with child," whispers Will.

"No matter, 'tis not thine," says the girl in perfect English.

Will halts in surprise, not sure whether to ask where she got her English or where she got her child.

"My grandfather was in the courtly train of the late ambassador to your land, and brought back maids, who both suckled us and taught us your lovely tongue. I know where I got my English, Sir, but not where I got my babe. No matter, for 'tis not thine."

Will wakes now entirely and shakes the cobwebs from his head. "I never knew a nine-month whelp conceived in one night," says he, "or not till now."

The girl shakes her head sadly. "For nine months I have grown to love this babe, and now must give it up to die. Last night I hoped the violence of our coupling might kill it — so that God would take that grave decision out of my hands — but now I see where it moves and kicks as lustily as before."

And 'tis true, too, for Will can see the shadowy form of the babe's tiny limb moving in the girl's belly as a leg moves under a coverlet.

He is sure this girl cannot be the same as the one he first swived last night, but then, he cannot remember how many nuns there were. Three, four, five, seven? Can a man be so forgetful?

The girl sheds a tear and sighs. "If only my babe could live. . . . I cannot bear to see it strangled in my sight."

Again Will thinks of Judith, Hamnet, and Susannah, whose fate he knows nothing of, nor has for several months past. He can see in his mind's eye their baby forms, as clearly as if 'twere yesterday. When Susannah was born in 1583, tiny babies frightened him with their floppy heads and drooling mouths, their infernal mewling and puking that a man could do naught to halt but only a woman knew the remedy for. Still, by the time the twins came, a year and some months later, babes terrified not him. He examined their tiny limbs with interest. He melted with paternal pity gazing into their baby eyes, so blue and impenetrable: seeing nothing, yet seemingly seeing all. He sniffed their baby necks, smelling like nothing on this earth if not like new-mown hay mixed with the gods' ambrosia. Susannah now was nine, the twins nearly seven. What he would not give to touch their little limbs again!

"If only I could save this babe," says the dark-haired child-woman. "If only I could send it away to lodge with strangers — if not with my own people. I would even have it baptized Jew, or sold as slave to a Mohammedon to save its budding life!" And then she bites her tongue, as if to bite back the blasphemy. "Better to have it baptized Christian, and to die," she quickly says in remedy, but Will knows that she feels the pulse of life so strong that she would save her babe at any price.

"What is your name?" he asks.

"Giulietta," says the girl. "My family name I dare not tell, for I disgrace my kin who are doges, dogaressas, procuratores of St. Mark, and others who nobly serve the Serenissima."

"Giulietta," says Will. "What a lovely name. . . ."

" 'Tis Juliet in your language," says the girl.

"I know," says Will, "and 'tis also the sweet name of a lady of Verona, who, 'tis said, died for the sake of a forbidden love."

The girl looks downcast.

"She was some kin of mine," she says, "but I should not tell that." Whereupon she suddenly gives a sharp cry, seizes her belly, bites her lip, and stifles further cries. "My pains begin," she says. "Look — I am starting to leak water like a wounded galley on the sea!"

And 'tis true, Will can see, her crystal fluids are leaking out of her, staining the velvet cushion whereon they lie, wetting even his own bare leg that rests near hers.

With a poet's reverence for life, whatever the cost, he says impulsively, "Come, Giulietta, where can we hide that you may have this babe out of sight of your murderous sisters?"

" 'Tis no use," says the girl. "If they find it, they'll kill it. . . . There is no help for it. . . ."

Then a flicker of an idea crosses her brow.

"I know a place!" she says, whereupon the pains take her again and she swoons. The poet fears all is lost now, that the girl will faint and the others will awaken before he rouses her again. But in a few minutes she recovers herself, though she pants and sweats mightily at the approach of birth.

"Come," she says, "dress yourself and help me do the same."

Quietly as he can, Will draws on his breeches, shirt, doublet, boots, and helps the panting girl into her shift, her robes, her wimple, even her boots. (The unicorn mask they leave behind, for no such frivolous disguise can help them now.) Stealthily, he carries his moaning burden down the worn and crazy spiral stair of the tower, fearing for his footing, fearing for her life, his legs, the babe's impending entry into this world of pain and joy. . . .

Halfway down the tower, the girl points to a wooden panel in the wall, barred with an iron bolt.

"Beyond this door is a wooden ladder," says Giulietta, "used only by stonemasons who repair the tower. There you cannot carry me, but I must go alone — for 'tis too narrow."

"Can you stand alone?" asks Will.

"I do not know," the girl says, "but I shall try."

Will seats her on a step, where she begins to pant softly, stifling her birth sounds under the white wimple. Meantime he sets about the task of opening the iron bolt, rusted by time, corroded by the sea.

The bolt is stubborn, immobilized by rust, staining the wood beneath it with shapes that seem made of dried blood.

Will heaves with all his might, using the strength of arms trained in killing calves in his father's yard when he was a boy. He says a silent prayer to his muse, whom he secretly conceives as Clio and Venus in one, and lo — the bolt moves! With a screech that tears his ears (and also the flesh of his fingers), it slides slowly back. The door in the tower opens. The wind from the lagoon accosts their faces. Outside, the day is gray and cold; the strange creature of the fog still sits atop the basin of St. Mark obscuring the sun, promising doom to all who venture past her misty claws. At the periphery of the harbor, little boats with little sails and little oarsmen glide up, seemingly emerging from the province of the fog-creature.

"Come," says Will to his panting, sweating paramour, whose eyes are closed in pain.

He helps the girl out of the tower and onto the ladder, where the wind whips her white habit, and she holds on for dear life. He doubts that she can make it down the tower's side, but knows past all reason that she would rather fall and die, trying to save her babe, than wait and watch her sister-nuns strangle it.

Rung by rung they descend the tower in the mist and fog. At each step, there is uncertainty and fear. Giulietta takes one step, stops, looks down, gasps for breath, faints a little at the height and her pain, then collects herself and takes another step.

"For pity's sake, do not look into the abyss!" says Will. "All things can be borne so long as one does not leap into the future, but walks deliberately in the present moment." (A fine one he is to talk of such things, he who frets alternately about his kin in Stratford and the beauteous Jewess in the ghetto — both of whom might be galaxies away.)

At the ladder's foot, there is soft earth and grass drenched by the rain: there Giulietta collapses in a gentle swoon, her strength, for the moment, gone. Will scoops her up in his arms and carries her for a little space along a rocky path toward the sea. There she revives again and draws breath long enough to mutter these words:

"A crazed hermit lives in this lagoon, on a small island, hidden half by reeds. . . . He is mad, and yet he loves me. . . . If we can sail to him, he'll shelter us."

Will looks about. The small bark that has carried them here from Venice is tied to the creaky wooden dock, which in turn is wreathed in mist. It is what the Venetians call *topo*, a little fishing boat gaily painted and bearing two oars, two sails — one lateen sail, one jib.

Will cannot sail, yet poet that he is, he has watched the boatman with an eagle eye on their sail across, and in the madness of the moment does not doubt his power to sail. Poets think they can do everything — deliver babies, sail Venetian barks, defeat death itself — and Will is no exception.

The abandoned boat lies here, tied to the dock, inviting use, and so he climbs into it, carrying the swooning girl, and puts her aboard, covering her gently with his tattered mandilion. Then he draws the oars into the bark (in case the sail should fail), unties the bark from the landing, and hoists the mainsail. Not sailor enough to know that he must drop anchor to steady the boat before he hoists the lateen sail, he is shocked to discover that the moment it is hoisted, the wind catches the boat and blows it with mighty gusts into the misty lagoon. The sailing, when the boatman did it, looked so effortless, but now 'tis clear that the wind has the upper hand, not the poet, and like a playful colossus, it is tossing the little *topo* here and there over the waters.

"Whither do we sail?" cries Will to the girl, whose eyes are shut in pain and who breathes like a dog on a hot day, though the day is cold.

"To Torcello!" says the girl. But truly the poet does not know where that place is, and they seem tossed on the lagoon toward an impending watery death.

The poet curses his stars, his stupidity, even his muse. If the babe comes soon, how will he help the girl, here in the boat, while trying also to sail? What stupidity to have commandeered a boat without knowing how to master it! Yet he feels somehow that the fate of this girl, her babe, portend somehow the fate of his own kin in Stratford.

Now, with a mighty gust from the open sea, they are blown across the lagoon, faster than Will can steer. Will surrenders to his fate. "I am thine," says he in a soft voice. "Thy will be done." And with that resignation, such peace takes him that truly he does not care whether his gods assign him to life or death. He hopes for a miracle, but does not expect one. In such a frame of mind, all blessings flow.

The boat scrapes bottom. Can these be rocks below? Then all is lost. But, mirabile dictu, it scrapes not rocks but only soft mud, grasses, and reeds that entangle the rudder, halt the tiller's play, and gently stop the boat on a mucky bank.

Will lowers the sail, picks up the girl, and carries her through the freezing water, which quickly soaks his shoes, and onto a grassy bank.

Ahead he can see a little house with a crooked red tile roof and black shutters. He carries the girl thither. She moans low and shivers along her whole body. He knocks at the door.

Presently it is opened by as curious a man as Will has ever seen. He bears a belly almost as big as the girl's, which he carries before him, his arms folded upon it. His gray hair flies this way and that as if he, too, had crossed the lagoon in the little *topo* — and his right eye looks toward Jerusalem whilst his left eye looks toward the Americas.

Mutely he motions the two into his abode, which seems, truly, the reflection of a disordered mind. Broken sticks of stately furniture, ruined altarpieces stolen from great churches (a Bellini madonna with a hole where her right eye should be), piles of peach and apricot pits in the corners, wine fermenting in an oaken cask, cheese in a stinking tub. Straw lies on the floor, piled into the semblances of beds. In the center of the room is a table with empty glasses, dirty plates, dried and rotted fruit, cheese parings, nail parings, mouse droppings, and even little mushrooms growing out of a tablecloth halfway gone back to the earth from which it, and all things, spring.

Without a word, but with several bestial grunts, the hermit helps Will place the moaning girl onto a pallet of straw, where she lies moaning, as if in a delirium.

Minutes pass. The two men keep their vigil, feeling useless and stupid, not knowing what to do to aid the girl. Will remembers Anne's two lyings-in, how the midwife was brought and the men banished; though screams issued from her birthing chamber (where she lay on the second-best bed), the men were called upon to do nothing but wait. Yet here they are, in the very room of birth, helplessly observing.

The girl moans, sweats, tosses her head from side to side in pain. The hermit rises to get some water from a pail, pours it into a cup for the girl, and holds it to her lips, whereupon she drinks thirstily. Will knows somehow that this is not right, but he can do nothing.

All at once the girl lets out a deep and bestial sound, seizes her belly, and gives a great heave with her whole body. Will helps to part her legs and remove her undergarments, and as he does, he is amazed to see a dark little circle emerging between her legs, then growing bigger and bigger as it strains the walls of her privy place, which flows blackish red with blood. It seems that the child's head splits that place consecrated to Venus, sending a stream of bright red blood into the darker clots that issue from her womb. Another heave from the girl and a little face appears, eyes shut tight, cheeks glistening with crimson blood like a little planet bathed in ruddy morning sun, then two little shoulders, arms, a little torso, a curled baby cockling, two little feet that have never touched the ground.

Will catches the baby as it squeezes out of eternity and into time. He cannot believe what his eyes behold, what his hands grasp, so beside himself is he with the miracle of it, the commonplace miracle that occurs each day, in each part of the globe, without ceasing to be miraculous.

Still attached to the mother by a blue and purple cord, like the girdle of a great Venetian's robe, the little man-child has not yet breathed nor screamed — and yet it seems alive.

Will slaps it on its tiny back; it gives a lusty cry, and as it cries, its mother rises up, sets eyes on the boy, smiles, grasps her throat and begins suddenly to vomit. 'Tis the fatal water the hermit hath offered, thinks the poet. And then it all happens in a rush: the child draws breath, the mother chokes on her own vomit, turns blue, and breathes her last while the two men watch, astounded that life and death can be as twins, born within moments of each other.

To save the child or save the mother? Will deliberates. Whereupon he raises the mother's form and seeks to slap her leaden back to give her life! 'Tis of no use. She's dead as earth. Will cuts the infant's cord with a cheese paring knife, clamps it with a string, praying to almighty God that it may live more providently than its mother died. The hermit runs out of the house in a frenzy, Will knows not where.

Meanwhile the girl, as blue of face as a sepulchral statue lying under death's pale flag, has breathed her last.

Will wraps the babe in his doublet, holds it close, then wipes away the deadly vomit from Giulietta's mouth.

"Now cracks a noble heart," says the poet. "Goodnight, sweet princess, and flights of angels sing thee to thy rest."

The hermit returns, leading a she-goat, whom presently he milks into a pail. With great pains, he dribbles the milk into a sort of bladder made for wine.

They give the babe to drink.

10

Shylock's Daughter

WHEN HE BROUGHT the babe to me in the ghetto, I thought him at first quite mad, for by now I had lived there long enough — only a few days, but in those few days also a lifetime — to know my role and those of my supporting characters.

"Aren't you afraid I'll sacrifice the child?" I say to this disheveled figure of a poet, with wild hair and wild eyes, who comes to me clutching a tiny baby.

"I have no fear of you," he says, "for I see in your eyes that you are good, but there are others to whom this child would be naught but a pawn or an innocent to slaughter."

It was a weekday morning in the ghetto, a market day, and the whole *campo* was teeming with people — fruit and vegetable vendors from the country (the pickings were scarce this time of year, but there were apples, squash, nuts, stored from the fall), Jewish butchers selling fresh-slaughtered meat, old-clothes dealers (or *strazzaria*), pots and pans vendors, Levantine spice merchants wearing their turbans and robes, dealers in used things, old things, broken things, stolen things.

Lined up at one end of the *campo* were the poor, who could not read, bearing their loan tickets (red, yellow, blue) telling them which bank to go to (Banco Rosso, Banco Giallo, Banco Azzurro). They carried little things, whatever they had to pledge: a torn shirt, an embroidered sheet, a brass cup, a silver spoon, a torn piece of tapestry, a blunt knife, a bent and battered dagger taken in who knows what mortal battle.

The din in the ghetto was fierce on such a day and the *campo* was alive with Jews, foreigners, children, animals. The poet had almost to scream to make himself heard above the roar of the crowd and no one saw or cared that in his mandilion he bore a babe, whose fate hung in the balance between Christian and Jew, between life and death.

I dragged him to a shadowed archway where we could speak in greater peace.

"Where did you get the babe?" I ask.

"I cannot say now," says the poet, "but if you'll but trust me for the nonce, I'll reveal all in time."

"Is it circumcised?" I ask.

"No," says the poet.

I am seized with fear.

"If the babe were to be found dead in or near the ghetto," say I, " 'twould cause a massacre of Jews — especially as Christmas approaches, and killing Jews this time of year is considered merry sport. You have truly put me in grave danger coming here like this."

"Then help me, Jessica."

"Why should I help — such a stranger as you are?"

I say this, but looking in his eyes I do not feel he is a stranger — this man who has summoned me back through the mists of time. Besides, I know that I must spare this child — if not for the child's own sake, then for my people's. So far, the Jews of Venice have been spared such frivolous massacres by Christians, but who knows what this child might do?

"There is a woman in the country, near Bassano," I slowly say, "where the hills are gentle and goats still graze — who would take this babe, circumcise it, and bring it up a Jew. She is the barren wife of a great Italian-Jewish banker who lives like a prince in a villa by Palladio but grieves that he has no son. Del Banco is his name."

"And would the child be safe?"

"If we can get there safely, the child would be safe indeed — as safe as a Jew can be in a Christian world. The brother of this rich Jew is doctor to the doge, thus the family has many privileges other Jews do not. . . . But many dangers must be met to go to them."

"Jessica, I have risked all to save this babe — my life, my limbs. Two Venetian lordings may come after me for gambling debts I cannot pay, and my noble friend will surely be enraged when he finds me gone."

"Why should I care?" I say, knowing I do.

Will looks into my eyes. "If you care not for me," he says, "then care for this babe, this innocent, saved for who knows what fate. Have mercy on his soul."

"And why do I owe him or you my mercy?"

"You do not. Mercy is never owed. It is a gift, the quality of which is never strained. It droppeth as a gentle rain from heaven upon the place beneath: it is twice blessed; it blesseth him that gives and him that takes."

These words move me. I remember my future life as in a dream; these words reverberate through time, strangely linking two disparate, yet similar, selves.

"My father has some business with this Jew of Bassano," I now say. "Perhaps I can prevail upon him to send me as his courier. . . . Go now. Hide yourself somewhere outside the ghetto's walls. Then meet me in the *campo* near the Frari church, when the clock strikes three. . . . *Now go!*" And I send him off, more wild-eyed than ever, clutching the babe, whom he clumsily feeds with a wine bladder of milk. I pray that it may live as I go to reason with my father, whose character by now I know.

How to describe living two lives at once? It is, after all, my sullen craft, my soaring art, to live one life in the quotidian (buying food, cleaning house, caring for kin) while I lead a more heroic life on the stage — speaking the lines of queens and courtesans, lovers and heroines. To hold two characters in mind at once, one's self and one's not-self, this is my art. And so to be Jessica-Christian and also Jessica-Jew seems less strange than it might be to one who followed a different calling. I am a player, after all, strolling through time. *That* is my religion. I remember the life of Jessica Pruitt as in a dream. Jessica Shalach is my present. But human beings are so made as to wake and dream all in one day and think nothing of it. We are such stuff as dreams are made of, and our little life is rounded with a sleep.

I understand my father better now, and in my better understanding understand his bitterness. Many Jews of Venice bless the doges, bless even the institution of the ghetto less than a hundred years ago, as something that protects both Jew and Christian. But my father's people were the privileged Jews of the Levant; my great-great-grandfather came to Venice as a pretended galley slave — who paid the captain fifty ducats for his freedom, thus he knew Venice in the days before Jews lived behind the wall. 'Tis said they traded on the Spina Lunga (called Giudecca after them) and had synagogues, where the friendly breeze of the lagoon could cool their summers, and windows that faced out toward the sea. Now they have these bricked-up towers and hidden synagogues. Since the ghetto was declared on the first of April, in the year 1516, Jews have been forbidden to live outside its walls, and only when they die do they exult in the breezes of the Lido, where the doge has given them sacred burial ground. To see the sea only from the cemetery — this is the fate of Venice's Jews in our age! Yet it is so much better than the fate of Jews in Rome or Florence that many count themselves quite blessed and do not even know the glory of the past.

Not so my father. His father was a patriarch amongst Venetian Jews; his late wife, Leah, an heiress from Castelfranco, and pure Italian for as many centuries back as any Christian. Thus he feels he is as much a true Venetian as the doge, and he resents the tribute he must pay. With this he justifies all — dealing on the Sabbath, keeping a gondola and liveried gondolier (though, of course, the gondolas are not so gaudy as in times past, since the Serenissima decreed they must all be painted black) — all excess. He is not like those marranos lately arrived from Spain, who count themselves lucky to be alive and out of the clutches of the Inquisition!

I know I can persuade my father of almost anything if I play upon these sympathies. . . .

When I go to him this morning, he is not in the ghetto but at the foot of the Rialto bridge — the new stone bridge opened just this year to replace the creaky wooden drawbridge that burned down last year. There, amid the Turks and Germans, the crush of foreigners from every corner of the globe, some few privileged Jews pay dearly in golden ducats to the Serenissima for the right to trade old clothes on the Rialto. My father, in turn, pays one of these Jews, whose name is Tubal, to share his place. There he sells to the foreign visitors to Venice such pledges as have never been redeemed by their poor owners.

Not all the goods are mean. Often a gorgeous doublet or a pair of fine-tooled boots comes to hand, or even a hand-painted fan, a ruff studded with Orient pearls, a pair of fur-lined gloves from France, a fur pelisse from Muscovy, a small painting by a great Venetian master. I love the Rialto with its shops of every description, its glorious fish market (with all the creatures of the deep staring up at me with questioning eyes), its passing gondolas rowed by liveried Moors, its great ladies with their little dogs, its bankers, traders, and merchants speaking in a babble of tongues, and its silent thieves, stealing from those bemused or besotted foreigners who have lost their way in the labyrinth of Venice.

When I go to my father, at first I pretend nothing is the matter. I rummage through his goods as a daughter will in her father's store, hoping to choose the best for myself.

This makes him laugh. "Once a daughter, always a daughter," he says.

In an indulgent mood, he lets me take three pledges that I fancy: a pair of gloves, earrings of Orient pearl, and a small painting by Carpaccio that was pledged some time past by an aristocrat, ruined by gambling debts. My father can refuse me nothing in this mood. Bitter as he is toward all the world, under his grumbling exterior he is sweet to his daughter. Though he may bark at me, still he is my pawn.

"What are ducats compared to a daughter?" he likes to say. "A Jew must oft have money to save his life, but what use is that life to him if he hath no family? Our ancient nation weaves a curious path twixt servility and pride, twixt saving and spending. We would hoard our gold to save our necks, knowing that at any moment the Christian curs may come to us, demanding tribute in exchange for our lives — and woe to the Jew who cannot pay. But money in its own self, for its own sake, is not the sap of life. It is grease for the wheels of commerce, but neither heart nor soul is warmed by its shine."

"Father," I say, "do you remember the promise you made to Del Banco in the *campagna?*"

"What promise, Daughter?"

"You promised that if a cloak of sable should come to hand — a precious cloak from Muscovy — you'd send it for his wife before the winter . . . and here I see before me just such a cloak." I hold up a sable I have found amongst his pledges. It is a fair-enough fur, though one moth has had his way with it.

My father looks. " 'Tis not good enough for Del Banco's wife," he says.

"But, Father, I can stitch it quite invisibly — this I know. And if I carry it to Del Banco in the country before the roads are wholly blocked with snow, he will be in your debt eternally."

My father looks at me gravely. "Del Banco's debt and Del Banco's ducats are nothing to my only daughter. . . . How should you disguise yourself on such a journey — you a Jewess and a lovely one at that?"

"By dressing as a Christian boy," I say. And from amongst my father's pledges, I pick out the very costume: breeches, doublet, hose — from boots to bonnet, all of it is there.

"Daughter," says my father, "with Leah gone, you are the dearest thing on earth to me."

"I shall be quite safe in my disguise. Besides, you gave your word. 'Tis December now, and already cold in Venice. 'Tis rumored the lagoon may freeze, as have some of the small canals. Imagine how much colder in the mountains. Soon, the snow will settle in the country roads, and try as you may, you cannot keep your promise."

My father knows that what I say is true.

"You have often said," I press on with my advantage, "that a Jew's only protection in a Christian world lies in keeping his bond to his brother. Del Banco oft has saved your skin. His brother is physician to the doge, studied at Padova, goes about outside all ghettos and doth not wear the crimson bonnet, nor even a piece of crimson cloth upon his hat. You cannot afford bad blood with such a family!"

"Your mother's family was as old as theirs — nay, older than the Caesars, or the doges."

"Father, you gave your word. Your word must be as sound and good as your ducats. . . . You may deal on the Sabbath, game like a Christian, go about in a gondola on holy days, but if you break your word, I shall not want to call you 'Father' more."

At this, old Shalach's eyes fill with tears, and I know that I have won my suit.

"Stay, Daughter," says he, but his eyes almost say "go."

"Go carefully then," he says at last. "Go carefully and may your mother's ghost go with you."

My mother's ghost did indeed go with me — my mother, Leah (whom, in truth, I never knew but felt I had), but also my other mother, who had married descendants of doges and kings (for all the good it did her).

We set out by gondola for terra firma, the mad poet and I and the little babe whose destiny had already been so strange and star-crossed. Who knows the destiny of any baby? Try as we may to make them safe from the world — safe behind locked gates, trust funds, and sheltering arms of expert doctors, expert nurses, and confused (for all parents are confused) parents — we never can guarantee their safety (or our own, for that matter). Our fates have plans for us to which we are not always privy. Nor are we privy to the meaning behind those plans — if there is one. We go on blind faith. We whistle in the dark. Even when it seems that all is safe and secure, howling chaos lives just behind the wall, behind the brick wall of the nursery, which truly is as thin and permeable as any Venetian fog.

Venice today still *feels* like an island. It has the claustrophobic social life of a cruise ship — the same people constantly remixed in different drawing rooms (or even the same drawing rooms) — the hot-house air of a very enclosed world, an island that gossip crosses in less than half a day. If you buy octopus on the Rialto at nine A.M., by noon all Venice knows what you are having for dinner (and the cannier members of the social set, or those who employ spies, know how your guest list reads). Gossip is as endemic and necessary on islands as on movie sets, a matter of survival. Stranded with the same few souls for what seems like eternity, it is essential to know where one stands: what parties one has been invited to, what parties excluded from, who one's friends are, who one's pseudofriends are, and who one's true foes. So the island fever of Venice remains — despite the causeways to the mainland and the railroad installed by the Austrians. But at the time into which I was sucked (as into the eye of a hurricane) Venice really *was* an island, and terra firma really was terra firma — reached only by gondola, and in December, it was a choppy and perilous ride.

Little whitecaps crowned the jagged waves. The babe squealed. The poet looked seasick (perhaps he was), and I, in my boy's attire, could pass for neither wet-nurse nor mother. But at least I did not pass for Jewess.

A gondola took us to terra firma — in this case, Chioggia. The gondoliers, for there were two, were traditionally foul-mouthed, and cursed at the weather, the choppy sea, the storm clouds, and the generous tips we gave them (which they found paltry — no, some things never change in Venice). They even cursed at the baby, though you could tell they didn't mean it — for Italians love babies, no matter how they pretend to grumble and no matter how puny and skinny those babies are.

This baby in particular had long thin fingers, little pink nails with silvery crescents at their bases, and toes that seemed not to curl at all; they flew out like tiny pink flags. Still, it lived. It sucked heartily at the bladder of goat's milk that kept it alive, and I was astounded anew (it had been hundreds of years, after all, since Antonia was an infant — literally!) at the strength of the will to live as it manifests itself in a newborn child. This baby, whom we had wrapped in the Muscovy pelisse for warmth, wanted so to live! All my broodiest feelings were rekindled by witnessing this.

Hundreds of years backward in time or hundreds of years forward seems, by the way, to make no difference. So long as people are people, some things remain remarkably constant: fear of death, a baby's will to live, love, seasickness, the difficulty of getting from here to there, from there to here.

Travel in these times was hardly easy. River routes were always preferable to land routes — for though there were still some few horses in Venice at that time, travel by *cavalli* was slow in the extreme. Locks separated the River Brenta (around which Bassano del Grappa nestles) from the salt water of the lagoon, and hoists were used to raise the gondolas out of the water, whence they were carried overland (if one had so contracted with one's gondoliers) to another lock at the mouth of the River Brenta. One could go either by way of Fusina or Chioggia to the Brenta, and then, as now, there were heated and differing opinions about the best route, the best prices, the best boatmen to choose.

All time is continuous and flowing, and it flows, I'm convinced, in a circular pattern. But it is easier to get from 1984 to 1592 than from Venice to Bassano by boat carrying a baby.

We had entered a time, after all, when navigable rivers were the most convenient way to travel and the Adige, the Po, the Sile, the Piave, the Brenta, fulfilled the functions that the *autostrade* do now.

There were ferries on these routes, but the poet had hired a private gondola because of his fear that we were being followed and because he was a stranger in a strange land, saddled with a baby, frightened for his life, and somehow he felt safer in the little gondola with two oarsmen than he would have felt in a public ferry.

His fear made me brave. If it is true, as has sometimes been said, that the human species is distinguished by its ability to be best when things are worst, then I am a charter member of the human species. For the worse things get, the better I am. All alone I can conjure up demons that terrify and transfix me, but in the face of real danger I become calm, magnificent, brave. Give me a boy's doublet, two assassins and a lover in pursuit, noble lines to speak, a baby to protect — in short, a heroine's role — and all is well with my world. But leave me alone in a cozy room with a clock ticking away the minutes and I may just go mad!

*

The Brenta begins in the Alps, empties into the Adriatic. Going up it in reverse from the ancient city of Chioggia, it meanders past Codevigo, Piove di Sacco, Stra, Vigonza, Piazzola, Cittadella, Sandrigo, Marostica, until it reaches the sweet city of Bassano with its covered bridge, its cobbled streets, its *osterie* selling *grappa* and Pinot Grigio, its gorgeous view of snow-covered Monte Grappa and the higher Alps beyond. I cover this territory as if covering it were as easy as drawing one's finger along a map. It is, of course, not. Even the best of dramatists (Shakespeare, for instance) takes you from here to there in a flash of inspiration — just by noting a scene change. Film editors do the same. One splice and we go backward or forward in time, from Venice to Bassano, from Bassano to Timbuktu, Kingdom Come to Ultima Thule — but not so the novelist, diarist, or biographer, who is anchored to the quotidian rules of geography and must explain the hows, the whys, the wherefores, of travel in every age.

By river, then, from Chioggia to Bassano. Imagine the chill wind, the little snow-covered hillocks, the half-ruined castles poised upon them, the riverboats we passed, the crying baby wrapped in sable, the cold, the cold. But more important — imagine what transpired between me and Will as we fussed over this baby that destiny had thrown into our laps. Protecting it, we fell hopelessly in love — this baby, neither his nor mine, yet given to us to care for and to shield from the harsh winds that whipped about us.

"Where did you get the child?" I ask again and again, but for the moment I ask in vain, for he will not tell me, being an honorable man and not confusing spilt confession with moral righteousness.

"I am his godfather," says Will. "That is, the father God appointed, and you, therefore, are his godmother. 'Tis an honorable enough post, more honorable methinks than being a natural father or mother, which is sometimes thrust upon one by a darkling shaft of lust whereupon our children become tickets in God's lottery."

I look at the baby. Tears fill my eyes, for I remember Antonia, taken from me in a cruel custody suit four hundred years from now. (My ex-husband will argue that my life as a vagabond, a strolling player, makes me an unfit mother, though he himself will become fit for fatherhood just by virtue of replacing me with another woman to care, resentfully, for my child.) Flesh of my flesh, blood of my blood, bone of my bone, the apple of my eye — taken from me with writs and motions, depositions, the expert testimonies of "expert" witnesses. . . . There will come a point at which I will decide no longer to resist, for as in that story about Solomon, I will not want to tear the babe in half to salve my own ego. And what remorse, regret, and madness I will live with then — you alone, dear reader, will know.

But what of this baby, whom we carry upriver to Bassano? This little boy who was born Christian but is being taken into the mountains to become a Jew? Babies have, after all, no religion but eating, no creed but sleeping. God to them is mother — or her breast. Was this baby godless, then — having only a goat's bladder of milk, a mad poet in a mandilion, and a mad actress wearing a boy's doublet?

In the busy market town of Bassano dusk is falling when, after five days of rugged river travel, we arrive at her wharves, beneath her covered bridge, in the shadow of snow-covered Monte Grappa. Bassano, like Castelfranco, like Asolo, like Cittadella, was once a town with many Jewish bankers, Jewish dealers in old clothes, who lived in uneasy peace with their Christian brothers. Not so when we arrived, for the Jews of Bassano were officially expelled in the early part of the century, and Del Banco's family had only kept their country seat by virtue of his brother's relation to the doge and the special dispensations granted to his family. He lived in the mountains part of the year, in Venice the rest of it. But he had retained the privilege of this villa (which, in title, belonged to the doge's family) because of the illness of his wife, to whom we hoped to bring this babe.

Italians were never ferocious Jew-killers or Jew-baiters — though sometimes a despairing, drunken Christian sinner would snatch a Jewish babe, baptize it with water from the gutters, and pronounce it Christian in order to save his own sinful soul (for so the Church promised). Jewish parents lived in terror of this. And there had been ugly incidents of attack on Jewish homes at beautiful Asolo some decades ago. It was a strange century for Jews in Italy — a country they had inhabited since Roman times, traveling from the Holy Land over old Roman roads. They would be tolerated at times to minister to the needs of the poor when no Christian pawn bank, no *monte di pietà*, was established in a town; but as soon as one existed, the Jews were no longer safe and they might indeed have to flee on a few days' notice — or else endure the establishment of a ghetto on pain of their lives and fortunes.

So it was a dangerous mission we were on, no less dangerous for carrying a baby who might betray us, no less dangerous for going to seek out one Jewish family in a Christian land. If it were known that we brought a Christian's baby to become a Jew, neither of us would be safe. Not I the Christian-Jewess, nor Will the Englishman who loved a Jew. It was for this reason that the poet and I spoke cautiously to each other as long as the boatmen were about — which was most of the time.

When we stopped to sleep at inns along the way, only then did we — who seemed but two brothers and a bundle, and slept in the same chamber — talk the night away as we ministered to the babe, coming to feel that its very survival was an omen for both our fates. Both of us were parents without our children; both of us far, far, far from home. Such camaraderie as developed between us was the camaraderie of fellow players, fellow parents, fellow travelers on the road of time. The love that had bonded us at first sight had space and time to ripen into something more — thanks to this babe — yet also thanks to this babe, we could not easily consummate our love. Or could not yet.

The poet told me much about himself, save where he got the child. He told me of his noble friend and his noble friend's proclivities. He told me of his struggles to establish himself as poet and player. He told me of his wife and children, his parents, Stratford country life. I could reveal all this here — but what purpose to my tale, which longs to rush onward like the mountain streams of the Veneto? Besides, if I told these things about this man of Stratford, what pleasure would I take away from how many book-bound scholars, whose greatest joy is to speculate upon this mythical man, providing him with professions he never followed, ancestries he never traced, even names he was never called! I'll not have that on my conscience. Let the Shakespeare industry flourish! I speak here not of "the Bard," whoever that may be, but only of a very lost and homesick young Englishman named Will who traveled a little way with me on time's continuum and then was wrenched away into eternity — or else I was.

At Bassano we paid our boatmen (and not without altercation), procured a new supply of goat's milk for the little one, and took horse into the mountains.

The poet was not much of a horseman, so I carried the baby, making a little sling for it out of linen and twine so it could rest against my chest, hear my heartbeat, and feel the heat of my body. I swear it comforted me to become a mother again in that alien time. Maternity is in my bones and blood — perhaps all the more because my child was taken from me when she still had that new-mown hay smell at the back of the neck, the divine trailing-clouds-of-glory smell that children lose at five or so, when babyhood ceases and the age of "reason" (or at least self-consciousness) begins. Also, I probably regret that I have never borne a son. This little orphan was my son for a time, I who wore boy's attire, yet felt in my heart like a mother again.

Once a mother, always a mother. This most humanizing act of the human species once done can never be undone. It reshapes the heart. It is a means of traveling through time. Even if one's child is snatched away (by death or an ex-husband), one remains a mother still. The identity is immutable — the opposite, in short, of an actress's role.

Del Banco actually lived nearer to Asolo than to Bassano, in the foothills under Monte Grappa, where the hillocks are as round and full as a nursing mother's breasts and little villas dot the country-side. Peasant cottages cling to the sides of mountains. Sometimes the roads are so steep a horse can't find foothold and one wishes one had a mountain goat. One looks in terror down a sheer mountain-side, grasps the reins, looks up, and moves on.

Fortunately, my mother had taught me to ride when I was little, and horsemanship, like motherhood, is an unloseable skill. Woman and horse, woman and baby, woman and dog, woman and man — these things are constant in every age.

As our horses walked along the broader roads, Will and I would talk. He had a poet's hunger to know all about my life — my education, my thoughts on poetry, philosophy, history. He wished to know also of my father and how his people came to Venice, for he was fascinated with the Serenissima, saw it as the crossroads of the world, full of people one would never (or seldom) meet in London — Jews and Moors, in particular, as well as Turks and Germans, Greeks, and Arabs. . . .

"How came your great-great-grandfather from the Holy Land?" he asks, while his horse treads the snowy path up a little hill.

"He came as many Jews of the Levant — as a shackled galley slave, though not a true slave but one who rowed his way to Venice and freedom, paying the captain for the breaking of his chains. Still, 'twas a dangerous passage, for these Jewish prisoners never knew whether or not they would be betrayed. They would join a galley in Beirut or Tyre, Famagusta or Alexandria, paying to be put into their chains, paying to be taken out. In the meantime, they rowed, like any prisoners, with shaven heads and shackled ankles, sitting in their own filth. When the wind dropped, the stench was unbearable, and the officers who strutted about the gilded poop with their nostrils crammed with spices, their bodies doused in scent, took to their cabins — for all the good it did them."

The poet is entranced by my tale. "Did many of them die?" he asks.

"They did. Of dysentery, of plague, of other diseases. And the Jewish prisoners never knew whether, having paid for their freedom, they would in fact obtain it. But so great was their desire to reach the Serenissima that they took the chance. We are a nation of wanderers, of vagabonds — perhaps that is why the theater suits us so."

"In their own filth," says the poet, seizing on this detail, as poets will. "Ships are but boards, sailors are but men, and there be land rats and water rats. . . ."

"All of Venice is a ship," I say, "floating upon the waters. There

160

are rats there, too — but, thank God, the cats are winning."

"Land rats and water rats," says the poet. "I should write that down."

"You won't forget it," I say with a twinkle in my eye.

"How do you know?" he asks. "Ah, Jessica, you seem to know more than a mortal should. . . ."

"Also, you," say I.

"I merely struggle on the path," says Will, "wending my way with words. I know no other currency."

" 'Twill pay back dearly, Will."

"How can you be sure?"

"History is on my side," I say, and I consider for a mad moment telling him where I come from — a strange future in which all things will change except his words — but I think better of it.

"Sometimes I think of you as Venus or Clio come to earth amongst mortal men," says Will, "for you are so wise. I swear I love you with all my heart. . . ." And he reaches out to touch me with his hand, stroking my cheek, then my breast, then the babe's head that nestles against it. For two who love with eyes, with words, the first carnal touch unlocks all else — and with it the entire future, fair or foul.

But do we two truly have a future, being in war with time as we both are? Whatever the answer to that question, this mountain touch changes all. A torrent of sexual longing locked up in me for so many celibate months is suddenly unloosed. My heart pounds in my bosom, my thighs grow moist, my skin craves his touch. Though he cannot see the eruption in my heart nor feel the pounding in my quim — or *can* he? — I swear I am embarrassed with him for the first time, as embarrassed as a little girl who has said something all the adults laugh at, and my face turns crimson.

"*Carissima*," he says, touching my hair.

The horses halt, stumbling slightly on loose rocks; for a moment we look down at the mountainside. My stallion shakes his head in its bridle as if he somehow feels the lustful vibrations that pass between me and Will. . . . Will's mare snorts in sympathy. Under the horses' stumbling hooves we hear the crunch of snow. The sky looks leaden as if, indeed, snow might come again. Then, suddenly, far below us in the valley, we see two horsemen, appearing and disappearing in the breaks between the trees. Will pales.

"Bassanio and Gratiano," he gasps. "God have mercy upon our souls."

We spur our horses on and begin to trot up the mountainside, for 'tis too steep to gallop. My heart is seized with fear. If we are caught and killed by the two lordings, the Jews of the Veneto all will be endangered by the corpse of the babe — and Will may never return to England to complete the life's work he does not even know is before him. If he alone is killed, then will I also vanish (since I am just a character in one of his plays)? Or is *he* a character in some delirium or dream of mine? No time for speculation now. We stumble upward, hoping to elude our pursuers on this rocky path.

Montebello — for that is the name of Del Banco's villa — lies far upcountry, above the snow line. In winter it is as remote as it is pleasant, and cool in the summer for which, truly, it was built. Del Banco stays there far past the summer season to give his wife good mountain air instead of the pestilential air of Venice. But his estate was not meant for access in the snowy months, thus the road is ill prepared for it. Rutted and rocky it is, with intervals of ice and frozen mud. The horses are recalcitrant, their footing unsure. We half trot, half walk, upward in fear for our very lives.

Suddenly we see a little farmhouse clinging to the mountainside. Shall we stop there and try to hide, or make for Del Banco's villa? The poet is in favor of pressing on, so we stop briefly only to water the horses. The *contadino* who owns this country shack gives us a piece of news that does not gladden our hearts: he tells us that an English lord has passed this way before us, raving and beating his horse, screaming bitterly at his retainers, possessed, in fact, like a madman.

"*Inglese furioso,*" the *contadino* says.

"Dear God," says Will. "Let us bring this baby to his protectors, Jessica, and flee forthwith."

I nod my head as I spur my stallion on, but in faith I do not know *where* we may flee — unless it be out of time and into eternity.

*

Montebello is a place that seems to perch on a mountainside outside of time. A Grecian temple serves as its facade, and mythic figures crown its eaves. Zeus, Hera, Demeter, Apollo, and Minerva rise, resplendent, from its roof; and stone satyrs frolic on its snowy lawns while Diana, the huntress, carved in dolomitic stone, protects its central fountain, dry now, and choked with ice and snow.

The sky still threatens storm, but here above the world the firmament seems pink, not leaden. Montebello sits above the fray, neither Jewish nor Christian, but outside all battles over the cutting of foreskins and the eating of pork. Will is as stunned as I am by the halcyon look of the place.

"If Jews cannot own land, how comes Del Banco by this country seat?" asks the poet.

"It belongs, in title, to the family of the doge, but Del Banco has the lease of it, which is as sacred as his ties to the Serenissima. Both his brother's doctoring and his great wealth serve to keep him safe. . . . Though not so safe that some new and hostile doge might not sweep it all away."

Will understands this well. "Nothing mortal is wholly safe," says he, "whether on land or sea. Why, what is pomp, rule, reign, but earth and dust? And live how we can yet die we must. . . ."

The poet is cheered by this little inspiration of his. It seems to buoy him forward on his horse and take away his fears.

"Poetry is our great consolation, isn't it," I say, "and you bear the word forward into the future."

He looks at me and shrugs with all modesty.

"I wonder mightily about this thing you term the future," says Will.

"That only proves you are wise," I say, "for fools never doubt their happy futures even as they cancel them out with foolish deeds."

Will gazes at me with love and longing, then casts his eyes upon Del Banco's unearthly country seat.

"Montebello," says the poet. "In England, we would call it Belmont."

11

Fancy's Knell

WHEN THE COFFERED DOOR to Del Banco's villa swings open on its great brass hinges, the first thing we hear is the sweet sound of the virginals playing in some distant chamber. Behind the door is the porter, who does not reveal himself to us for the nonce. I clutch the baby in my arms. We have fed it just after dismounting from our horses, and yet it squalls and fusses in discomfort — and I, being a woman, feel responsible for its welfare.

Suddenly, the servant who has opened the door emerges from behind it. 'Tis no man, but a bent and witchy-looking old woman! I swear 'tis Arlecchina, or her doppelgänger! She mocks me with a cackle that seems to reverberate through time, and her two coal-black eyes stare out from under her coal-black velvet wimple. The baby lets out a fierce howl as if reacting to her proximity.

"So now you know the virtue of the ring," she says, looking me in the eye with a manic gleam. "*Vieni, vieni.*" She beckons with one bony finger; then she throws wide the portal, and her toothless retainer scurries up behind her to take our cloaks and wraps.

I am dumbfounded by this appearance of Arlecchina and her consort — yet also, I wonder if I am not imagining it. Is Montebello like some dream wherein all the creatures from one's past appear, in different costumes?

The music of the virginals plays on. Dimly, through an open door, we hear a female singer singing the words to the song in English, accented strongly with Italian:

Tell me where is fancy bred,
Or in the heart, or in the head?
How begot, how nourished?
    Reply, reply.
It is engendered in the eyes,
With gazing fed, and fancy dies
In the cradle where it lies.
    Let us all ring fancy's knell.
    I'll begin it — Ding, dong, bell.
    Ding, dong, bell.

"For whom have ye brought this babe?" says Arlecchina, trying to snatch it from my arms. I hold him fast.

"For the *signora*," I say. "Pray, call her."

Arlecchina makes a hideous face at her retainer and sends the plump, blond man scurrying off into the far chamber from which the music wafts.

Will and I stand there for a moment face to face with Arlecchina, while the baby shrieks as if he would drown out this faery music.

"Prithee, close the portal," says the poet to the witch, "for 'tis cold, 'tis cold."

What he does *not* say is that we three are pursued. Perhaps the old witch knows this already, for she seems to know everything. She stares at me and smiles evilly, her witchy right eye larger than her left. Suddenly I see something that I have not noticed before (in that other life, or is it the same life with different costumes?): Arlecchina has a goiter that bulges on the right side of her crepy neck.

"Let no one beg the ring, Jessica," she says in a voice that crackles like dry wood in a fire. "No, not for three thousand ducats — for you may have need of the ring."

I look at once at my fingers, searching for the magic object, which I have nearly forgotten. It is still there, on the third finger of my left hand, and its transparent crystal twinkles over the auburn strands of hair beneath, which are still twisted into a love-knot.

"Words fail," cackles Arlecchina, "time must have a stop; babies cry, then cry no more; poets scribble, then fall silent; the clock ticks, then is smashed; but rings pass from hand to hand, from age to age; begged, borrowed, stolen, belonging to no one, rolling through time into eternity, taking our lives with them." And, having uttered these portents, Arlecchina lets out a long, resonant cackle, slams the heavy, coffered door at our backs, pivots on her heel, and slithers off in the direction of the music.

As she lifts her heavy black skirts to slip away, I can see that she is wearing *crakows* on her feet, those long-toed phallic shoes whose *poulaines*, or points, curl upward then seem to turn back on themselves. Her petticoats are blue, with silver crescent moons upon them; and though her back is still bent as a sickle, she is walking without her usual staff. Is it truly Arlecchina, or do I dream her? How will I ever find out?

"Of what ring does she speak?" asks Will, whereupon I turn to look at him quizzically, for I have forgotten for the moment that he has not always been with me and thus does not know about the magic ring. Suddenly, out of the corner of my eye, I see an owl loosed from under Arlecchina's skirts! It darts up toward the painted ceiling of the villa, which is resplendent with angels poised upon rosy clouds.

"Did you see that?" I ask Will.

"See what?" he says.

"The owl from under the old witch's skirts."

"No," says he. "Ah, Jessica, you are tired. Oft when I am tired, I seem to see animals or birds in the corners of my eyes. 'Tis all illusion, tricks the senses play upon us." And he reaches out to stroke my cheek. The moment his fingers touch my flesh, I am on fire with longing for him, despite the long journey, the crying baby, the appearance of the witch, the ring, the owl. Abruptly, the mortal music ceases.

We wait for what seem endless ticking moments for Arlecchina to return. The marble floor we stand on is a chessboard upon which we play out the knight's moves of our lives. Oh, to be a pawn! Oh, to take two steps forward, two steps back, to castle the useless king, uselessly, while the queen rules the board screaming "off with their heads" — and only the gallant snorting horses with their quivering nostrils and glossy manes express the complexities of our lives.

"We are destiny's pawns," says Will, reading my thoughts, as poets will.

"Destiny's knights errant," I say, whereupon the babe lets out a howl as Arlecchina returns — followed by Signora Del Banco.

How can I tell you this, it is so strange? Signora Del Banco, with her masses of silver hair heaped upon her head like the puffed sail of a great galley, looks astonishingly like Lilli Persson! True, she is wearing a pearl-studded, sixteenth-century Venetian bodice; true, she commands this villa and its servants as if she perfectly belongs here, yet still she seems so like Björn's wife that I want to call her "Lilli," though I restrain myself.

Her great green eyes fill with tears when she beholds the baby wrapped in sable. "Welcome, little stranger," she says, clasping the babe to her bosom. And I know beyond all doubt that this woman feels herself to be its mother. Will knows it too.

"Money cannot breed like this," says she, rocking the babe in her arms.

Arlecchina smiles her twisted smile and looking at me knowingly, says, "Yet many have sold their souls for ducats, and their babes, too — as the young gentlemen surely know." Her words stab me in the heart, for I think of Antonia, whom I did not sell but whose fate is presently as unknown to me as if I had.

"Begone!" Signora Del Banco says to the witch. "Make their chambers ready. These gentlemen are to be our guests tonight, along with the English lord. We shall have masques and revels for them to celebrate the babe, whom we shall presently circumcise according to our Jewish laws and call Leone — after Judah, that lion's whelp."

"My father's name," I gasp.

"Then are you, too, a Jew?" asks Signora Del Banco, still thinking me a Venetian boy. I swear I don't know what to answer. Jew, Christian, man, woman — what am I truly? Just one burning human soul, one flame, one puff of white smoke — who wears different disguises in different times — seeking to ascend toward heaven. And yet, if it is most difficult of all things on this earth to be (and most perilous), then I shall choose to be a Jew. For a Jew is one who goes willingly into the flames rather than renounce her burning faith, and such heroism would I choose.

"I am a Jew," I say, pleased enough with the words to repeat them. "I am a Jew," I reiterate, "and my friend is a poet."

"Welcome to you both," says Signora Del Banco. "Welcome to Montebello, where both Jews and Christians are safe."

She cuddles the orphan babe in her sheltering arms as we follow her to our chambers and Arlecchina's cackle resounds through the marble halls.

The villa has vaulted, plastered ceilings, some richly decorated, some ornamented only by a mask upon the keystone. We follow Signora Del Banco along a hallway whose ceiling bustles with depictions of Cosmic Harmony and Eternal Wisdom, enthroned amid the gods and goddesses of Olympus. To my eye, the work seems reminiscent of Veronese's, yet the brightness of the colors and the perfection of the paint outdazzle even the restored and repainted murals I have seen in other Palladian villas. Of course, I realize with surprise, these paintings are quite new. I am used to seeing the art of the sixteenth century through the metamorphoses wrought by time's pentimentoes and retouchings. Now that time has abolished itself for me, the paint seems too bright — almost vulgarly so.

And what curious murals embellish this villa! At every turning, one sees false, half-opened doorways with painted servants lurking behind them, false balconies with painted courtiers poised upon them, false terraces with painted lutanists plucking their painted strings, false porticos with painted feasters and dancers. Everywhere the eye alights it is promptly fooled! The painted people seem almost more real than the *real* people, and the real people of this villa seem none too real themselves.

Presently we arrive in what appears to be the guest wing of the villa, where the poet and I are given adjoining rooms. Mine has a great canopied bed that stands upon a platform and is hung with tasseled emerald damask. The columns of the bed are fluted, with Ionic capitals, and the furniture in the room is quite plain: a large chest, several simple wooden chairs covered with worked leather, and a trestle table with a brass brazier under it for warming frozen toes. The walls in this bedchamber are also covered with murals. Painted Corinthian columns flank painted porticos that reveal, beneath their arches, pleasant painted gardens.

Near the bed there is a disturbing trompe l'oeil doorway in which a female figure stands, as if on guard. Despite her laced bodice and winged ruff, her hennaed hair, her high *zoccoli*, and the fluttering fan she holds in her right hand, she looks like my mother when last I saw her alive — or do I imagine this? I think suddenly of Browning's "My Last Duchess." My Last Mother, I want to say, but bite my tongue, not wanting to betray how alien I am here, a refugee from other, future times.

Maids are sent to help us undress and wash, and also to bring us our costumes for the revels to come. I am given the attire of the Innamorata in the commedia dell'arte troupe (as if my boy's disguise had fooled no one), and the poet is given the costume of Harlequin, or Arlecchino — an irony I cannot fail to notice.

Fearful though he is for his very life, Will (who is a player to his fingertips) is thrilled by the Harlequin costume he finds spread out on his bed. The costume is perfect in every particular and executed with great skill and cunning: the black half-mask with its separate chin-piece; the patched suit suggesting a parti-colored fool, a tatterdemalion, a motley to the view; the black ballet slippers, the soft cap with its dangling hare's tail, even the traditional bat, hung around the waist with a thong of leather.

Will can hardly wait to try on his costume and play his role, but first we must rest after our long journey and wash away the dust of the road. As we fuss about in our adjoining chambers with the half-open doors between them, I think how happily Will and I travel together — as if we had been partners for many lifetimes. This naturalness, coexisting with passion, must be love — a love such as I have never known, for it is both utterly secure and perilously risky. "Who chooseth me must give and hazard all he hath," I remember, risk being the very essence of love as defined by the poet himself.

But what of this sense of rightness, this comfort, this feeling of being at home at last, united with the other half of one's self? This is more than I dared ever hope.

Suddenly Will runs in to me, wearing his motley. He turns for me, showing it off. He drops his mask, then puts it back on, doing a little dance around the room, miming the perfect Harlequin. Then all at once he banishes the maids in a stern, masterly voice. They flee from the room bowing and tittering. My heart pounds as if it should fly out of my bosom. Then it happens — all in a rush — he takes me in his arms (I still dressed in my boy's doublet), holds me fast, and kisses me with molten sweetness.

"Jessica, Jessica," he says, enfolding me. The tight rosebud between my thighs, furled for so many celibate months, wants nothing more than to explode, but my mind races ahead as minds will. Perhaps when animals mate it is all a matter of blood and nerves, scents and synapses, vessels filling and vessels emptying (although sometimes I doubt even that); but humans love within the context of that great convention "Love," that well-worn metaphor "Love," that gaudy tapestry "Love" woven through the ages by the poets and artists, dyed in our nerves, imprinted on our brains, accompanied by sweet familiar music.

Oh, I had loved and lusted, loved and "Loved." And sometimes I was not sure whether I had loved "Love" or the man in question, myself and my role as Innamorata, or just the adrenaline rush of love, that most powerful of all drugs, that highest of all highs — kickier than cocaine, more euphoric than opium, dizzier than dope. For sometimes we create a lover out of a parti-colored fool just to feel that rush again — and when the rush is over, we look at him and laugh, asking ourselves why.

But at its truest, love is altogether another matter: a matter of gods and goddesses, of spirits merging, of a holy communion in the flesh. And one never knows, before making that leap of faith, whether one will find pure spirit or mere motley, holy communion or sexual aerobics, gods and goddesses, or goats and monkeys. "Who chooseth me must give and hazard all he hath" — the essence and the test of love.

"Jessica," the poet says, "I must have you."

"Dear my love, you took me with your eyes some days ago — it is inevitable your limbs must follow. . . ."

And here I confess I am torn — whether to break off (as in the good/bad old days of grundyish censorship) or whether, indeed, to describe our carnal amour as he himself, that most carnal of poets, would have done. Shall we pause and let the readers vote? After all, who would dare describe love with the greatest poet the world has ever known, the poet who himself defined love? To detail organs, motions, sheets, wet spots, would be too gross, too literal, too finally deflating! It is quite one thing to imagine the poet of poets abed with his convent Juliet or his bisexual earl — but for a mere player like myself to go back in time, bed him, and then tell tales out of school? Fie on't! Was Will Shakespeare good in bed? Let the reader judge!

Exciting it certainly was, for sex was dangerous then — and therefore more piquant. Sex most dangerous is most rare. If nothing can come of it (neither plagues nor babies), then perhaps there is no existential risk and the mystery is less.

We knew when we made love that this act might be our last on earth. The earl, his patron, followed hot upon our love, and Bassanio and Gratiano had surely come to Montebello by this hour, raving of pounds of flesh. It was only a question of time before they caught up with us. Thus, we made love in the hopes of making time, our enemy, stand still.

When we came to it — to bed, that is — when we peeled off each other's clothes (my boy's doublet, his motley), when we ran trembling fingers along each other's arms, backs, legs, igniting each other's skin — we were caught up in a sort of natural disaster, an act of God, a shipwreck, a typhoon, a tempest over which we had absolutely no control. It was as if meteorites showered the earth, or the moon was sucked into the sea; as if a tidal wave swallowed a whole convoy of Venetian galleys, spreading crimson silks, gold coins and frankincense and myrrh upon the churning waters.

And what did he say to me after we had made the beast with two backs again and again, after we had devoured "cormorant devouring time" with our hungry mouths, our hungry hands, our hungry thighs? Did he quote one of his own sugar'd sonnets, or compose a new one to commemorate this moment? No — that would come later. He quoted instead a rival poet, quoted him with envious admiration.

It lies not in our power to love, or hate,
For will in us is over-ruled by fate.
When two are stript, long 'ere the course begin,
We wish that one should lose, the other win;
And one especially do we affect
Of two gold ingots, like in each respect.
The reason no man knows; let it suffice,
What we behold is censur'd by our eyes,
Where both deliberate, the love is slight;
Who ever loved, who loved not at first sight?

"If only I could write like that!" said a spent and languorous Will —
but not too spent and languorous to be envious. "Tell me, Jessica,
am I a knave to sometimes wish such a splendid poet dead?"

"Beware of wishes, Will." I laugh, hugging him tighter and muss-
ing his thinning auburn hair.

"Were he to die," says Will, "I would be the greatest poet of my
age."

He hesitates a moment, repents of his words, then adds, clearly
not meaning it:

"Or maybe not."

"Do not wish Kit Marlowe dead," I say, "for it might come to
pass."

"Marlowe? How knowst thou it is Marlowe that I quote? Those
lines are still unpublished, a mere fragment sent in a letter to my
lord to flatter him out of his ancestral gold."

"I only know that wishing another poet dead is the same as wishing silence to one's muse. For we are all part of God's unearthly
choir, and to silence one is to silence all. Silence Kit Marlowe, and
you perhaps silence your own muse. I promise, Will, in time he'll
be no rival to your verse, while you, perhaps, will rue the day you
wished him dead."

"Yet his fame outburns, outshines mine — and he is but my age.
I swear it galls —"

"How can you know God's plan for him? Perhaps he burns more
brightly because his light will be the sooner spent."

"I am nearly thirty — and a failure in the eyes of all my kin! At thirty Alexander was already dead, and Antony had bedded his Cleopatra."

"So have you bedded yours," say I, smiling slyly. "Besides, Antony was already an old soldier by the time he came to Egypt and found her dying. He was almost fifty to her forty, an old man. . . ."

"What a subject for a tragedy!" says Will.

"You must write it, then."

"If I live," says he. "Or else damned Kit Marlowe will — and make Mark Antony a Ganymede!"

"Hush," say I. "Our revels await."

And so the revels begin! Drunk with love and danger, flushed with love, we are ushered into the great ballroom where the revelry will take place. The room is bright with candles. On the walls, painted giants hold aloft painted balustrades and balconies. Another set of feasters and revelers graces the walls — painted people echoing the real people who fill the room, greeting and bowing to the strains of the music: virginals and viola da gamba, lute and cornet, trumpet, organ.

This may be a Jewish household, but few Jewish laws are here observed — for everyone is masked and disguised in a manner that would cause a pious rabbi to wring his hands in grief. Women dress as men, and men as women; and all the masks of the most clever and ingenious Venetian artisans are on display. Women with the heads of unicorns, courtiers with jesters' masks topped by ringing bells as well as suns and moons, fabulous insects and butterflies, lions with solar manes blazing round their faces, tigers with golden spots, zebras with silver stripes. Even the valets and porters, the waiters and sewing maids, are gorgeously dressed and masked. On a real, not painted, balcony, Arlecchina — who wears no mask but her own terrifying face — reads the tarot cards; courtiers come to her, crossing her palm with sequins and ducats to hear their future fates.

Will and I mingle in the crowd, amazed by the beauty and excess of the costumes yet still on our guard because we do not know which of our enemies lurks behind which mask. My mask, as befits the

Innamorata that I play, is a simple black velvet loup, which only covers my eyes, the better to offset the whiteness of my skin. Will wears his Harlequin mask, and it gives his face a pantherlike appeal. He is a trifle wicked, I know now, and wildly mischievous abed — now puppyish, now playfully violent, now tender. My thighs ache for him and my heart seems ready to explode whenever he touches me. There was no way not to fall in love with this man; it was written in the heavens, spelled out in the starry constellations in whose fire all loves are foretold. And now all my resolve, my independence, are of no account to me — and I am tethered to him, thigh to thigh, by raging lust, the poetry bred in the blood, God's plan to trick us into reproducing our own kind, at any cost.

I am musing thus when the musicians start to play and various dances begin. The masked courtiers now disport themselves to the sounds of viola da gamba and lute, virginal and organ. I recognize the *pavana*, the *pavaniglia*, the *gagliarda* (all danced two by two), and then the *villanico* (danced by four). Will and I dance the *pavaniglia* together, then stroll about the periphery of the throng, warily checking the crowd for a familiar gait if not a familiar face, then join another couple to dance the *villanico*. Our partners both wear golden ruffs and capes of plum-and-gold brocade. The woman's pushed-up powdered breasts shake as she dances, and the man's golden codpiece has been stuffed to make it appear that he is endowed like a beast of burden — an ox or plowhorse. Her mask is the full moon; his the blazing sun. Suddenly he drops his mask and it is none other than Björn Persson who winks at me! I gasp. He pulls his mask back on.

"Björn!" I whisper.

"I am Del Banco, Signorina," says the blazing sun, "and this is my lady." Signora Del Banco whispers through her mask, "Do not fear, the babe is well." But I do not see this lady's face behind her silver moon-mask, nor her hair beneath her pointed, silver hat topped with a twinkling crescent.

We dance together for a while, we four, and when the music stops, we part. Will and I now wander in the crowd, looking for the English and Italian lords but hoping not to find them.

"Perhaps, having delivered the babe, we should flee," says Will, "for we will be safer even on the river than here." But as the night is dark, there is no thought of fleeing until morning; besides, our host and hostess are never far away and they seem to watch us through their masks. Indeed I am glad of that, for the very thought of parting from the baby boy fills me with pangs of dread. In only a few days, he has become like my own child, and though I know I must leave him someday, I do not want to think about that parting now, for it makes my breasts ache and my heart as well.

We are not the only commedia dell'arte players in the room, for in the crowd we also see more than one Brighella with his brothers in knavery Beltramo, Finocchio, Scappino, Flautino, and Truccagnino as well as various Pagliacci, Pulcinelli, Pantaloni, Capitani, and Zanni. I am not the only Innamorata — nor is Will, I presently discover, the only Harlequin. There are different Harlequins in different motleys throughout the room — and even on the painted walls. Their costumes are various. There is Harlequin the jewel merchant (with gems sewn all over his coat and breeches), Harlequin the Emperor of the Moon (with silver breastplate covered with moons in every phase), even a strange transsexual Harlequin (Diana in a skirt and farthingales and feathered headdress dripping crystal crescents like tears). It would be easy to lose each other in this masquerade, so we hold hands even as we dance or stroll about the room, though it is not the custom of the times in which we find ourselves.

After an hour or two of dancing and music, food is laid on — such fanciful food as I have never seen: pies baked with live quails' eggs that hatch before our very eyes; marchpane palazzi filled with marchpane clarissimoes of Venice, wearing marchpane cloaks and golden candy hats that can be crunched between the teeth; whole roasted oxen and pyramids of roasted hens; glazed ducklings covered in sugared fruits that mime the mosaics of San Marco. The *valletti* who bring in the viands are all dressed as perfect Pantaloni — so that they, too, appear to be part of this commedia dell'arte masquerade. The forks they bring are of the finest beaten gold, the platters of worked silver, the napkins of embroidered linen, and all the table hangings of gorgeous golden damask. The musicians play on as the masked revelers crowd about the feasting tables to sample

these delicious delicacies, and Will and I are warier than ever now —
for many lift their masks a little in order to eat, and we both hope
and fear to recognize our pursuers.

Suddenly, a reveler dressed as Brighella — the rascal, the gigolo,
the light-fingered, facile-tongued intriguer (who does not so much
steal from people as he may be said to find objects *before* their owners have lost them) — appears behind us and taps Will on the shoulder.

He is dressed like the classical Brighella from Bergamo: a military
coat (though of what army we cannot discover — nor, probably,
can he), breeches with golden braid, a leather pouch and dagger at
his waist, a soft biretta with a turned-up brim. But it is his olive-
colored mask that betrays him most: sloe eyes, hooked nose, sensual
lips that half invite, half sneer, a brutal, bristly chin (the beard is
sparse and scraggly), and the waxy mustache of a confirmed fop.
This Brighella has a russet mustache and beard, but that misleads
us only for a few seconds — for the hair that cascades down his
back is flaxen and appears to be as much his own as the red mustache and beard are part of his mask, through which he whispers to
Will these familiar lines:

> "Whoever hath her wish, though hast thy Will,
> And Will to boot, and Will in overplus.
> More than enough am I that vex thee still,
> To thy sweet will making addition thus.
> Wilt thou, whose will is large and spacious,
> Not once vouchsafe to hide my will in thine?
> Shall will in others seem right gracious,
> And in my will no fair acceptance shine?
> The sea, all water, yet receives rain still,
> And in abundance addeth to his store;
> So thou, being rich in Will, add to thy Will
> One will of mine, to make thy large Will more.
> > Let no unkind, no fair beseechers kill;
> > Think all but one, and me in that one Will."

He recites — nay, he hisses — the lines with ascending menace, as
if they spoke not of lust but of murder, not of the pounding of the

177

poniard in the thighs but of the passion for the dagger drawn from its sheath and dripping blood.

"Harry . . ." Will whispers, knowing his friend.

"Will to boot, and Will in overplus," says Harry, dropping his Brighella mask just long enough for us to see the sweet, maidenly girlish face, the eyes of blue cut-crystal, the pale tresses and the pale cheeks.

"And this must be the Jewess. Madam," says he, bowing with what seems like subtle mockery, "I hope the mirror this monster hath stolen pleases you. It belonged once to my lady mother. . . . May it reflect your beauty even as it did hers." And then to Will: "May I observe that even thievery will not save your parti-colored skin, for you are doomed? If Bassanio and Gratiano do not feed you to the wolves, strip of skin by strip of skin, then surely Shalach will. He raves in Venice of his long-lost daughter — it seems he hath gone mad with grief of her. He claims you stole a sable skin of him. No ducats can assuage him for his daughter. I doubt not that he will be here soon."

"How can that be?" I say. "He blessed my going."

"Blessed on Sunday, repented Monday, swore vengeance Tuesday, rode on Wednesday, rowed on Thursday, climbed on Friday, killed on Saturday," hisses Harry. "Many men go mad for loss of their daughters and their ducats. Marry come up, Will — thou art more of a fool than I thought to steal my mother's glass. 'Thou art thy mother's glass, and she in thee calls back the lovely April of her prime' — or so you wrote in that third bartered sonnet. A man who will write sonnets for money will do anything at all — even steal family heirlooms, the crack't mirrors of a legacy. Go to — thou art no more than a riming beggar. Dost this lady know what manner of man she hath bedded?"

"Bedded?" say I. "Sirrah, I protest."

"Lady," says Southampton, "I was there, watching from behind a painted door. I mean to be there again — this time, not watching."

He grasps my arm quite harshly and begins to drag me a little way to show he can.

Will protests. "Harry!" he whispers, stunned by his friend's revelations.

"Harry me no Harrys, Will. This lady will I have in forfeit for your debt — else I feed you to the wolves."

"Feed me, then — but spare her."

"Why should I spare her, or the babe?" asks Harry.

I gasp, "How knowst thou of the babe?"

"It is my business to know lecherous business," says Harry. " 'Twould be your business too if you loved a beggarly poet who gambled like a lord, whored like a player, and cowered like a Jew. Come! Or I let Bassanio and Gratiano know which knaves you are behind your masks."

"And which knaves are *they?*" I demand.

Harry points to two masked dancers not far from us. One is dressed as Pagliacco, the other as Pulcinella. The Pagliacco slips down his mask for a moment and winks at me. He looks like Grisha Krylov! Pulcinella's face I cannot see.

"Come," says Harry. " 'Twill not be so bad. I am a tolerable lover — if not so earnest as my poet friend, then at least more skilled in lechery. . . . What? Is rime all? The quim rimes not with the cock, yet they get on together. I've never had a Jewish quim and I'm told they're hairier withal and juicier. . . . What say, Will? Is't true? Doth the lance-of-love slip through to Egypt on a churning sea? Doth it smell like raw fish or burnt mutton? Certes, 'tis not pork. . . . Come!"

12

Beauty's Doom

THE POINT OF HIS PONIARD in my bodice convinces me to come along. Thus am I half prodded, half dragged, out of the balustraded ballroom with its groaning feast table, its masks and costumed courtiers, along the painted trompe l'oeil halls of the villa.

My *zoccoli* clatter on the chequered marble floors; the painted people on the walls seem to smile and sneer as I move along the halls prodded by Harry, followed by Will.

Above us the ceilings are alive with mythological battles, rapes, judgments, feasts, and fancies, even as I am dragged toward I know not what similar fate.

Harry takes us first to his bedchamber — grander than either Will's or mine, and graced (or perhaps I should say cursed) with a huge marble fireplace whose opening is the height of a tall man and whose form is that of a grotesque head with a gigantic open mouth. It breathes fire at us; its marble teeth are blackened by wood smoke, while its huge globular eyes look up toward who knows what horrific vision of things to come. Here, Harry seizes cloaks and blankets, rudely gives them to Will to carry (as if he were no more than the most beggarly of manservants), and prods us once again out of the chamber and into the hall. Again, our Brighella hustles us along.

"Whither are we going," asks Will, "and why?"

"I do not wear my heart upon my sleeve — for daws to peck at," says Lord S. as he hurries us along. "I tell not where I go nor what I plan. I am not what I am." He laughs like a commedia dell'arte

villain, then hurries us out of the bedchamber and along the chequered hall again.

Halls open into other halls; painted people wink and stare, feast
and revel, as we three hurry past. Occasionally we meet a masked
flesh-and-blood reveler who has gone out, perchance to piss in the
snow — some wandering Harlequin or Pantaloon or Pulcinella feeling nature's need beneath his motley and mask. Sometimes we pass
another Harlequin and another Innamorata kissing and culling in
the hall, or even furtively fornicating beneath voluminous skirts and
farthingales. Harry hustles us on.

Out we go, finally, into a covered passageway where plows and
carts are kept, rakes and pitchforks, thence into a snowy, moonlit
garden all crystalline white with bluish purple shadows painting the
snow under a full moon. On such a night, I think, when the sweet
wind did gently kiss the trees, did Troilus mount the Trojan walls,
and Thisbe o'ertrip the dew, and Dido waft her willow wand, and
Medea gather enchanted herbs — but no, 'tis not true, for though
the moon is full, the winds are bitter cold, and though Jessica, with
an unthrift love, hath stolen from the wealthy Jew and run as far as
Belmont, here there is no haven either, but menace in the frigid air.

Harry pushes and prods me into a boxhedge labyrinth, where
loose pebbles nearly trip me in my *zoccoli*. We three scramble through
the maze, rats in a trap, three blind mice whose fates are linked,
although we know not how. Is there a Minotaur at the center, or
are we three together our own Minotaur? How can one tell?

Through the elaborate labyrinth we go and out the other side,
whence it appears that we are heading for a *tempietto* that stands,
surrounded by dreaming poplars, at the other end of the garden.
The little temple has Corinthian columns with swags of fruit and
flowers connecting them, and a pediment upon which Grecian goddesses go about their Grecian business. Thither we are prodded,
through an iron gate and up a brick stair, until we stand before a
studded door with heavy, walnut coffers. Harry has the iron key.
He turns it in the lock and the door creaks as it swings open, releas-
ing the damp, ecclesiastical smell of snuffed candles, old incense,
mildew, mold.

Hurrying us within the temple, Harry locks the door behind us and rushes ahead to light a few votive candles, whereupon the chapel is illuminated: a round and womblike space flanked by empty, pedimented niches. Where, in a Christian holy place, would stand statues of Jesus and Mary, John the Baptist and St. Peter, there are empty damask-curtained arches, and in one central niche the carved doors of the *aron*, with a beautiful, brass oil lamp hanging before it. Unlike the Venetian synagogues, which are rectangular, this synagogue is circular — as though it had previously been a church, hastily converted to the Jewish faith.

I gasp. To be here in our masks and disguises is sacrilege enough without even knowing what mischief Harry plans.

"Jewish meat is best enjoyed in a Jewish temple," says Harry, spreading the blanket before the bimah and dragging me down to the floor with him. He tears off his olive-hued Brighella mask, tears off my black velvet loup, then covers my face with ravenous kisses. Absorbed though he is in his raging lust, nonetheless he looks up to see what his motley friend intends.

"Watch me plunder your dark lady," hisses Harry.

Will lets fall a tear, not knowing yet what he should do. Poet that he is, he hesitates before he acts, and hates himself for hesitating.

" 'Thou dost love her because thou know'st I love her,' " says a taunting Harry. "Ah, Will, if thou and I are truly one, then — sweet flattery, she loves but me alone!"

Here, he pins me down, throws up my skirts, tears away my undergarments, and presses his flaming lips to my nether ones, darting a frenzied tongue in that purple place, which so resembles a hungry mouth.

I confess I am stirred as much as I am disgusted. Perhaps that is why I scream, whereupon Will falls upon Harry's back, raining blows upon his flaxen head. Harry laughs and quotes poetry: " 'That thou hast her, it is not all my grief. . . .' " And the two men scuffle for me, touching each other as much like lovers as enemies.

This, I think, is at the very crux of love: it is all between the men, and we women are merely the lures and the excuses.

The two men pummel and pound each other, roll round and round in their motley and military attire, screaming curses, quoting poetry. Mayhem and murder mixed with verses, the fate of the human species: half beast, half angel, wholly conflicted. But which half will win? The beast or the angel? The poet or the murderer?

Harry brandishes his poniard, holds it to Will's throat. Will, as Harlequin, has the lesser weapon, merely a bat or cudgel, and pinned beneath Harry's knee as he is, he cannot use it.

Holding the dagger to Will's jugular, Harry says, "I kissed thee 'ere I killed thee!" then plants a lingering kiss upon Will's lips, more passionate than any he has given me. The kiss goes on and on as if in slow motion. Time seems to stop. My head is alive with lines of poetry that Will will never write, iambs unscanned, images unmade, suns, moons, stars, extinguished even before they are born in fire. I feel like God seeing the potential for a human life, then cutting it off at the bloody root. Poetry is divine but it requires a living hand to write it, eyes of fleshly jelly to read it, a waggling tongue to voice it, unsplit vocal chords to thunder it through the universe. The divine bleeds through the mortal, and now, with Harry's poniard beginning to cut his throat (and three red drops of blood springing through the line of white flesh on his neck), Will, my lover, my Harlequin, will never climb the towering stairs of verse that fill my mind: a colossal city, built for a moment in the brain and then demolished, vaporized, as if it had never been.

A gust of cold wind; the creak of hinges. The door swings open and behind it stands Arlecchina, brandishing a rusty key and cackling. Two revelers run in behind her; they are Pagliacco and Pulcinella, and they have come to seal my beauty's doom.

"The pound of flesh the whoring beggar owes!" screams Pagliacco in Grisha Krylov's voice, whereupon these two fall upon Harry, tearing him away from Will and commandeering his knife.

"Flay the beggarly poet alive!" screams Pulcinella (in a voice that seems to belong to Gaetano Manuzio). These two brigands begin to strip Will of his motley clothes preparatory to stripping him of his skin — a trick the Venetians have learned well from their erstwhile enemies, the Turks.

"Poetry must bleed to be real!" shouts Pagliacco, with his Russian accent. And now, having Will almost naked, Pulcinella puts the purloined poniard to Will's thigh and begins to strip the skin.

I can feel the knife in my *own* thigh — so close is our bond, our troth — and in desperation, I turn to Arlecchina, who still stands like a hideous sibyl, watching this display of cruelty.

"Help me, Arlecchina," I plead.

"Help me no helps," says she, "ye have all my magick round your finger!"

The ring! I have forgotten the ring. Whereupon I draw my frozen hand into the light and gaze upon it. It twinkles mystically around its knot of hair; I grope for the perfect wish, with no words wasted. So much rides upon this wish: Will's life, Jessica's, Shylock's, Romeo's, Juliet's, Othello's, Desdemona's, even Hamlet's and Lear's, all those other lives within those lives. Even my own life as Jessica Pruitt, since Jessica Pruitt could not truly be born if there were no Jessica Shylock for her to play!

Silently, clenching my heart, my bowels, my teeth, I call down all the powers of light and darkness into this one crystalline ring: *"Let Will Shakespeare live to write!"* I shout into the ring. And suddenly, raving out of time, in runs Judah Shalach, my stage father, ranting of his purloined daughter!

Now the men are mad with blood and mayhem. All want to kill Will; all want to kill each other for the sacred right to kill Will — as if the death of a poet were a sacrificial act, more precious even than the many deaths that litter the planet daily. Pagliacco will kill Pulcinella ere he lets him kill Will; and Harry will kill them both. Even Shalach, the subtle and self-mocking Jew who knows the uselessness of Jewish violence in a world of Christian bloodshed, is crazed to have Will's heart out, now that he sees the other brigands bent on the same act. The men are flushed with battle, their faces filled with blood as if they were in heat, in lust, in love. Pagliacco draws an imaginary line on the floor and dares Pulcinella to cross it. He does, as he is meant to do, and the battle heats up, whereupon Harry leaps into the fray and Shalach creeps upon him with a glittering stiletto, probably a pawn. He stabs at him but misses.

"Arlecchina!" I cry out again, as if for my mother.

"Let the men kill each other," cackles Arlecchina, "*that* is the final female magick. The lions die, the lionesses live forever."

"But live alone," say I.

"But live," says Arlecchina, cackling. "And younger lions come." She tosses me the rusty key. I catch it in my ringed hand. "Lure the poet, lock the others in," says she. "I vanish." And in a moment she is gone, as if she has indeed vanished into the air.

Now Shalach has put away the stiletto and is beating Pagliacco with a club; while Pulcinella is engaged *corpo a corpo* with Brighella, or Lord S. For one moment Shalach looks at me and leers, and I suddenly see beneath his grizzled beard, his scarlet hat, the face of Per Erlanger, my old lover! Yessica, Yessica, he seems to say.

Will lies before the bimah utterly stunned, as if he cannot believe the men have stopped shredding his flesh and are, instead, attacking each other.

"Come, Will!" I call, but he lies there like a dead man. I run to his side and seize his bleeding hand, wrap him in the blanket Lord S. has brought, and drag him along the chapel floor. At the last possible moment he comes to his senses, and, in a daze, follows me out of the *tempietto*. We slam the door and lock the brigands in, then flee into the snow.

What can we be thinking? We are thinking we will return to the villa and find the feast and revels still in progress, but some new mischief is now afoot, for as we make our way back to the central villa, we see courtiers running out into the snow — Harlequins, Brighelli, Finocchi, Flautini, Pulcinelli, Pagliacci, Pantaloni, Capitani, Zanni, Innamorate — all fleeing the ball like so many Cinderellas hearing the clock strike midnight.

We have left the men dueling in the temple, and now we encounter this throng of revelers screaming, pushing, jostling in the moonlight.

I see Del Banco, with his sunlike mask, at the head of all the revelers.

"The villagers have come!" he shouts. "It was foretold."

And sure enough, behind the revelers — in angry ranks and bearing pitchforks, rakes, hoes, and other homely agricultural implements — come the *contadini* of the Veneto, screaming death to *gli Ebrei!*

I stop Del Banco long enough to ask him what the matter is.

"They claim we sacrifice a Christian child," he says, then struggles onward with his courtiers.

"And where is the babe now?" I ask after him.

"With the *signora*, safe for now." Whereupon he turns and runs with his costumed guests.

For a moment Will and I join the roiling ranks of fleeing revelers, for want of another place to go. Swept into the crowd, I kick off my *zoccoli* and run in stocking feet beside my beloved Harlequin. We cannot return to the *tempietto* where the men still fight, nor can we sneak back into the villa now — but surely this flight will soon be terminated by the pebbles and rocks beneath my feet, the difficulty of running on such stony, snowy ground.

"The labyrinth!" says Will. "We may hide in the labyrinth." I nod at once — and so, shrinking stealthily away from the crowd of revelers, we hide behind a hedge and creep backward to the cover of the maze. We do so not a moment too soon, for one angry *contadino* has just seized a reveler dressed as Pantalone, slit open first his satin doublet and then the skin beneath, as if it were no more than the thinnest silk. Blood stains white satin, then moon-blue snow; shrieks reverberate in the clear mountain air.

I see the mad, blood-crazed face of one who thinks he kills his fellow man for an idea, though it is no such thing; it is blood lust finding an excuse, murder without a cause, unless that cause be murder's very self, the human need to spill red blood upon white snows, the beast leaving its mark.

But slitting a gullet is not enough for this rogue. He must have humiliation as well as death — and so he draws the fat heart out of this Pantalone's breast and all the bloody entrails from his belly.

This spurting show of blood inflames the other peasants, who fall upon the closest revelers in a fury — stabbing at their eyes, necks, gullets, like men possessed.

Will and I cower behind the hedge, hiding our eyes, wishing not to see this display of cruelty and yet perversely wishing also to see it. I peek between my fingers to behold one peasant stuffing chicken feathers in a reveler's wounds, another stabbing at the eyes of a Zanni he presumes a Jew.

"See how the eye's vile jelly drips," says Will. "A universe, an ocean, is in those eyes when they behold the world, yet how like dew or nothing are they when a poniard pierces them. We are made of dust and water, dreams and tears. We can cross the ocean, prove the world a globe, yet not contain the beast beneath the skin. What a piece of work is man: how noble in bearing, how like a god in reason, yet how treacherous and mean against his fellow."

"Let them all kill each other," I say in disgust, "only spare the babe."

"Aye," says Will. "Somehow we must find it before these villains do."

"Come!" I say, taking Will's cold hand and sneaking through the snow in stocking feet.

13

Hairbreadth 'Scapes
and Most Disastrous Chances

BACK, THEN, to the villa we creep, entering by a stairway near the scullery and up a flight of secret servants' stairs.

"There must be access to the mistress's apartments somehow through the servants' wings," says Will. "Have faith, keep climbing."

What choice have I but to keep the faith — in equal danger whether in the present or the past. "My fate is in your hands," I mutter to that benevolent heavenly mother who guides my footsteps through the world. I feel cold marble on my bare soles and keep climbing.

Up a stair, along a narrow hall, and up another stair we go. It is dark, with flickering candles placed at lengthy intervals along the wall. Will snatches a taper from a wall sconce and bears it like a brand; we march forward in the darkness, haloed in the light of one sputtering candle. My skirt rustles; my frigid feet pad along the floor, silk stockings long since in tatters. My breath comes short, for I am breathing shallowly out of fear. Remembering my craft, my study of yoga and dance, I take deep breaths to ease my fear and encourage Will to do the same.

"Fear and faith cannot coexist," I whisper to Will, "nor can fear and deep breathing."

I hear him start to breathe like an apt pupil — and just at that very moment I hear a baby cry.

"Listen!" I whisper to Will.

" 'Tis the babe," Will whispers back.

We run along the hall, following the baby's cry. It leads us to a chamber, regally appointed with carved chests and a canopied bed hung with cloth of gold. There, in a corner of the room, in a carved walnut cradle with a golden quilt, lies the baby lion cub, little Judah. Signora Del Banco herself rocks the cradle.

She looks up at us, her face transfixed by terror.

"Go!" she commands. "You jeopardize his life!"

"Alas, Madam, 'tis you who do so — remaining here," says Will.

"Where can I go?" says the *signora* in despair.

"Why, back to Venice and the protection of the doge," I say.

"Montebello was my haven," says the *signora*.

"No more," say I with true sadness, for if Belmont is gone, then is there any place of safety on this earth? And at that very moment, who should appear with raised pitchforks and hoes but three *contadini* from the *signora*'s own estate, screaming that *gli Ebrei* have cursed the harvests, bringing early frost, snow and ice, hard upon a summer and an autumn of plague and pestilence.

"The child!" screams the *signora*. "Spare the child!"

"We mean to baptize him a Christian," shouts one peasant, rushing toward the cradle. Whereupon Will unsheaths a purloined poniard, picked up amidst the carnage, and, before I even see a flash of steel, unseams the villain from his nave to his chops. Blood spurts even over the baby in his golden quilt and I make haste to snatch the bloodied little one whilst Will holds our attackers at bay.

Again it is my fate to stand back and watch the men fight. Will can hold his own with one fierce *contadino* while I cower in a corner with my baby lion, plotting our escape. The other eludes him and runs to take revenge, plunging his shiny dagger deep into Signora Del Banco's gold-encrusted stomacher.

She falls backward onto the floor, groaning, her face as curiously serene in death as Lilli Persson's is in life, her blood slowly beginning to seep through the gold embroidery and beads beneath her heart. "Farewell, sweet mother," I mutter whilst Will dispatches her murderer with a swift stab to the eyehole. "Would I could kill Kit Marlowe thus," he hisses.

I hold my tongue from moralizing about the deaths of poets, knowing that a man as tender of heart as Will must have a straw opponent in his mind to murder ere he can slay even his own would-be assassin.

Three dead men and one woman decorate the glistening marble floors with the crimson frescoes of their blood before we take off for the stables, with the babe, to reclaim our horses.

"Oh, this out-Kyd's Kyd!" shouts Will, still mad from murder and in a sort of high hysteria.

In the stables, there is riot and misrule. Horses rear up and neigh under the moon as if they knew their owners' fates. They stamp their feet, they snort, they seem to smell the bloodshed. With a sort of harness of silk ribbons torn from my Innamorata's gown, I tie the precious baby to my breast once more. I put Harlequin's soft cap with its dangling hare's tail upon the little head for cover, while Harlequin himself saddles our horses and makes ready to depart. Oh, I am sad at Signora Del Banco's death, but gladder than glad to have the little boy again!

And once again we are off, with the babe in tow and without even a bladder of goat's milk to stave off the little lion's hunger. I think for one daft moment of a story I heard once, in another life, of a woman somewhat past the age for bearing whose breasts began to give milk just because a babe suckled at them. Such marvels are known on earth if not in heaven. Could such a miracle happen to me? I wonder. For I know that a mother always thinks like a mother, no matter what her age, and that the care of the baby always comes before the hairbreadth 'scape.

"Onward!" cries my Harlequin as our horses set their hooves once more along the mountain path that leads down from the villa.

It is bright moonlight still, bright enough for the moon to lead our way, and we can see the hills — rounded as little mounds of cream, stuck with candy trees — as we descend. But as we go lower into the hills a mist, or *nebbia*, seems to envelop us, as if to protect us from our pursuers. The air becomes suddenly warmer and the fog comes in so close that we can see nothing either to the right or to the left of us as we descend the steep path. We know that somewhere beyond the mist are our pursuers, and just immediately off the road — to which we carefully keep, guiding our horses — is the steepest of drops. Even though we cannot see the cliff, we know it is there, and however much we are drawn to it (death in such a manner sometimes seems simpler than the life of disastrous chances we lead), our instinct to protect the baby overcomes even the cliff's siren song.

Down we go in mist. The mist turns from gray to pinkish and clings about our shoulders. It rises from the ground like a creature seeking to take shape out of chaos and become incarnate; it seems to have a life of its own. Was it summoned by a witch to shield us?

Abruptly I look down at my finger and see that I still wear the magic ring with the hair knot. "Thanks be to Arlecchina," I mutter to my amulet. And no sooner are those words loosed from my throat than a clap of thunder breaks and the whole sky is illuminated by a jagged flash, painting its neon z's across the air. The baby squalls, Will's horse rears up, and the heavens begin to pour with rain and hailstones. We bend our heads under the sky's assault and rein our horses in.

Each time the lightning comes, we can see the little hillocks lit up from behind, the wind-whipped olives and poplars, cherry and apple trees, seeming to cling to the hillsides, as if they were in danger of being blown away. We know we cannot stop in any *contadino*'s house, bearing the babe as we do, so we press on in the storm, bedraggled in our costumes and soaked to the skin, praying that the baby will not take a chill and die.

The rain and hailstorm are brutal; we slog on down the mountain. Suddenly, in a burst of bluish lightning, Will sees a sort of barn or shed clinging to a curve of a hill below us. We make for it, as our only hope. Dismounting, entering, shaking off the rain, we find a kind of barn or stable filled with farm animals of every description taking shelter from the storm. Cows and goats, pigs, and even chickens jostle on the straw floor in the darkness, and they are not a little alarmed by our entry, horses and all. Nonetheless, we claim our part of this place.

Aha, I think, if I can milk one of these goats, the babe can live another day. Thus Will and I set about peeling off our soaked clothes, hanging them up to dry while our eyes adjust to the darkness, and we begin to think of how to commandeer a goat and milk it into the baby's mouth.

Have you ever milked a goat in darkness and tried to aim the stream into a crying baby's mouth? Ah — there should be medals on earth for such a feat! But, alas, keeping babies alive is deemed such a small achievement compared to killing assassins, warriors, Turks, or even *contadini* who are bent on killing us! The world values bloodshed above giving life — else why would women be honored less than men? Yet I know, when I hit the target of the baby's mouth in the dark, that I have accomplished a feat that causes all the angels in heaven to choir in unison. Thus together, Will and I feed our little Judah, whereupon, huddled like puppies, we three drift off to sleep.

Dreams take me for a while — I am so tired. And my dreams are fretful. Antonia is in my dreams, and her father, the Ur-WASP, a man of my own class and caste whom I married, thinking he would bring me safety, whereupon he conspired with my own brother to steal both my inheritance and my child. I wake up with a jolt, thinking of that other life, my heart pounding in terror. It seems I have been dropped into this world, as if I have slipped through a crack in time, and elsewhere, back in not-yet-existent New York and Los Angeles in the not-yet-existent 1980s, a whole world goes on without me — as if indeed I were dead and nobody knew or cared. Yet, *do* New York and L.A. really exist if I am here in 1592? Can both times exist simultaneously — parallel universes, time flowing forward in one and backward in another, and I the only wanderer, the only vagabond who can pass between them?

"My love," says Will, "what startles you?" The animals low and shift on their straw pallets; the smell of rain, of barnyard, of manure and sodden clothes and uncleaned baby, is nearly overpowering.

"Why so pensive?" asks my lover, this sweet man who can both unseam an enemy and feed a baby, his head filled with poems through it all.

"My daughter," I say. "I had a daughter once — nay, I have a daughter still, though in another country. . . ." Out of deep superstition, I do not finish the last sentence of the quote — "and besides, the wench is dead." Will does not ask for the particulars, as though he knows I cannot tell them.

"I, too, have a daughter," says he. "Nay, two daughters, one a twin. They are as dear to me as all my sonnets, all my poems, my few paltry plays, e'en Kit Marlowe's fame. . . . I miss them, too, and sorely."

"And your son?"

"A man's son is so much a part of his own self that it seems somehow Hamnet is here with me e'en now. This baby could be my Hamnet. No, more than that — Hamnet is within my heart, my flesh, my bone. When I kill, he kills. When I love, he loves. When I rage, he rages. . . . Sleep now, gentle Jessica, for only sleep knits up the raveled sleeve of care."

And so we curl toward each other in sleep, but before we do, Will reaches out to stroke my breasts, my hair, my quim.

"No loathsome canker lives in this sweet bud," he says, opening the rose between my thighs, bedewing it with his honeyed tongue. Before long, we have been led by our fierce blood into a fierce coupling. "Jessica," he cries, plunging into my depths with his soul's saber, "let me come home." And he slides into my center with all the passion of the gleaming knife for the dark sheath.

Whether it is the presence of the animals, the babe, the sense that he will lose me soon, or all the bloodshed we have witnessed, he is like a bedlamite tonight, mad-eyed, raving, snatching this last lovemaking as if it were his ultimate chance to couple on this earth. My mind is mad with lines of his own verse, unwritten now, yet seeded in the embryo of time, for times as yet unborn. The pen, the penis, the rosebud of the quim, bear the poem even as they do the babe. The muse is, after all, no virgin, but a Venus seeking her Adonis. Both are breathing here, here in this manger amongst the beasts of the field.

I am torn betwixt elation and sadness, ecstasy and despair. I feel Will's hardness within me, knowing that never again shall I find my mate, my husband out of time; and I almost want to die here, now, with him, rather than be parted ever.

The animals low and moo, grunt and breathe, as though they were part of our sensual act. I can feel their breath upon me as well as my lover's even as we embrace and roll apart, embrace and, at long last, sleep.

My dreams this night are kind, as they can sometimes be even in the midst of dire emergencies.

I am home again, on Park Avenue, in that same childhood apartment with the birds on the ceiling of my room. But this time my mother is alive and well and she is waltzing gaily with my ten-year-old Antonia. Together they are reciting Sonnet Nineteen, alternating lines, leaping and dancing. I hear the lines of the sonnet echo in my head as perfectly as if I were waking:

> Devouring Time, blunt thou the lion's paws,
> And make the earth devour her own sweet brood;
> Pluck the keen teeth from the fierce tiger's jaws,
> And burn the long-lived phoenix in her blood;
> Make glad and sorry seasons as thou fleets,
> And do whate'er thou wilt, swift-footed Time,
> To the wide world, and all her fading sweets;
> But I forbid thee one most heinous crime,
> O, carve not with thy hours my love's fair brow,
> Nor draw no lines there with thine antique pen.
> Him in thy course untainted do allow,
> For beauty's pattern to succeeding men.
>> Yet do thy worst, old Time; despite thy wrong,
>> My love shall in my verse ever live young.

The sonnet being done, we three embrace. I feel the sweet bulge of my mother almost as though she lived, and I smell, even in my dream, my daughter's lovely little-girl-on-the-verge-of-nymphet smell.

All is well, I say to myself in the dream. All is well.

Bright sun. It is morning. The demons of the dark are burned away. Somewhere off in the distance a church bell chimes, echoing and seeming to ricochet amidst the hills. The animals moo and baa, scratch and cluck, cluck and crow. Outside the shed, the day seems bright and warm. The baby squalls, is fed from the milky way of the goat's udder, then burps and smiles his first true smile. For that one moment, watching those baby lips turn upward like the promise of life renewed, it seems impossible to believe that all is not right with our world.

We take off once again through the Asolean hills. Where all was fog and dark last night, there is now a brilliant landscape of rounded hillocks, peasant houses with red tile roofs, olive trees, poplars, cypresses, and vines holding out their arms to dance across the hillsides. Little *torres* dot the gentle bumps of hills, and now and then a ruined medieval citadel, or *rocca*, crowns a precipice. The towns nestle in the valleys and the church bells peal as if they did not proclaim death to the Jews — or indeed to anyone — as if they were as utterly benign as the baby's first smile.

We ride along like Mary and Joseph and baby Jesus in some quattrocento painting, painted with tiny brushes in jewellike pigments ground from semiprecious stones. Down the mountain path we continue till we come at last to a wider path, then to a valley, then to a somewhat flatter road, which follows alongside a pretty river on which barges, *barche fluviali*, and gondolas ply their trade.

"We must steal new clothes," says Will, realizing we are come to a populated area, "and a gondola — and a goat so the babe may eat."

"Where shall we go?" I ask, knowing there is nowhere we can go. "Back to Venice? To Padova, Vicenza, Milano? Or else to England — sweet England with her low stone cottages, her half-timbered houses, and her burning green lawns? Shall we away to Warwickshire, there to hide in the hills?"

"Ah, Jessica — would that we could discover the Americas and make a new life with the babe."

I think of the "Americas" I know — a whole continent consecrated to greed, and given over to the rape of nature and the death of art. If Will knew what had become of this New World, he would be as sad as I, so I am glad I cannot tell him.

"Back toward Venice," I say, "along this sweet river. And on the way, we'll think of what to do and how to beard the dragon of our fate." I think to look down at the ring again, but truly I am afraid to do so, for it has such unpredictable, capricious powers. Instead I whisper a psalm, remembered from my childhood:

> "I am poured out like water,
> and all my bones are out of joint:
> My heart is like wax;
> it is melted in the midst of my bowels. . . .
> Save me from the lion's mouth:
> for thou has heard me from the horns of the unicorns. . . ."

Whenever I am most perplexed about my life, I pray, asking that my future be revealed to me although I know not, for the moment, how. Perhaps God is a woman with milky breasts, perhaps a vengeful bearded patriarch, perhaps a dancing satyr, perhaps a maiden in a helmet with a sword in one hand and scales of justice in the other, perhaps a Triton with the waves at his command, perhaps a wood nymph piping through the wild, perhaps a seething fog seeking to become incarnate. . . . Whatever God's form — and I know God takes different forms at different times in our lives — it is the union of our soul with God's that alone makes life bearable. And when we can no longer bear this sublunary turmoil, we fly up then to God's all-encompassing bosom.

I need not tell you how Will stole the boat and the clothes from two drunken gondoliers who were sprawled out on the riverbank in the morning sun, drinking the pale white wine of the Veneto, and sunning themselves in nothing but their open linen. Nor need I tell you how he stole the goat from a farmer whose property lay farther downriver toward Padova. The farmer had so many goats that he probably would not miss one for some time, but to Will and me this she-goat was as precious as if it were a unicorn.

Thus attired as boatmen, rowing a stolen gondola containing a stolen goat and an orphaned baby, we continue down the Brenta toward Padova, then down a smaller river toward Fusina and Venice.

Stately villas dream along the banks. With the weather as warm as it can sometimes be in the Veneto in December, we feel somehow suddenly blessed, lulled into a state of false security, as if this river idyll could last forever.

Will tells me of his plays and poems, swearing he has done nothing of consequence yet — some English history plays, the start of one erotic poem of the sort that university wits like to keep beneath their pillows and refer to in their venery, a few "sugar'd sonnets" for private eyes only — but he swears that if he lives, he will amaze and astound the world. Especially with plays he shall write of Italy and its wonders.

"Do you prefer playing the part, or writing it?" I ask.

"The player can ruin the writing for a time," allows Will, "but the writer hath the last laugh always. Certes they try to change all you have done. Players are stubborn, cussed beggars. . . . They try with all their might to make the author into a mere shade of himself, a ghost, and when the play begins no one is more despised a creature than the poor author. Ah, someday, Jessica, I shall, by my troth, write a ghost's part and play it myself! For that is all we are good for once the play begins — mere ghosts of intention, stalking misty battlements by night. . . ."

I laugh, thinking of *Hamlet*, which I know is to come, but Will does not — not yet.

"I wish with all my might that you live to write such wonders," say I.

Dreaming with my baby in the sunny gondola whilst Will rows with a gondolier's twist to his oar, I think of my mother again, of her suicide, and of Antonia, my wise and subtle ten-year-old who goes to Chapin with a knapsack on her back, endures a stepmother who speaks as though her jaws were wired together, and loves her father, as all daughters must — at least at ten — although she knows he is not my friend. If only I could bring my world and Will's together! That he might know Antonia — and I might know his babes as well. Perhaps I could save Hamnet's life were *I* his mother!

Mad — all mad. How can the dead conspire with the living? And yet, in truth, they do so all the time. Even in my own family, the dead kept the living in an iron grip. My grandfather reached icy fingers from beyond the grave, controlling all of us through the mechanism of his dreadful will. It was his will that indirectly caused my mother's suicide, his will that inevitably took Antonia from me, his will that knitted Pip and my ex-husband together as allies, although they mistrusted each other every bit as much as Grisha Krylov and Björn Persson.

Sometimes freedom is just a matter of changing perspective. In another frame of mind, with stronger self-esteem and less of a tendency to sabotage myself, I might take on the battle to win back both my daughter and my inheritance — possibly even win it. It was not that Pip and Antonia's father had any more legal right to the money or to my grandfather's dream of a foundation than I had, it was only that they had busied themselves with sucking up to the trustees and executors, with putting themselves in the drivers' seats while simultaneously discrediting me as a much-divorced, itinerant actress with a lurid psychiatric history. These maneuvers — or perhaps my own sense of powerlessness — had enabled them to take both Antonia and the Bostwicke booty from me. Perhaps, if I ever got back to New York — if New York still existed, that is — I would change all that. Antonia deserved better than a mother who gave up a fight. For her sake as well as mine I ought to have done things differently.

It was certainly something to dream and scheme about while rowing down the Brenta, past Palladian villas whose golden stones and columns are reflected in the ripply mirror of the water — and the more I dreamed and schemed, the more I became convinced that somehow I had to get back to my own time and begin to change the course of my life. But that, of course, was much more easily said than done.

I look at Will, who rows the gondola by now like a true Venetian, and looking at him, my heart breaks. Love this strong can warp the universe. For is there any other force but love that can obliterate time? The longing of a woman for a man — or a man for a woman —

can cancel centuries, wipe out eons, cause the universe to arch back upon itself like a glittering snake devouring its own tail.

"Will, I love you with all my heart. Whatever becomes of us — never forget that."

He looks at me and his golden eyes fill with tears.

"Love is not love," he says, "which alters when it alteration finds. Oh no, it is an ever-fixed mark which looks on tempests and is never shaken."

I gaze at his strong body, which has given me so much pleasure, his eyes, the windows of his soul, which have given me so much joy — and I am weak with longing. Again, death seems sweet to me compared with parting from this man. To die and be together through all of time seems reasonable and right. But a small insistent voice in my head whispers: *Antonia, Antonia, Antonia*. Motherhood calls me back to life. I have two children now to ground me — Antonia and little Judah — so death is a luxury I cannot afford.

"I wonder what has become of my father and your patron?" I ask Will.

"The devil take them!" says Will, rowing furiously.

"The devil never takes people exactly when we wish him to," I say, rocking my little one. But I am also wondering what has become of that unlikely pair.

I can almost see Shalach and Southampton, those two uneasy allies on the road, fleeing Montebello in the storm brought by Arlecchina's ring. But while we hide in the manger from the hailstones, they press on and by now have come to Cittadella. They have taken horse rather than boat toward Venice, linked together by their rage against us and their vow to take revenge on Will, no matter what the cost.

I see them riding over the hillocks, anti-Semite and Jew, neither wearing his proper attire — Southampton is by now a rather bloody and tattered Brighella, and Shalach wears a black hat in defiance of the ghetto's laws. What do they speak of? The conversion of the Jews? The queen of England? The doge of Venice? The establishment of the Venetian ghetto? Men need have nothing in common but an enemy to ride together, haunch to haunch. Nor need they speak to be allies. These two have a common cause: Will's skin. That itself is bond enough.

Will's skin. I look at Will's skin — his scarred chest (nearly flayed of its pound of flesh), his forehead, glistening with sweat — and I am overcome with longing for him. My knees part slightly as if to receive him. His wounds speak to my own. If I leave this lover and go back to my time, what lies in store for me but loneliness? Since I first knew my stubborn craft, my sullen art, at seventeen (when I played Juliet to a Romeo who, alas, turned out to be resolutely gay), I have known that the life of an actress wedded to her art is hardly calculated to bring happiness and joy in love. Some few find it. The rest fling themselves from man to man as if their lives were complex square dances, with changing partners the order of the night.

What awaits me in either New York or Los Angeles is a sort of sexual Sahara. Married men, gay men, narcissistic actors wanting caretakers who act like mommies but look like daughters, studio executives spoiled rotten by the sexual smorgasbord that is Hollywood, captains of industry who require a full-time call girl–decorator–caterer to fly around the world in Lear jets as their schedules demand.

Just thinking of all that, I want this river idyll never to end, for Will and me to stay here in this stolen gondola forever, drifting, but going nowhere. Oh, I know there have been saints who died in religious ecstasy never to return to the world of men, bodhisattvas who renounced the call of the sublunary spheres, shamen who disappeared into the desert forever. But the true calling of the hero or heroine who follows a vision-quest is to descend into the underworld, into the labyrinth, up to the vaulted heavens, out of time, only to bring back a boon for all of humankind — and such a hero would I be. I want to rock in this timeless gondola forever, but I know that is impossible. It is as though Demeter and Persephone have had their roles reversed, and my daughter, my Persephone, calls me back to earth.

But what of Judah, my little lion? Which world does he belong to? That remains to be seen.

14

A Hell of Time

AN ABANDONED VILLA sleeps along the bank. Its golden stones are rusticated, so as to suggest antiquity, and it has turrets, columns, windows that are glinting rosettes, and windows that are slates of polished gold in the setting sun of the Veneto. It appears strangely still, its garden overgrown with weeds and vines, vines climbing its stones as if to repossess the turrets. Perhaps mad dogs guard its battlements, but we are determined, nonetheless, to stop here — at least for a while — so we tie up our gondola at a half-rotted river dock and step ashore.

No dogs bark as we alight, and no servants rush out to greet or repel us. With the baby in my arms and the goat in Will's, we find a wobbly purchase on the rotting dock, then trudge up the weedy, graveled path to the main house.

There are crumbling steps before the portico; these we climb, passing under a classical frieze of gods and goddesses, nymphs and shepherds, heavenly hounds and harts. We are astonished to find that the door is not locked, but stands ajar. We enter, goat and all.

The central hall of the villa shows signs of a hasty departure — though when this departure occurred, it is not possible to say. Muddy boots are flung about the floor, dead leaves, clumps of earth, dropped weapons, a torn cloak. A sudden tumult of wings alarms us and we look up to see, in the vaulted ceiling painted like the zodiac in the night sky, a horned owl madly flapping.

"Is it an omen?" asks Will. "And if it is, then of what?"

The owl zooms down perilously close to the baby's face as if it meant him harm, then wings its way into another chamber, seeming to lead us there.

"Chase it, Will!" I cry. "Chase it out of the house!" For I remember folk tales of owls come to carry away babies, and suddenly am in terror that this is no ordinary bird, but an evil spirit come to take my child.

Will seizes the torn cape from the floor and runs after the owl with it, flinging dusty windows open and trying to shoo the bird out into the wood beyond. It flaps and swoops, soars into the eaves, dives down, and seems to taunt us. This monster bird means us ill — of that I am sure. Will feints at it with the cloak, now like a bullfighter, now like a maddened housemaid with a dust mop. The owl still flaps, forcing us to chase it through many chambers, chambers full of unmade, hastily abandoned beds, chambers with abandoned trays of rotting food, chambers with ball gowns hastily cast off and discarded coats and breeches.

At last it leads us into what seems an alchemist's laboratory with limbecks and retorts, braziers and bottles, dusty books full of secret formulae. There it alights upon a limbeck full of some glistening substance that seems to gleam with all the colors of the rainbow. The bird appears to indicate this elixir with its beak, then soars to the ceiling again, flapping and calling. (Or does it cackle? — I swear it seems to cackle.)

"Open the window, Will!" I cry. And as he does, the owl dives down again, alights for one terrifying moment upon the baby's back, causing him to scream in terror, then flies out the window into the wood. Clutching my little lion, I follow with my eyes to the very edge of the greenwood, where the bird pauses for a moment, then in the wink of an eye seems to metamorphose into the bent figure of an old woman in blue and silver skirts. She turns and winks at me, cackling, and I see — or think I see — Arlecchina's glittering eyes.

"Did you see her?" I ask Will, but he is not even looking out the window. Instead, he is holding the rainbow-colored limbeck in his hands and contemplating it.

"To drink or not to drink?" he asks. "Perhaps this elixir contains all future poesy and knowledge of our fates — or perhaps it contains death. What say you, Jessica?"

"I say put it down. That bird was sent for evil not for good, and if *she* indicated that elixir, then surely it will poison you. There is danger aplenty in the world without elixirs."

"Oh, what creatures women are!" says Will, staring at the limbeck as if hypnotized. "All of life and death may be in this glass, yet you would not taste it. See how it catches the rainbow in its rounded bowl." He raises the limbeck to his lips. "See how it glints, promising knowledge." He tips it at the edge of his mouth. "See how Christ's blood streams in the firmament. . . . One drop would save my life — nay, half a drop." He is about to receive the rainbow sacrament upon his tongue. . . . Whereupon I knock the devilish limbeck out of his hand and smash it to the floor. But not before some drops sprinkle on his hand, and Will — that wayfarer in hell, in heaven, that poet seeking a holy vision — hastily laps them up.

His eyes burn as if he sees another world. Time seems to stop for him. The rainbow fluid flows about our feet. A gust of chill wind rushes in via the open window through which the owl departed. Will stands transfixed. Then the babe starts to whimper, waking him back to this world.

"What did you see?" I ask Will as his eyes seem to focus on the room again.

"Ask rather what did I not see. I saw things too wonderful and terrible to comprehend. . . . My Hamnet dead; my lord condemned to die; the mortal moon, my queen, eclipsed; my father dead with a gentleman's escutcheon on his tomb; my elder daughter made a doctor's bride; my younger a vile seducer's; battles and loves too awesome to behold; tragedies and comedies full-blown, needing only my pen's transcription. . . . I even saw Kit Marlowe dead and damned! Jessica, lick this hand that is full of the wisdom of the spheres. Perhaps some drop remains. . . . Humor me, my love. It will not hurt you — that I swear."

On a mad, possibly suicidal, impulse, I lick his hand, but either Will has imagined the effects of the elixir or no drops remain — for I cannot see such wonders as he swears he sees. Yet in my mind there does spring full-blown the vision of a theater, made like the Old Globe that stood in Southwark once, and bearing my grandfather's name. Antonia and I are acting on the stage. She plays Juliet, and I her nurse. Where this theater stands or who has built it I do not know, but it seems as solid as the stones of the villa in which we find ourselves.

"Have you seen the future?" asks Will.

I shake my head.

"The future has seen me," I say. "But what it means to do with me, I cannot tell."

We are tired. The babe is tired. And so, without further ado, we find the abandoned bedchamber that most suits us and prepare for sleep.

When the babe is fed and rocked and lies sleeping in my arms, Will looks about the bedchamber with a shudder and says, "This strange, abandoned villa puts me in mind of the plague that rages still in London — for there, all those who can, forsake the plaguey city for their country seats, leaving fine houses abandoned in the town."

"And what of the poor?"

"The poor?" says Will. "In times of plague they toss on their straw pallets rattling their last, and stinking like corpses even as they live. Sometimes whole families perish all alone, or else those who come to nurse them steal their goods and chattels, making away with whatever they can. I think of my kin in Stratford and I quake with fear. . . . What horrid visions that rainbow fluid conjured — horrid and beauteous at once! I fear for my Hamnet and my daughters. . . ."

"Sleep, gentle poet," say I, "for you will need your strength if we are to row our way back to Venice."

He curls himself next to me and the babe on the great four-postered bed and begins to drift, thinking of plague and parenthood, plague and poverty. He whimpers and draws close to me. I have two babies now, I think. Nay, three.

I think of his plight and somehow it lightens my own. He with his kin in plaguey England; he in thrall to a noble lord who values him as if a poet were a plaything; he not knowing he is destined for great deeds, but only feeling his mortal chains — his wife, his children, his unworthiness — and not yet having the certainty that he will soar into the empyrean on the wings of his verse.

Lying back with the baby and thinking of my daughter, a new feeling rises in me: a feeling of my power to change my life. Oh, I have often felt my power on the stage; but off the stage, in the world of men, I have felt curiously castrated, reduced to little girlhood, even babyhood, and buffeted about by the big people. Now, I begin to sense that the power I command on the stage can also be mine in life. It is as though slowly, inexorably, my strength has been growing in me and I now know without a doubt that I will go home and claim both my child and my inheritance. The thought comes to me that a woman whose child has been taken from her — whether in a custody suit or because she gave it up for adoption after a star-crossed pregnancy of youth — walks the world like a ghost. She feels almost transparent, as if she lives in a curious double exposure with the shapes of shadowy streets and buildings showing through her skin, as in some old movie with ectoplasmic protagonists. I have known women who lost the fruit of teenage pregnancies to adoption in the days before legalized abortion, and they have walked the world this way, feeling like specters until somehow they established contact once again with these lost children. For a child once made, borne — and born — is part of one's soul, the bond severed at one's peril, the peril of becoming a walking ghost.

Will sleeps. I put the babe beside him in the bed, leave my two sleeping boys, and rise to undress. I am uneasy, unquiet, as if I know somehow that this idyll cannot last and we are to be wrenched apart. But oh, if only I could stay with him and also have my life, my daughter, my little son, Will's poems, his plays. . . . Impossible. He must go back to England with his lord and write the poems and plays. I must retrieve Antonia somehow and build that theater bearing the Bostwicke name. . . .

My ears prick: someone has entered the villa. I am certain of it. Can it be Arlecchina? Or, worse, Bassanio and Gratiano? Or worse still, Southampton with Shalach by his side?

The sound of boots along a hallway. I stand frozen for a moment, waiting to meet my fate — then creep out into the hall to meet it fearlessly. I wish I had a dagger or, at the least, a club. I hold my breath and pray. And then around the corner comes a very tattered Brighella with no one by his side.

"Good evening, Madam," says he, bowing low. I have been so convinced he rode with my father that I am surprised not to see Shalach there as well.

"Where are the others?" I ask.

"Ah, thereby lies a tale," says the Earl of S. "Bassanio and Gratiano are dead — which is not such a pity considering that our dear, impecunious Will owed them a thousand ducats. We have made a nice profit, have we not, out of their mutual murder — for the fact is that they killed each other at Montebello. May they rest in peace. And your father, Lady, is not such a swift horseman as am I. Now I comprehend why Venetians are famed for their ineptitude on horseback — for 'tis an old jest to say 'He rides like a Venetian,' meaning he cannot ride — but I, Lady, can ride you. And not like a Venetian, but like an Englishman!"

Whereupon he grabs me by the arm, whips a silken kerchief from his coat, and binds my mouth with it. Then, with a red cord, he binds my hands — and shoves me, kicks me, prods me, to another chamber.

What he means to do with me I know. What I do not know is how I shall respond when this tattered commedia dell'arte villain, my love's lover, throws me upon another tossed and crumpled bed, strips me of my boatman's clothes, and presses his mouth to my neck, my breasts, my navel, my quim. Against my will, my blood begins to heat. Against my will, I desire him. This brigand of the road covers me with his sweaty body, grazes my cheeks with his rough beard, forces himself into my steaming, almost liquid center. "Can you doubt that I love you, Lady?" he inquires into my ear, pouring his words there as he will pour his seed into that other place.

This is a dream, a nightmare, every woman's most desired — and feared — debauch: the forbidden lover. (Is he my brother, Pip? Is he one of my mother's motley husbands? Is he — heaven forbid — my own sweet father?) I open like a torn flower. I scream more in pleasure than in protest. The tattoo of blood builds to its crescendo, and as it builds I see, in my mind's eye, that I am mastered not just by Brighella and Southampton but also by my brother, all my stepfathers, my own father, and my grandfather! Thus every woman makes love to a dozen men each time she opens her legs — and when she comes, it is with all the phantom lovers of her childhood.

Footsteps down the hall, then double footsteps. Will appears, the baby in his arms, followed by Shalach, muddy from the road. Both stand open-mouthed for a moment, watching this display of purloined lust. Whereupon Shalach groans like a beast and tears his hair.

"My own flesh and blood to rebel!" he groans.

But, instead of falling upon my attacker or upon Will, who holds the baby, he tears me away from the Earl of Southampton and bids me clothe myself.

Now he seizes the babe, grabs me by the shoulder roughly, and drags me — half naked, clutching for my clothes — out of the bedchamber, down the halls of the villa, and outside where two horses await.

Will and his patron follow as far as the portico, making no move to stop us. They stand transfixed like figures in a play. Are they no more than spear carriers, members of the chorus? Who can tell? Is it here that our two worlds fracture and break apart?

As in a delirium, I mount the horse, strap the babe once again to my bosom, and ride, ride, ride with old Shalach riding behind me flinging curses into the wind. "I will have my bond!" he screams. Or is it "I will have my babe"?

We ride as in a nightmare. The landscape of the Veneto flies past us — apparitional, blurred, dreamlike. I struggle for breath but can hardly catch it; I grasp my baby and I ride.

Where is Shalach taking me? Why has Will made no move to stop us? Why has Southampton let us go? These questions torment me as we ride up hill, down dale, fleeing our fates.

All sorts of terrifying visions fill my head. If we take this babe back to the ghetto, how will we, or it, be safe? Whole communities of Jews have been put to the sword for less than one purloined Christian baby. I know we are in danger — and now, with Montebello gone, how do we know the hysteria of the anti-Semitic mob has not spread to Venice and the crowded confines of the ghetto itself?

We ride, we ride. Shalach is indeed a poor rider, like most Venetians, and there are many moments when I feel sure I could outride him and elude his grasp. But I do not. Why? Because I know not where to go. With Montebello gone and no sure way to get home to my own time, I feel compelled to stay within sight of my stage father. It is all I know as an actress. If one world does not claim me, then another must. If the quotidian life of the twentieth century cannot hold me, then Shalach and his sixteenth century must.

Sometimes, as I ride, I seem to hear flapping wings above me; but looking up I can see nothing, so dense is the fog. I think of Arlecchina and the ring. Dare I even gaze upon it here? Better not, I think. Another thunderstorm like the last one might dispatch us all. The babe would surely perish in the cold — and I myself might not endure it. But I know that in some way Arlecchina is behind all this mayhem and debauchery. She is the witch, the muse, the midwife to our fates. But whether she is trifling with us to no end, or prodding us along toward some glorious destiny, is not yet clear. What fertile seeds will spill out of the gourd of time? What will be revealed?

Riding thus in the fog, I think of my life and my death. "Death, as the psalmist saith, is certain; all shall die." But if I were to die today, would it be too soon? I have borne Antonia, played some few roles I am proud of — but I have completed neither Antonia's education nor my own. And I have not claimed the legacy that should be mine. Not just the legacy of lucre, but the legacy of art. Nor have I borne a son. The two acts are oddly intertwined, for there exists a curious, disputed codicil to my grandfather's will that states that any son of mine could claim a lion's share of income from the layered trust.

Best not to think of this! But if somehow I could get back to my own time and take the baby with me, I'd have the key to all: the

Shakespearean theater with the Bostwicke name and grandfather's disputed booty. Even more, I'd now know what to do with it, for I'd build a theater to perform Will's plays — Will's plays, which do not yet exist!

But what if Will should perish? What if even now Southampton slays him in a fit of pique? Or what if he should drown while sailing home? Or die of plague or fever? And what if the babe and I should perish? Oh, strong magick is needed and needed now — perhaps even stronger magick than Arlecchina herself possesses. The magick of the muse alone will do!

We gallop on. From time to time I outride Shalach, whereupon he frantically gallops behind me, trying to catch up. Each time he almost catches me, he shouts a more desperate promise. "I'll raise the babe as my own grandson!" he shouts on one occasion. And, on another, "I'll permit no harm to come to him!" Thus has my WASP knack of horsemanship saved me even in a Jewish world! Toward Fusina we furiously gallop — where a hired gondola awaits. And thence by choppy sea from Fusina to San Marco, thence toward Cannaregio and home.

The ghetto is as we left it: the teeming *campo* with the poor lining up to pawn or redeem their pledges, the din of the street vendors, the children playing, the water carriers, the old-clothes men, the foreigners from every corner of the globe, the tourists in turbans, coronets, yellow hats, red hats, come into the ghetto to gawk, to pawn their chattel, or to buy a jewel, a painting, or a sweaty old garment (with a jewel or painting sewn into its silk).

The ghetto has not changed, but we have. For we have seen the threat that lurks like a sleeping beast outside its walls. We know that at any moment raving Christians can storm its walls, screaming of plague, bad harvests, ruinous rates of interest — all of which will be blamed upon the Jews.

For this reason, Shalach is determined to circumcise the baby as soon as possible and claim him as a grandson and a Jew. No word passes between us about my adventure with the Christian Englishmen. Whatever his deepest feelings, Shalach is prepared to act as if he forgets my indiscretions. Did they ever occur? Who knows? Such acts of passion have the quality of dreams. The more they move our deepest selves, the more we cancel them to consciousness. Shalach will claim this baby as a Jew — that will be his revenge.

He looks at me and his watery old eyes bear a father's mixed blame and blessing. He cannot hate me, no matter what I've done. He could reveal me as a harlot to the Jews in the *campo* and see me stoned to death by my own people (with the women, no doubt, taking the most perverse delight in my destruction), but he will not do so. Instead, he will claim this baby as his heir.

Oh, dear Will Shakespeare, when he finally came to write his Jewish play, was unerring about Shylock! For all his grumbling and bitterness, he remains the most interesting character in the story — a tragic hero like Lear, a great soul despite his defects. Even at the end, when Portia (that Miss Priss, that WASP debutante) grants him the flesh but not the blood to go with it, and calls in a forgotten law against the alien to do him out of his ducats, our sympathies remain with him. For Shylock, and Jessica (with Antonio a poor third), seem finally the only real characters in the play. To Portia's debutante, Bassanio's fortune hunter, Gratiano's rake, Lorenzo's anti-Semite, only these three appear as complex beings, full of the terror and wonder of life. Against our wills, we leave the theater feeling Shylock's deep humanity. And Jessica's. How did the playwright know to put it there?

He knew.

Life resumes in the ghetto — but now, with little Judah to account for. Shalach will brook no questions about the baby's origins, and my maid and all the other womenfolk assume that I have gone away to bear a bastard babe and brought it back into my father's house. They gossip about me behind their hands, say how they always *knew* I hid a pregnancy beneath my stays, but I care not — nor does my father. It is astonishing to see him melted by grandfatherhood, to see him spending hours cooing at the baby, neglecting his counting house. The other merchants whisper and wish him ill.

But since Shalach is relatively rich, and since the commonest people in all ages grovel before money, he is permitted his eccentricities. The poor must conform to laws, but the rich are allowed to be above them. Both within and without the ghetto, human nature is equally inhuman when it comes to gold.

Life goes on. The wet-nurse feeds the baby and it grows. Time slows to a crawl as life revolves around this infant life. Will and Harry seem almost like figures in a dream. Montebello all but fades from memory. California and New York, Antonia and her father and my brother, Pip, again become but memories of another life. The baby holds me captive in his power. He coos to me, gurgles to me, smiles at me, and all of history is held in abeyance as I play my greatest role.

A son! We fall in love with our daughters but we adore our sons. If women have any weakness on this earth, it is that they put their sons before themselves!

Well, then, if I am doomed to stay here as Shylock's daughter, I shall enjoy my son, who, with his radiance, obliterates all other worlds. The winter creeps along and Christmas is almost upon us. I stay indoors, worshipping at the altar of the baby's cradle.

One gray morning I awaken to the shouts of revelers in the *campo* below. I run to the window and look down — and there, milling about the open well, I see dozens of Venetians in their masques and dominoes come to haggle with or taunt the Jews. Real terror grabs my heart, for this baby has become my will to live.

I see one reveler dressed as Pulcinella grab a Jewish boy by one foot and dangle him above the open well as if to drop him in. The boy's mouth gapes wide in silent horror. The screams of all the Jews for the last six thousand years are in that silent O. The boy's mother rushes forward in despair, and in that moment, the reveler puts the boy down as if only a jest were meant. But the Jews coagulating in the square know differently. Christmas time approaches, then carnival; it is a most dangerous time for Jews.

A chill rushes through me. My hands tremble and I begin to sweat. At first I think it is the fear of what I've seen, but as the day wears on, I feel giddier and giddier and my vision dims. I grow weaker with fever and my armpits swell. In my groin there are two tender lumps, and my stomach alternately heaves and cramps violently.

Plague, I think — and then laugh at myself for being melodramatic. Even in twentieth-century Venice I believed I had plague. Impossible. I stagger across the floor to the baby's cradle — and it is there that I collapse.

All health is alike; all illness particular. I shiver; I cannot get warm. My back aches, and all my limbs feel bruised and sore. I cannot look into the light of day, or even at a candle in the room by night. My eyelids droop and yet I cannot sleep. My stomach heaves and a boiling stinking purgatory pushes from my guts. I stagger up and fill the chamber pot beneath my bed, praying that no one sees me, hears me, smells me. Then I stagger back to bed. The soreness in my armpits grows. My fever rises and it does not break. I hear someone say, "Thus are harlots punished," but I cannot tell who the speaker is.

And then I am away at sea. I lose consciousness and rock in an ocean of feverish dreams. I am five; the benign birds on the ceiling of my room have changed into enormous, bloody-beaked pterodactyls from the Museum of Natural History. They are buzzing about the ceiling, opening and closing their beaks as if they are about to swoop down on me and pluck my eyes out. I scream for my mother and with that scream awaken, not knowing where I will find myself. The writhing columns around my bed alert me: I am still in Shalach's house in Venice, and when I open wide my eyes I see Arlecchina standing before me.

She looks down at me with glittering eyes. She lifts and strokes my icy hand.

"I made a promise to your mother long ago," she says.

"Which mother?" I croak, my throat dry from fever, my mouth full of cotton wool.

"The one who lost the will to live in Venice, the one whose suicide brought you back again and yet again, the one whose death you have been fighting all these years."

"What promise?"

"To protect you from all harm — your children, too. Jessica: the baby boy is yours. I give him to you in whatever time. Time does not exist. It is a fiction we invent to please ourselves. Just as life is. Just as death. We can move through time at will, but most of us do not know this. You of all people understand that the dead are not powerless. There is no death, but only a change of worlds."

"By what magick will you send me home?"

"Your own, Jessica, your own."

And she is gone. My fever grows like a monstrous red creature filling the room, a silken tent of red through which the noon sun shines, a glowing coal imbedded in my forehead.

Del Banco's doctor brother is sent to minister to me with leeches and bleeding bowls, potions and poultices, powders, salves. A rabbi is sent; another doctor. Suddenly all the faces in the room around me wear long-nosed chalky masks — as in a play of plague. I remember an errant line from my Shakespearean research some weeks (or is it centuries?) past: "The cause of plagues is sin, if you look to it well; and the cause of sin are plays; therefore the cause of plagues are plays." Good God, I think, I am really dying! Is this how it happens — like a pantomime, or a masquerade, or a bad play with shoddy, tattered, rented costumes? You keep expecting a reprieve, and then you die with half your work undone? Inexorable as childbirth or a baby's cry, death stalks the chamber where I lie.

I drift, I drift. A day passes, a night. Masked figures come and go in my darkened chamber. They take my blood, swaddle my forehead with rags soaked in bitter herbs, apply leeches, apply poultices, give me potions to drink. The little suckers of the leeches sing to me; they sing to me of death. Sometimes I swim (nay, struggle) into consciousness raving (in English) that I need sulfa drugs or antibiotics — whereupon the beak-nosed watchers think me mad, or entering the last delirium of death.

"Hear how she speaks in a barbaric tongue!" whispers one chalk-faced wraith.

"The dead are not powerless!" I cry in English.

Behind their masks they cluck with pity and with condescension. *"La morte viene subito. . . ."* they say.

*

215

How many hours or days I drift I cannot tell. My great four-post-ered bed becomes a boat, rocking in a stormy sea. My mother is clinging to its side, her eyes hollow from the grave, her flesh in tatters around her cheekbones.

"Do as I say, not as I do," she whispers.

"What?" I croak.

"I release you from my death," she says, and then she floats away.

Pip appears, a little boy with gray shorts and a blue blazer that says BUCKLEY SCHOOL.

"I always worshipped you," he says. "I wanted what was yours — especially love. I got the money, but they all loved you. And so I still had less. . . . I've never had enough." He cries like a baby and floats away, shaking his fists at the waves. And then Antonia appears wearing her green school knapsack on her back. She unzips it and extracts for me a little bag of gummy bears such as I have sent her when she was sick.

"Take them, Mummy, they will make you well!" I pop a gummy bear upon my tongue, then reach out my arms to hug my darling girl, but she too churns away on that boiling sea that takes all my relatives: mother, brother, all.

"Am I really dying?" I ask myself. I cannot die; too much remains undone. The whole first half of my life, I understood nothing; everything was wasted on me. Now that I have finally become someone on whom nothing is lost, shall I have to pay with my life? I suddenly want so terribly *not* to die. I who have worn my life so carelessly till now, who have courted suicide with one eye open, want nothing more than life.

Dear God, be with me now. Dear God, give me a little time to change my life. And then, out of the depths of some memory I did not know I possessed, these lines come to me:

> Beauty is but a flower,
> Which wrinkles will devour:
> Brightness falls from the air,
> Queens have died young and fair,

> Dust hath closed Helen's eye.
> I am sick, I must die.
> Lord have mercy on us!

Two courtiers approach my bed.

"Hush, Will," says one. "Don't be a frightened puppy." I recognize Southampton's voice, and the tone in which he speaks to Will tells all: Will has submitted to him for the sake of a thousand ducats — that disputed debt canceled by the deaths of Bassanio and Gratiano. I wonder if Will knows this or if the earl still holds the debt over his head like a sword of Damocles.

Then comes Will's voice, heavy with irony: "Being your slave," says he, "what should I do but tend, upon the hours and times of your desire?"

"Then hate me when thou wilt," says Harry, "but for God's sake, play not your motley japes about the dying wench. . . . See where she faints with fever and expires."

My eyes flutter open. Before me I see Will restored to his former state of fashion — the balding young Englishman abroad. And Harry has dropped his Brighella mask and goes about the world once more in his own flaxen hair. I see he looks on me with lust — and love.

For a moment, I am lucid and I understand it all: Will's love for Harry, and his love for me. Harry's love for Will, and his love for me — all intertwined, impossible to untangle. When two brothers love the same woman, is it each other that they love? Or the woman? Or is it both? *They* do not know the answer to this riddle. Do I?

"Farewell, gentle Jessica," says Will. "Thou art too dear for my possessing. . . ."

"He means we sail for England on the morrow, having redeemed my mother's glass." I see where it glints in Harry's hand like a harbinger of doom, for it is cracked now, God knows how. "No matter," says Harry, seeing me eye the crack, "a new glass will be found in England. 'Tis the silver back I crave, the beast with two backs as 'twere."

My heart sinks; I know I will never see Will again, yet I also understand that he must go home with Harry to write his plays and poems.

"I release you from my death," I say to Will, whose face now seems as cracked with sorrow as that glass.

"My love is as a fever longing still, for that which longer nurseth the disease," he says, looking at me with liquid eyes that seem to understand my gift to him.

Harry proffers a golden goblet whereof he bids me drink: "*Un goccino, per piacere.*" I bring my lips to the cup and take a drop on my burning tongue. My head swims and I drift again into the sea of fever. And then — or do I imagine this? — he is suddenly beneath my coverlet, pressing his girlish lips to my feverish quim.

"Come, let me suck the fever out of you," he says, raising his head above that tropic country, then diving down to graze its shores again. As he does so, Will plants his lips upon my blistered lips; two brothers joined by the electric current of one woman. For one mad moment, I exult in having them both applied to my body like poultices, and even in my illness I begin to come — riotously, as in dreams.

And suddenly I am out of my body. I have left it behind and I am rising now, hovering above it near the ceiling and looking down at Jessica who lies there on the carved walnut bed, caged by four writhing columns. What a beautiful young woman, I think, to die so soon. Her hair is chestnut brown with titian red-gold streaks; her eyes are brown, flickering to gold. She wears the garb of a wealthy young Jewess in the ghetto and two young Christian foreigners genuflect before the orifices of her body, then rise and flee the room like thieves, forgetting their pocket mirror, which still lies on the coverlet, catching the dregs of sun in its broken face.

A commotion in the room when they have gone. Maids rushing in. Then a doctor, then a rabbi, then a distraught old man with a grizzled beard. He looks upon the dead wench.

"Is this the promised end?" he howls. "Howl, howl, howl, howl! O, you are men of stones. Had I your tongues and eyes, I'd use them so that heaven's vault should crack. She's gone forever! I know when one is dead and when one lives. She's dead as earth. Lend me a looking glass. If that her breath will mist or stain the stone, why then she lives!"

The rabbi takes the mirror from the bed, puts it beneath the dead woman's nose. No mist, no motion. She is dead as earth, and now they draw the coverlet above her head and offer muffled prayers.

I watch all this like a spectator at a play, as if I were not in that body and that body were not dead. I want to tell Shalach that he has slipped his role and accidently spoken King Lear's lines, not his own, but I cannot speak for I am not really there. I seem to drift over the room, alighting now upon Jessica, now upon the baby, bidding my farewells. It still does not seem possible that I am dead. But when, presently, a coffin is brought and they lift the woman into its depths and arrange her in its womblike, red satin interior, I know the terror of being buried alive.

Now I am in the coffin, my heart pounding as if it meant to burst; now I am being carried down a crooked stair, jostled horribly, nearly dropped, then hastily caught again. Now I hear the sounds of the *campo*, feel a gust of wind through the box's slats. Now I am carried to the edge of a canal (for I hear water lapping), now lowered into a boat, and now we rock gently as we are rowed along canals. This gentle motion calms me for a time and lets me catch my breath. Is it possible that Arlecchina lied? Was that her last cruel joke, a false deathbed promise to a dying waif? And what of the ring? I have the ring still — but cannot move my hand to look on it. Nor can I see out of these earthen eyes!

We row, we row. Now the water grows rough. We must be in the basin of San Marco, rowing in the direction of the Lido. I can feel the chop, hear the curses of the boatmen as I take my last long sea journey toward burial in the sacred ground of the Venetian Jews. Thinking of that I become really fearful again — fearful of suffocation, for I know I am not dead. Or am I? How can I tell any longer what is real and what is not, what is life and what is death, or even what century or what place I shall be buried alive in — if burial is to be my fate.

I wish again upon the ring. Of course I cannot see it, but I can feel it around my finger like a burning wire. I visualize it in my mind and appeal to it and to Arlecchina for help. The boat suddenly begins to rock quite furiously. Waves spill over the side. The boat-men scream and curse. A storm seems to ensue and hailstones pelt down on my coffin lid, ping, ping, pinging on my little roof with an almost cozy, comforting sound.

The waves are wild now, and the boat rocks harder and harder. With a sudden crash of thunder and lightning, the coffin is capsized into the boiling basin of St. Mark and floats away from the scream-ing boatmen.

A dream of floating, floating, floating on the sea. The coffin rocks as if it were a cradle, and that cradle in the waves. Once, at a health spa in the desert, I whiled half a day away in a flotation tank, held up by Epsom salts: thus it is to be in a coffin in the sea. Fear is suddenly gone. If I must die, I am blessed at least to die in the sea. I give myself into the Nereids' hands, hoping they mean me well.

How long I drift thus I cannot tell. I imagine myself floating past the islands of the lagoon, past Mazzorbo, the island of the nuns, past Murano, Burano, and then past the point of the Lido toward the open sea. Buoys clang. Seagulls swoop down on my rocking coffin-boat, their curious claws landing on the wood with a scraping chicken-scratching sound. And then, suddenly, one furious wave grabs me at its crest and dashes me, box and all, toward the shore. I duck the box the way a young Malibu surfer once taught me how to duck a surfboard. In the tumult of the waves, I lose my *zoccoli*, my stockings, my skirts, my petticoats, even my boned, bejeweled bodice, to the churning sea. And Arlecchina's magic ring marries the Adriatic as surely as the doges' rings once did. So sweetly does it slip away that I do not even notice when it plights its troth with the sea. I swallow mouthfuls of salt water, but still I swim with all my strength for shore.

Suddenly, rocks and pebbles scratch my bare soles. I rise out of the sea — head, shoulders, breasts, navel, quim, thighs, legs — na-ked as Botticelli's Venus. My long dark hair is knotted with sea-weed; bits of sand and shell are under my fingernails, in my navel, between my molars. I inhale deeply and my nostrils thrill to the smell of Venice.

I look up. Even in the *nebbia* I can see the misty turrets of the Excelsior; and before it the naked beach, its summer tents all gone. And lying half buried in the sand, with no note inside it but only murky seawater, is that telltale sign of the twentieth century — a greenish bottle bearing the name of the patron saint of mineral water: San Pellegrino.

Epilogue

The Horns of Unicorns or Tender Heir

I AM LYING in bed at Lorelei's house in Dorsoduro. I have the front bedroom on the second floor facing the canal, and I can hear the gondoliers joking and shouting in the old boathouse near the Campo San Trovaso. Bells ring. The ceiling shimmers with the old woman's squinny — *fa la vecia*, as the Venetians say.

Motorboats race by, making the greenish water of the canal suddenly almost white. Seagulls fly in from the lagoon, rest briefly on buoys in the Guidecca Canal, then dip and dive near San Trovaso before alighting upon the tiled chimneys of the French Embassy, looking seaward, their beaks tasting of salt.

Out at the Lido, in the Antico Cimitero Israelitico, the old Jews sleep — perhaps even Shalach sleeps — for the oldest graves there date back to the quattrocento and are wild with moss and ivy, their weathered Hebrew letters gold with lichen, green with moss. The tarnished gold coins of the lichen are now their only wealth. By some curious Venetian irony, the graves of the Jews are undisturbed while the Christians, who are buried in San Michele, receive only a twelve-year lease, then suffer the indignity of having their bones dug up and flung upon the bone island. Thus Venice is still comparatively kind to her Jews, who have learned to shrug and gesticulate like proper Italians — which perhaps they are. Or then again, perhaps the Italians have learned to shrug from *them*. Some say, in fact, that the Italians are one of the lost tribes of Israel, now so intermarried and genetically muddled that one cannot tell where Jewishness leaves off and Italianness begins. No wonder that Jews and Italians still greet each other like brothers and recognize each other all over the earth as members of the same tribe.

I wake up feeling peaceful, with a sense of utter safety and security — shall I call it bliss? I am in Venice. The time is now. Mother has been laid to rest. Antonia, I am sure, is well. I know I shall see her soon.

Suddenly, the doorbell jangles my reverie. I hear Lorelei running to the door in her velvet palazzo slippers; I imagine her blonde curls tossing as she runs.

"*Chi è?*" she calls, then opens the door without waiting for an answer. I hear garbled speech, hers and a man's. Then the door slams again and I hear Lorelei's feet on the stairs, running up to my room.

She knocks on the door. She peers in. From her expression of concern, I can see that I have been ill for a long time. But I am not ill now.

"Come in!" I call.

"A man came, with an envelope for you. . . . He says it's a script. He says that Björn will call you later about the start date of the film. Here." She hands me a gray envelope. "*Vuoi un caffè?*"

"I'd love one," I say.

Still sitting in bed, I tear open the envelope. Inside, there's a script in a plastic binder. The title page reads:

Serenissima
a film
by
Björn Persson

property of:
Björn Persson Productions, Ltd.
3rd draft: Jan. 1985

Heart pounding, breath coming short, I flip through the hundred or so pages of the script. All of it is there: Harry, Will, Shalach,

Jessica, the gambling, the ghetto, the *cortigiane*, the costume ball, the pogrom, the hairbreadth 'scapes and most disastrous chances, the *nebbia*, the baby, the plague, the coffin, the sea, the rebirth.

I flip at once to the first scene where Will meets Jessica in the ghetto, she staggering on her *zoccoli*, he twisting his auburn beard, his one gold earring glinting.

"Who ever loved, who loved not at first sight?" he says, quoting his rival and looking up at the lady who is to be his muse on earth. I long to read on, to relive the adventure, to lose myself in a reverie of love so strong it can wrench time back upon itself as if it were the merest Möbius strip. . . .

But I must close the book for now, because in one corner of the room, in a bassinet trimmed with blue and silver ribbons, the baby, my little lion, cries.